Cover design by Nina Patel

Edited by Kate Keysell Copy Editing

Books by Peter Larner

Lost in a hurricane
Deathbed Confessions
The Unfolding Path
Farewell Bright Star
Covenant of Silence
Covenant of Retribution

Compilations

The Jack Daly Trilogy
The Covenant Chronicles

To Betty

I hope you enjoy the story.

HARPOON FORCE

Peter x   January 2018

Acknowledgements

The History of the Irish Guards in the Second World War
By
Major D. J. L. Fitzgerald, M.C.

Published by Gale & Polden Limited, Wellington Press, Aldershot 1949

Dedication

Dedicated to the courageous men of the
2nd Battalion Irish Guards and especially to
Guardsman 2720093, John Joseph Donoghue.
Member of the Harpoon Force,
captured at the Battle of Boulogne, May 1940
and served five years as a prisoner of war.

Winston Churchill said:
"Never give in, never, never, never."

This is the story of what happens when courageous men decide not to give in.

HARPOON FORCE

PETER LARNER

1

Saturday 19 May 1934 — London

Organising his own hanging was proving to be decidedly more difficult than Jonjo had first imagined. Closing the door to the privy was essential if his body was not to be discovered by anyone who simply happened to walk through the backyard gate. And now he found he required something sturdy to stand on. It needed to be capable of being kicked away and therefore to fit between the toilet basin and the lavatory door. A beer crate left over from Easter fitted the bill perfectly, but the empty beer bottles needed to be removed first.

The mechanism for a hanging was more complicated than the Meccano set he had received for his fourteenth birthday in March. Although, why anyone should consider a Meccano set a suitable gift for Jonjo was beyond the recipient's imagination, which was itself the nucleus of his success. His flair for storytelling was the talent he was most proud of, unlike arithmetic, which is simply the result of logical deduction. The disturbance he caused at the last school awards evening should have impressed this fact upon his parents.

Having won prizes for both maths and English, Jonjo was denied one of these through a rule that disallowed a student from receiving more than one prize in the same year. This, in itself, was not a difficult concept for the unselfish Jonjo to accept. But to be given a geometry set, complete with compass, for his victory at maths, instead of a copy of Franklin W. Dixon's *The Secret of the Old Mill*, made no sense to the disappointed boy. Were the teachers mad? Handing his story book to the runner-up in English, the spotty, bespectacled Arthur Willetts, only added insult to injury. Although, in fairness to the teachers, there must have been a reluctance to award the maths prize to Walter Stimpson, who had come second in that subject, because they couldn't have been certain that sharp objects such as a compass would be safe in his house. His father was injured in the war and allegedly he still had pieces of shrapnel in his head. Doubt was cast on his intellect and judgement when he had told the headmaster that multiplication should be banned from school as it gave the pupils a poor sense of proportion. So, Arthur became the surprised recipient of the English prize, while Walter was left trying to add up why his second in maths did not warrant an award.

The Meccano set had never been suggested by Jonjo. Indeed, having just forfeited a book he clearly coveted, one would have thought that *The Secret of the Old Mill* would prove very acceptable, or even the ideal present. But to parents and teacher alike, it seemed success in the more practical skills of engineering and maths must take precedence over English. In practice, Jonjo's father believed that a book would last only as long as it took his son to read it, whereas a Meccano set could be constructed, deconstructed and reconstructed endlessly. It was like comparing an everlasting gobstopper with a bar of chocolate.

Jonjo felt like screaming, for in his mind, science should never triumph over art. He was left to wonder whether his parents really knew him at all. But the ill-chosen present and the lamentable judgement of the teachers were not the cause of his current distress. The decision to end his life was not a final narcissistic supplication to be better understood. No, the plan to hang himself was not borne out of self-indulgence, but from an overwhelming sense of self-loathing. In fact, in his mind, the act was never considered to be suicide but, moreover, an execution; punishment for his poor judgement on that ill-fortuned day.

Jonjo balanced precariously on the beer crate, which, itself, stood a little more firmly on the wooden toilet seat. The rope had been tied around a rusting black water pipe that stretched across the ceiling and he was making a noose as shown in his *Boy's Own Annual*.

Jonjo put the noose around his neck and wondered whether he should say a short prayer, when suddenly the tip-tapping of high heels could be heard on the street outside. It wasn't his mother, as she wore high heels only on very special occasions and she was not yet aware that this was to be a memorable day in her life. As the woman approached the Thompson house, the click-clacking paused for a moment and then continued along the short path to the front door. The boy tried to distribute his weight evenly on the wobbling beer crate to stop it making a noise and a hush fell on the sombre, yet absurd scene.

Violet Martin lived only two streets away, but there was no reason for her to be in *this* street unless, of course, the rumours were true. The curtains of several rarely used front parlours twitched in the houses opposite. Old Mrs Podolski thought about telling her that the Thompsons were out but then her cats would probably escape, so she kept her counsel on the matter, something that Ada Blackbrow might have considered sensible when she chose to spread gossip about Violet's recently bereaved son.

Impeccably dressed and not unattractive, Mrs Martin was a formidable woman who spoke her mind and cared little about the consequences of her sharp tongue. She was mature beyond her thirty-four years and her fearless reputation had little to do with her physical appearance. The aura of menace and intimidation she projected was unrelated to her stature or size for, in truth, she was a diminutive woman, but one of rare confidence and presence. She was universally disliked. Well, perhaps not universally. Her husband didn't dislike her, of course. He feared her, perhaps, but he liked her, even loved her at times, when he thought about it. Not the occasions when he had to think about it of course, such as birthdays and anniversaries. To forget such an occasion would have resulted in divorce or worse.

She was always beautifully turned out for, in her view, presentation was paramount. Manners might maketh the man, but an appealing appearance was what mattered in the female gender. Violet marched, out of step with the world, prepared to answer anyone who questioned her status or position. That position was above everyone else in the neighbourhood. She wore the best clothes, her husband was a white collar worker and they lived in the east end of London because she wanted to, not because she couldn't afford a more salubrious location. Violet knew what her neighbours thought about her. They thought that she believed she was better than them. But she didn't *believe* she was better than them, she knew she was. Woe betide anyone who spoke ill of her family, because the gossiping women who lived thereabouts didn't call her 'Violet with an n' without good reason.

The purpose of her visit to the Thompson household was clear. She wanted to find out if the rumours were true. Had her son slipped, as his friends had said, or was he pushed, as the gossips had recently suggested? She didn't make the short journey with vengeance in her heart but she certainly had no thoughts of forgiveness in mind, for she was an unforgiving person at the best of times and these were definitely not the best of times. She was unaccountably calm in the circumstances. She simply needed to establish the truth about how her son and only child had died that morning on the way to school. Her own mother used to say that Ada Blackbrow knew everything about everyone and nothing about anyone. Violet's mum understood the essence of knowledge. Ada knew as much about Jonjo or any other neighbour as she did about King George or Winston Churchill. What she knew was simply what she had heard from other people and was almost exclusively recycled scandal, made less veritable by its retelling. More often than not it was untrue, except in this case, of course, it wasn't.

Gossips love to put someone on a pedestal and the higher the pedestal they build, the harder the individual falls. A good-looking, popular and accomplished student, Jonjo was gifted at sport and, in Ada's view, an exulted and spoilt only child, who never wore hand-me-down shoes. The temptation to play a role in his downfall was too great for her to resist.

Ada Blackbrow was one of just five people who knew about Jonjo's malfeasance. She saw the shadow that darkened his young soul. Jonjo had worked that much out when he heard the rumour himself. Only Ivy Frampton and her friend Lily Maguire knew the truth for they had accompanied Violet's son, Andrew, and Jonjo on the journey to school that fateful day. Jonjo knew that Ivy would not tell a soul, but he was just as certain that Lily would tell her mother and she would, in turn, tell her own mother. And Lily's grandmother lived next door to Ada Blackbrow.

The click-clack of the high heels stopped and Jonjo heard the knocker on the front door slam. Violet was entirely conscious of the twitching curtains across the street but didn't bother to look round. She banged the heavy cast-iron knocker again and waited. There was no answer so she looked through the front window, past the aspidistra, into the parlour. Smoke drifted upwards from a cigarette butt that had recently been left in a large ashtray. Someone was at home, so she slammed the knocker again, attracting even more attention from the neighbours. Her patience lasted for less than a minute. She would not be ignored and so she opened the back gate, walked past the privy, through the yard and down the side of the house. She strode past the scullery and looked through the window. She was just about to try the door when she heard a strange creaking noise behind her. She retraced her steps and realised the sound was coming from the outside lavatory. Nothing could deter Mrs Martin in her present state of mind, not even the idea of finding Mr Thompson sitting on the outside privy. She assumed the door would be locked and was surprised when it opened on her first attempt.

The sight of Jonjo standing on a wooden beer crate that was balanced on the toilet seat shocked even the redoubtable Violet Martin. A rope was looped around his neck and attached to a large water pipe in the roof of the outbuilding. The boy was just about to rock the crate off the seat and leave himself hanging. The only reason he had not done so already was because he had heard someone come in through the back gate. She placed her hands firmly on the beer crate and shouted at him to remove the noose and get down immediately.

'What on earth are you doing?' is what she wanted to ask, but in a quieter tone than the situation demanded because, strangely, she found herself remarkably calm. Instead she said nothing, but led the fourteen-year-old back into the house, along the passage and sat him down in the front parlour. It smelt musky in the room because, apart from a brief visit by the boy to smoke a cigarette that morning, it hadn't been used since last Christmas. She thought about opening the window but remembered that the entire street was watching and listening. Whatever she did next had to be done in a temperate and measured manner, not accompanied by the normal haranguing with which she was associated.

Asking the boy what on earth he was doing was an unnecessary question. It was obvious what he was doing and why he was doing it. When it came to it, Violet Martin didn't need to ask whether the rumours were true. The truth was self-evident by the dramatic scene that had greeted her on arrival. Her first words needed to relax him but the non-sequential and incongruent question simply served to unnerve him even more.

"How long have you been smoking?" she asked as she sat down and lit a cigarette. She spoke not as a dissenting adult but as a classmate might do in the playground. She thought about offering him one but waited for his answer.

"Today," he replied, with his head bowed, too nervous to look directly at her.

She put the packet of cigarettes back in her handbag and resolved to talk about anything except his attempted suicide. He didn't speak, so she continued in an off-hand manner, as if she was only casually interested in his answers.

"I saw you sitting on the kerb by the road the other day." She paused. "At the place where Andrew was killed." He nodded, but she wanted to know why. A moment's silence lapsed before he realised she was waiting for an answer to the unasked question.

Jonjo sat quietly for a moment wondering how much he could trust her. But her pragmatic and engaging manner put him at ease.

"I was timing the cars as they passed." He paused and she looked at him questioningly.

"Counting the seconds between each one," he continued.

Violet stood up, pulled back the net curtain and stared directly back at a woman peering from her window in the house opposite. The other curtain closed quickly and Violet returned to her conversation.

"Timing the cars?" she asked, remembering what he had said a moment earlier.

"We're doing averages in maths at school," he added, as if she should see the significance of such a comment. But she didn't speak, for she was still trying to remember the name of the nosey neighbour opposite, in order that it could be mentally recorded in her little black book.

"The average gap between cars was twenty seconds along that road. If it takes one second to pass, there is only one chance in twenty of being struck by a car if you step out."

She wanted to ask if he had thought about stepping out himself instead of resorting to hanging, but she didn't do so, as it would introduce the subject of suicide. If he wanted to hang himself, then he would have considered stepping out in front of a car. She felt sure he was mature enough to see the irony or poetic justice of such an act. She wondered, for a moment, why he chose to hang himself instead, but knew it would be in deference to the innocent car driver. Absolution for Andrew's death could not come from implicating someone else in his own suicide.

"So, the odds are twenty to one," he added, almost as an afterthought.

"Does your father gamble?" she asked, wondering how he knew about betting odds. She wasn't deliberately trying to change the conversation but was genuinely interested in other people, even though she despised the majority of them.

Jonjo considered the question, if indeed it was question. It was impossible to guess what she would say next. Although, in fairness, it is difficult to anticipate what kind of discussion might naturally follow a boy's suicide attempt. But he rather expected it to take the form of an inquisition and that would certainly have been the case had his own mother found him in the same situation. But Mrs Martin was so different from his mother or any other adult he had ever known. She was unique and unpredictable. The very obvious subject of suicide had been ignored completely in favour of a discussion on smoking and gambling. He had to answer the question but wondered what might follow.

"He does the football pools," he declared, wondering if that counted as gambling. "He shuts himself in the kitchen every Tuesday evening after dinner and fills in his pools coupon. He spent nearly five hours last week trying to decide whether Preston North End versus Arsenal was likely to result in a draw."

"And did it?" she asked.

This time her question was so bizarre that he didn't understand it.

"Did it what?"

"Did it result in a draw?" she asked as she puffed smoke into the stale air and placed her cigarette in the ashtray.

"No, of course not. Arsenal are the league champions and Preston are rubbish."

"So why did he think it would be a draw?" She sounded remarkably interested in football for a woman but, in fact, she was interested in people.

Jonjo realised he had to answer but was still trying to understand how he had come to be in the parlour having a discussion about football with Mrs Martin, who had recently lost her son through one moment of stupidity on his part.

"I suppose he thought that, as they were already champions, Arsenal would have nothing to play for, but they won 2-0." He paused. "He did exactly the same thing last year when Arsenal played Wolverhampton Wanderers in the last game of the season but Arsenal won 7-0."

The comment marked him out, in Violet Martin's mind, as someone of rare quality, an individual who could learn from other people's mistakes and a person who understood the weakness of making the same mistake twice.

Jonjo waited to see what strange direction the conversation would take next. And, for Violet's part, she was pleased he seemed to be relaxing in her company.

She stubbed her cigarette out in the ashtray and looked directly at him. "I think one error of judgement can be forgiven," she said, adding, "but anyone making the same mistake twice deserves anything that befalls them."

It took him a few minutes to realise that she might be talking as much about him as his father. Was she forgiving him for killing her only son? It seemed unthinkable. She was a remarkable woman and he could not let this moment pass. He wanted to raise the issue of Andrew's untimely death and he sensed a hint of clemency in her voice.

"I thought about going to confession, but couldn't."

"Why?" she asked, realising his comment was an admission of guilt.

"The priest would have to tell my parents."

"Priests can't tell anyone what you say to them in the confessional, John, everybody knows that." It was the first time she had spoken his name and the first time anyone, other than a teacher, had called him John for a long time. He looked doubtful about her last statement. He knew what she said was a universally held truth, but it seemed unreasonable that any priest would demand a penance of three Hail Marys and let him leave the confessional box after such a damning admission. Then, in the same offhand manner in which she had conducted herself throughout, she presented him with the opportunity to lay bare his infirmities.

"You can confess to me if you want." Her smiling countenance concealed her true sadness but she suddenly realised that one young boy's death could not atone for the death of another, even one she had loved so much. In that moment, she turned the extreme pain that she felt for the loss of her son on itself, giving it purpose, dedicating it to something, or someone, else. A truly selfless act deflects pain and, although that pain never departs, it is subdued by its new purpose. Her curious behaviour began to influence him. If a woman who was old enough to be his mother could conduct herself in such a bohemian manner, then why shouldn't a fourteen-year-old boy do so? The invitation was met with an immediate response on his part as he felt strangely compelled to participate in this extraordinary parlour game.

"Forgive me, Mrs Martin, for I have sinned." He spoke quietly, choosing each word individually, rather than reciting it, childlike, as he had done at every confession he had ever made. "I killed Andrew. I killed your son. I pushed him and he stumbled in front of a car. I didn't mean to push him; well, I did mean to push him, but just a foolish shove, a prank. I didn't realise there was a car behind us. It all happened so quickly, I couldn't react. The car spun him round awkwardly and he fell backwards, hitting his head on the kerb."

He spoke in precise detail, as if he had relived that moment over and over again, which he had, of course, each time he closed his eyes. Mrs Martin sat quietly listening to him.

"I would give anything to change that one moment in time, Mrs Martin. I can't live with myself. I can't live with the disgrace that my family will suffer, when the truth is revealed. That's why I wanted to kill myself, Mrs Martin. Is that too selfish?"

She waited a moment before answering him, knowing he was hanging on her every word.

"Selfishness is not living as *you* want, but expecting others to live that way too. You should do what you want, John, it has always worked for me."

It was a liberating statement and this time she sounded more like a favourite aunt than a classmate. But, even for an extraordinary conversation such as this, she really had surpassed herself. Mrs Martin seemed to be actually endorsing his suicide. She had heard the rumours about Jonjo from her son; that he was the one all the other kids looked up to at school. She knew his rather impractical attempt to kill himself was the product of an unacceptable failure on his part. It was not a cry for help. He was alone and nobody would have arrived to save him had she not done so with the unplanned visit to the Thompson's house.

"There is no immunity to failure, John," she said as she stood up and took the ashtray outside to empty it. As she passed him in the hallway, she handed it back to him.

"Put it back." She paused. "Exactly where it was, John," she said looking directly into his eyes. She obviously meant the ashtray because life could never be put back to exactly where it was, ever again.

"Shall I tell my mum that you called?" he asked as she stepped out of the front door.

She looked at the twitching curtains. "Yes, John," she answered contemplatively and walked off down the street.

2

Wednesday 20 May 2015 — Beadsman's Cross

Of course, there *were* no ghosts in Woolly Fold Wood. It was no spectre or spirit that caused the greenwood to die and the birdsong to cease so abruptly that hot summer day. Those particular creations of Tonka's vivid imagination were the result of a thousand bedtime stories told to him by his grandad. I know, because I'd heard most of them when I had slept over at his house as a child. No, ghosts and buried treasure were not products of the legend-laden breezes, as Tonka referred to them in a poorly contrived scary voice when the lights had been turned out, but a consequence of the eventful life and creative mind of his grandad, the sagacious veteran of countless adventures, John Joseph Thompson.

With no grandparents of my own, it had become natural to call him Grandad, because that's how Tonka always addressed him and the old man didn't seem to mind. Jonjo, as he was known to his contemporaries, along with a few other nicknames, was always old in my eyes; old enough, it seemed, to have served on a pirate ship and fought alongside Leonidas at Thermopylae. At the age of eight, we didn't know where Thermopylae was and it had never occurred to us that he would have needed to be nearly 3,000 years old to have been there when three hundred Spartans fought valiantly against 300,000 Persians. We should have questioned, too, the fact that none of the three hundred Greek warriors had survived, yet here was Grandad telling us the tale.

We are the product of our experiences, my old teacher Mr Kelly would say, but a good essay needed to be the product of our imagination, too, if we were to get more than six out of ten for our English essay homework. History is often elevated or reduced to a date; 1066 and all that. The Battle of Hastings lasted for less than ten hours and yet the gallantry of one day is aggrandized with the laurels of a year, a year that remains in the memory of the masses forever. The steadfast Norman towers that litter a conquered land remind us of that moment chosen from all years to record the fall of Harold Godwinson and the Anglo-Saxons of which we consider ourselves the descendents.

"History is made each day," taught Mr Kelly, an English teacher who knew the importance of history. "All factual writing and most fiction too is simply the recording of events, authentic or otherwise."

Yes, Mr Kelly, history isn't about the lives of captains and kings, but the ordinary days that make up the mosaic of life. It is less about the ill-conceived declaration of war and more, it seems, about the spontaneous actions of the common man. Godwinson or Harold I is remembered, but the Norman archer who despatched the fatal arrow is not, much like any foot soldier of war.

Each day, it seems, is much like another; the same number of minutes, the same number of hours. The sun rises in the east and sets in the west. But each day is decreed to record something, a moment selected from all millennia to set down a birth, a death, a tragedy or a wondrous event. In everyday life, occasionally, a particular event outside our control dominates proceedings. And, somehow, we find the time to suspend all the normal requirements for that day and allow that event to take precedence. And so it was on Tuesday 19 May 2015, just five days before Jonjo was going to return to his own and very real Thermopylae.

The telephone rang, a fairy got its wings, life's journey took a small detour and the day chosen from all millennia received its own laurel crown.

"Who was that?" I called to my wife, Ludo.

"Old Mr Anderson," she replied.

"Why is he calling us?" I asked about the elderly man, who knew my late mother and used to accompany her to church on Sundays.

"Because we are probably on his 'friends and family' list of people he can call for free," she answered, a little cynically.

She was probably right, I thought. Who else would make it into his top five? The barman at the British Legion, Mrs Griffith, Mrs O'Brien and Father McNally, of course.

"What did he want?" I called, a little too antipathetically, but Ludo had entered the room, taken the newspaper from my hands and sat down opposite me. She wore the expression of a sad puppy.

"Tonka's grandad has died," she said, knowing very well that the news would sadden me and I should receive it without distraction.

I sighed and looked vacantly at the floor, trying to remember one of the times I had spent in his company before it disappeared into the black hole that enslaves all but a few memories.

I immediately knew I should go to the Thompson household. Tonka would be there. He would probably be drowning in a sea of inanities. I couldn't let his grandad begin his last long march to the strains of 'he had a good innings' or something similarly pitiless. So, rather than take the car, I walked to the house where Jonjo had lived with his son and daughter-in-law, on the outskirts of Evestown. The journey gave me time to think.

I suppose I had first met Jonjo when I was about eight years old. He was fifty years older than me and, at that age, he already seemed like a very old man. Now, nearly thirty-five years later, he didn't appear very different. Old is old to a young child.

On reflection, I knew very little about Jonjo. Indeed, to know anything at all, I would first need to separate the fact from the fiction. Obviously he wasn't a pirate and he hadn't fought alongside Leonidas. But he did serve in the war, the Second World War. It was strange that he hadn't talked very much about the war that he did actually fight in but was more enthusiastic about relating his service in the American Civil War or at Agincourt. I recall someone saying that he was a prisoner of war for a long time. Perhaps that's why he didn't talk about it very much, because if he had spent five years as a prisoner of war he couldn't have seen much action. I'm not sure Tonka knew much more than I did. His grandad had been upset when Tonka signed up for the army but was equally proud when he was accepted into the SAS.

What do we know about our grandparents? Indeed, how much do we know about our parents? When they pass that midmost point of their life, that time when an appetite for knowledge and thirst for intelligence is supplanted by a more worthy desire for wisdom, they become lost to the next generation. We have little knowledge of their lustier youth, except what their merry and disingenuous contemporaries might have us believe. In our immaturity we see nothing of the true man and only a faint recollection of their bold endeavours. So, if we know so little of our fathers, in truth we know nothing at all about our grandfathers. For, by the time we begin to search for the roots of our own existence, it is too late and, in just two generations, our previous self is lost to us.

Yes, we are the sum of our experiences. And, the earlier these appear in our development, the more indelibly they are imprinted on our character; but the more obscure, the more difficult for future generations to recognise. This was obviously true of Tonka. Even though he had followed his grandad into the service of his queen and country, the very world that provided such similarity had produced two quite different circumstances to prompt such an act and two different worlds in which to fulfil that decision. And yet, if we are disposed towards it, we have a greater opportunity to know our grandparents than our parents did, because everyone is living longer now and we have the aid of photographs. Times are different. How was it for Grandad, born into the world of the 1920s? They were harder times and I assume that generation was therefore made more resilient to hardship.

I arrived outside Grandad's house to find the front door ajar and mentally berated myself for not using the time more wisely. I hadn't considered what I was going to say to Tonka. His grandad would have known what to say. Grandad would have taken him away, far away from the sadness of bereavement, to a land of adventure and wild surmise. The stories he enjoyed telling the most, probably because Tonka and I never tired of them, were the tales of his pirate days. The battles between the Jolly Roger and the enemy ships would begin with cannon fire and then, led by his captain, the Crimson Pirate Axe Egan, Grandad would commence hand-to-hand fighting, his sabre clashing with the hook and sword of Blackbeard. The Crimson Pirate, aided by Grandad, always won of course, before speeding off to the remote desert island where they would bury their treasure.

"X marks the spot," Grandad would say as he drew maps of imaginary islands surrounded by blue ocean.

"Hello, Jack," Tonka said as he wrapped his muscular arms about me. "I just phoned Ludo and she said you were on your way. Thanks for coming."

I could see he regretted adding the final part of his greeting. He knew I would be there with him as soon as I heard the news. The relationship we shared was greater than that of any ordinary friendship. Neither of us had brothers or sisters, nor did we have cousins, so we were as close as family. As boys we had stayed over at each other's houses, although mainly at his, with Grandad as a very willing and unpaid childminder in the early years.

In Grandad's day, it was not uncommon for families to have ten or even twelve children, but not the Thompsons. Grandad had only two children, his daughter, Vera and Tonka's father, Joe. When Vera died of cancer, Joe effectively became an only child and then he and his wife, Ann, had only one child themselves— Mark John Thompson, affectionately known as Tonka from the age of six, when he managed to break an 'unbreakable' Tonka toy. He never did know his own strength. But physical strength is of little use when someone loses a close friend. And that was the situation Tonka found himself in, because Grandad was a close friend and had been since he was born. Indeed, it was Grandad's military career that had inspired Tonka to join up shortly after he left school. Tonka told me once that his dad had wanted to name him Andrew, but Grandad had objected to it and, eventually, Joe conceded to his father's wishes. It was his grandad who had first given Tonka his adopted name, after seeing a TV advertisement for the unbreakable toy.

"How old was he?" I asked, as I had never thought about it before. When you're young, old is old and Grandad was always old.

"He was ninety-four a couple of months ago," Tonka replied.

"He's up there with Ivy and his daughter, Vera, now," said Tonka's mum as she placed a tray of tea and biscuits on the table. It was impossible to have a cup of tea without a biscuit in Tonka's house, or rather, his parents' house.

"Hello, Son," Tonka's dad said to me as he hobbled into the room, saying he thought he'd heard the kettle boiling.

"Sorry to hear of your loss, Mr Thompson," I said, conscious of the lack of originality in my condolences.

"He had a good innings," Joe replied, predictably.

"What's wrong with your foot?" I asked, noticing that he was limping heavily.

"I'm going under the surgeon's knife next week," he answered, adding with a grimace, "bunion."

"He's been waiting for months for this operation," Ann pointed out. "Now this has come along."

"Don't worry, Mum. It will be alright," Tonka assured her. "We can arrange the funeral around Dad's operation. I'll take care of it."

When Tonka said he would take care of something, you could rely on it happening, so his mother didn't question him further, but merely encouraged him to speak to Father McNally about it because she knew her father-in-law would want a full requiem mass.

"How's your job, Son?" Joe asked me as he lifted his sore foot up onto a dining chair that had been strategically placed close to his armchair. Nobody sat in that armchair, only Joe. Not even Grandad had sat there. It was a statement of respect for the man of the house.

I knew what he meant by his question. He wanted to know if my job was secure, because when he was younger job security was paramount for the working man.

"Fine," I said and Tonka gave me a glance. I didn't feel the moment was right to unload my current employment problems onto the Thompson family at their time of grief. The magazine I had been working on had just ceased publication and I was relying on freelance assignments for an income. It had been regular work but all fairly mundane.

Tonka, too, had been relying on temporary office work since leaving the SAS. He had received offers of permanent employment from two of the agencies but wasn't sure what he wanted to do with his life. He had avoided the lure of some highly paid security work in the Middle East and Africa, mainly under the influence of his girlfriend, Gabriella.

Temporary jobs meant he could work almost when he wanted to and so he arranged for some time off as soon as Grandad was found in his bed, peacefully asleep forever. He knew there would be a lot of arrangements to be made and his dad was immobile and his mum had never learnt to drive. Tonka was pleased to have the responsibility anyway. He wanted to do this last good deed for Grandad.

"I need to pick the death certificate up in the morning, Jack," Tonka said. "Then go to the undertakers to make the arrangements."

He didn't ask for company but I offered it anyway.

"Make sure you get Father McNally for the service," his mother instructed him. "He wouldn't want a stranger putting him into the ground."

Tonka nodded to assure her he would look after everything.

"He'll want 'Thine be the Glory' and 'Soul of my Saviour'," she added and her suggestion received no objections from Joe.

"Yes, Mum. And Jack can do a reading and I'll say a few words." He said it as if he had already told her this several times before.

His father remained silent. As long as Ann was happy he was fine. She'd become like a daughter to Grandad after he lost Vera and Ivy.

"You're not writing anything down," she added as a postscript.

"God gave me a memory, Mother."

"Just wait 'til you get older," she said. "'Cause, he takes it away again." She regretted speaking ill of the Almighty and made the sign of the cross.

The room went silent for a few moments as we each reflected on our memories of John Joseph Thompson.

"Have you had many visitors?" I asked, remembering that the front door was ajar.

"Popping in and out," replied Joe. "Word gets out quickly around here."

"He was hardly cold before Mrs Griffiths knocked at the door," said Ann and thought about making another sign of the cross. "And Father McNally came immediately to administer the last rites, except he was dead already, so he couldn't receive the holy sacrament."

Silence returned to the room for a moment.

"Mrs Griffiths said the priest can give the deceased a special blessing from the Pope. A plenary indulgence, she said, but I don't know if he did. Do you think I should ask?"

"Father McNally won't mind you asking, Mum," replied Tonka sympathetically.

"It's just that I don't know if I'm supposed to know these things. You know, as a Catholic."

"Mum," Joe finally said after a few moments and we all thought he knew the answer. But he didn't, he just wanted to change the subject. "Mum is borrowing a wheelchair from Tom Anderson and taking me down the British Legion club tonight." He paused, looking at Tonka and me. "If you should fancy joining us."

"Of course," I replied, although I was fairly sure Ludo wouldn't be able to attend, unless she could arrange a babysitter for Giacomo and Elissa.

"Extreme Unction, it used to be called," said Ann.

"What did?" asked Joe.

"The last rites. When we were kids; when it was all in Latin. It was called Extreme Unction."

"Extreme Unction isn't Latin," said Joe, confidently.

"I know it isn't," said Ann, getting a little agitated. "Mrs Griffiths said that, in the old days, you couldn't make a deathbed confession; the church didn't accept it. You had to die in a state of grace."

"That was hundreds of years ago," insisted Joe. "They've changed their mind now, though. Can't make it too difficult or we'd have nobody in the church. Anyway, Dad couldn't have made a confession, he died in his sleep. Peacefully in his sleep, the doctor said."

"What would Grandad have to confess anyway, Mum?" said Tonka, who had noticed her agitation. "Mrs Griffiths talks a lot of nonsense at times. Grandad didn't need to make a confession and he wouldn't need a plenary indulgence either. He served his country dutifully, he was a good man. What could he possibly have had to confess?"

"He was a tough old dog was your grandad, but a bit of a softie," replied Ann as she stood to pick up the tray of empty cups. "I can't imagine he killed anyone in the war."

"Dad was a survivor," offered Joe, lamenting his passing. "The way he survived five years in a German prisoner-of-war camp was proof of that, and that long walk. Walking around Poland in the middle of winter for four months. It made him capable of facing anything life threw at him, like the loss of our Vera. It nearly killed me and it certainly killed my mother," he added, looking at Tonka. "But you just couldn't knock him down."

"Well, he got it from his own father," added Ann as she made her way back to the kitchen. "He fought in the First World War; came back, unlike a lot of 'em. Then he got over the influenza that swept the country just after that. Made of stern stuff, are the Thompsons. I mean, look at our Tonka there. Strong as an ox."

After a brief discussion it was agreed that I would join the Thompsons at the Legion and Gabriella would enjoy a girls' night in with Ludo. These decisions were all made without consulting the two ladies concerned but neither would want to interfere with any arrangements to toast Grandad.

~~~~~

That evening, Gabriella arrived at our house just as I was leaving and told me not to worry about how late I arrived home. Beadsman's Cross, where Ludo and I lived with our two children, was about one mile from Tonka and Gabriella's house on the outskirts of Evestown. Their house was my old family home, which they had bought when my mother died a couple of years ago.

I wasn't sure whether Tonka and Gabriella wanted to have children. It wasn't something we discussed. There was no talk of marriage, either, although that didn't necessarily mean they wouldn't have children. Of course, I always knew they liked children, not just because of the way they were with Giacomo and Elissa but, when you have kids of your own, you innately know if other couples like them too.

Then, one day just over a month ago, when the two of us were having a beer at the local pub, Tonka had said they wanted to have children, but didn't want an only child like him. The premature death of his Aunt Vera meant the last three generations of Thompsons had effectively been only children. Their wish to have children together was, of course, good news, except Tonka was the same age as me, forty-three, and Gabriella was two years older. At that age, to have one child would be difficult, but to have two was extremely unlikely. I sensed the word 'together' resonating in Tonka's head as soon as it was spoken. Tonka already enjoyed a special relationship with his stepson Bodgan, having been singularly responsible for reuniting him with his mother Gabriella only five years ago. Gabriella had been raped as a teenager in her homeland of Romania and became separated from her son under the brutal Ceausescu regime. Encouraged to escape to Britain by her parents, she didn't see him, or know where he was for over twenty years. Now, back in the UK, my best friend was determined to treat Bodgan like his own son but that relationship couldn't replace the desire, in his own heart to share a child with Gabriella.

The delicate subject had not been mentioned since that conversation in the pub and I didn't feel comfortable asking whether he was making any progress with the plan. I knew he would tell me when he was ready. Not surprisingly, he didn't raise the matter at the club that evening. Instead we reminisced about Grandad and discussed more mundane issues such as our careers. Freelance reporting was paying quite well, but it lacked any purpose or direction and it was hardly an upward step in my career development.

I confessed to Tonka that I mostly enjoyed investigative journalism and felt there was a gap in the market that some enterprising person might consider filling. Both newspapers and TV were keen on articles exposing criminal activities but didn't have the resources for long-term projects that were often a complete waste of their reporters' time.

"Surely such projects would be just as unprofitable for any news agency that tried to fill the gap?" suggested Tonka.

The key, I told him, was to be able to identify the worthwhile projects and dispense with any others before any extensive investment in time and money was made. One hour and a few drinks later, I found myself suggesting that between my journalism acumen and his experience in the SAS, we could be the perfect partnership to fill that gap.

"Be honest, Jack," he asked, "you're really just seeking a bit of muscle in case an investigation turns nasty, aren't you?"

I assured him that this was not the case. "Christ, Tonka, everyone knows you're much smarter than me. Cleverer, more intelligent and able. Anyway, I'm not suggesting we take on the Mafia."

"Good," he replied, "because I'm sure your brother-in-law, Sebastiano, is a member of that organisation."

My proposal generated considerable discussion that evening. I reminded him about the success we had enjoyed solving the mystery of Woolly Fold Wood and tracing my ancestors back in Ireland.

"We have a good track record," I told him. "And, anyway, if I just needed some muscle I would have to offer the job to my family first and approach Sebastiano."

In the end, nothing was resolved and both of us realised such a matter should not be something we agreed after six pints of beer. More importantly, we were not devoting enough of our time to consoling his parents, although they seemed to have sufficient company with neighbours and parishioners from the local church.

As I clambered into a taxi outside the Legion that night, Tonka told me he had been planning to accompany his grandad to an anniversary service at Boulogne in four days' time. I could tell he was quite upset as I left. It may have been that he wouldn't be spending Sunday with Grandad as planned, but the large quantity of alcohol we had consumed certainly added to his melancholy.

It was Ludo who first suggested that I should accompany Tonka to the event in Boulogne. I didn't pay too much attention, nor did I give it much consideration. Instead I dismissed the idea because I had never served in the armed forces, so probably wouldn't be allowed or entitled to attend. Also I wasn't a relative of someone who had fought at the Battle of Boulogne, which was what the event was commemorating. But Ludo must have mentioned the idea to Gabriella because when I met Tonka the following day the plans were already taking shape in his mind.

3

Thursday 2 May 1940 — Wellington Barracks, London

The need to squint his eyes suggested to Jonjo that the sergeant needed glasses. As he stood to attention in the parade ground of Wellington Barracks, trying to remain expressionless, he remembered Ivy wearing glasses with a pink plaster patch over one eye for most of their final year at primary school. He assumed that Sergeant Donovan tried to do without them for practical reasons, rather than appearance. Like football, Jonjo guessed, glasses must be a disadvantage in combat situations. He desperately wanted to tell the sergeant that Ivy had been soon able to dispense with her spectacles but he was worried about the consequences of such an unsolicited comment. Being deterred from giving sensible advice was one of the many questionable contradictions that Jonjo found in the army. He immediately regretted using the word 'army', even in his thoughts, let alone saying it. He had been told by Sergeant Donovan many times that he was not in the army, he was in the Irish Guards and he was not a private, but a guardsman. And Jonjo was lucky to be one, too, that's what the sergeant had said.

Jonjo had been encouraged to speak up in class at school. Such audacious behaviour was frowned upon in the Guards. And it wasn't for a guardsman to give a sergeant advice, even if it was well meant and could improve the long-term eyesight of the sergeant concerned.

Jonjo was bemused by the fact that individuals with a questioning or inquisitive mind were less likely to succeed in the Army. But that much had been made clear to him. Acquiescence, compliance and, strangely, submissiveness were all qualities that Sergeant Donovan ranked highly in his recruits. Conversely, a curious mind caused him to squint his eyes, even though his face was only inches from that of the individual he was talking to. On at least two such occasions, that individual had been John Joseph Thompson and that was two occasions too many. The sergeant had been very surprised that Jonjo had made the same mistake twice, as few people did with Donovan. As he stood to attention, long after all his colleagues had returned to barracks, a distant memory returned to Jonjo. He visualised himself with Mrs Martin sitting in his front room on that strange day. Looking back now, he could see she was a very attractive woman, even if she was old enough to be his mother. And she was so different from any other woman of her generation he knew, incredibly unpredictable.

She sat opposite him, with her legs crossed and the pencil line in her stocking showing below her dress. It was like it had happened yesterday. She was stubbing out her cigarette and telling him that she thought one error of judgement could be forgiven, but anyone making the same mistake twice deserved anything that befell them. The wrath of Sergeant Donovan is what befell Jonjo and now it was raining.

The only saving grace was that standing to attention in the pouring rain when everyone else was back in barracks drinking hot tea was less of a punishment to Jonjo Thompson than it would be to most new recruits. His head was so full of thoughts that he had no difficulty occupying himself. Sergeant Donovan would have preferred him to reflect on his stupidity and misplaced forthrightness but Jonjo probably wouldn't make the same mistake a third time anyway.

Jonjo was less concerned with Sergeant Donovan than he was about the war and, in particular, when he might see some action in that war. When he signed up, legislation prevented anyone under twenty years old from serving abroad. So he assumed that once he reached the required age he would be despatched on the next available ship to France or some other foreign country requiring assistance in defending their borders against the advancing German army.

The reality turned out to be considerably different and the priority appeared to be how to mount king's guard in St James's Park. The sergeant had told him that it took forty-five minutes to complete the changing of the guard at Buckingham Palace and it normally took forty-five hours to learn how to do it. In his opinion, he believed it would take Jonjo forty-five years, although he didn't express that thought with quite such eloquence. Persuasiveness, yes, but not eloquence; eloquence was for officers; persuasiveness was his remit.

His suggestion about considering spectacles had been Jonjo's second error of judgement in his relationship with Sergeant Donovan. It was his eagerness to enter the fray that had caused Jonjo's first run-in with him.

For his part, Jonjo merely wanted to ensure that the sergeant knew he was over twenty years old and was ready for front line duty.

"That," Donovan had responded, "is a matter of opinion." And it seemed guardsmen were not allowed opinions. Donovan had made it clear to the new recruit that it was ability, not age, that would earn promotion to the front line.

Like Churchill, Jonjo sensed a noticeable lack of urgency in the country's response to the overtures of a manic Fuehrer. This was apparent when he first voiced his desire to volunteer and the apathy continued after he joined. On many different levels, the world was divided in 1940. There was, of course, the conflict between the fascist power of the German-Italian axis and the rest of Europe. But there were other divisions of less consequence and, on a more domestic level, there was also discord between truculent mothers of a patriotic persuasion who could see no reason for their sons not to enlist at the earliest opportunity and those of a contrasting view. The latter group consisted not of conscientious objectors as the zealots declared, but those whose maternal instinct was to defer or prolong the inevitable farewell to their beloved sons for as long as possible.

And, in Jonjo's view, the government in its noble desire to maintain calm had itself shared the inertia of the second group. Jonjo had been ready to volunteer before the hostilities began, but his mother insisted he waited. Her strategy succeeded, at least temporarily, because when conscription began only single men aged between twenty and twenty-two years were called up.

"Never you mind," Mrs Thompson insisted. "Mr Chamberlain knows what he's doing."

Like so many others, Jonjo did not share her opinion in this respect and, when the Norwegian campaign fared badly, he decided to volunteer.

Even then, Mrs Thompson's view, or at least the one expressed to her son, was that we should avoid doing anything simply because we can. What, thought Jonjo, like treading on an ant or pushing your friend on the way to school?

"I'm doing it because I should, not because I can," he replied.

She only acceded to his wishes because, in his doubtful wisdom, Mr Chamberlain had declared that nobody would serve abroad until the age of twenty. That would at least get Jonjo to his next birthday in March.

And so young Jonjo volunteered and joined the Irish Guards. His mother cursed her husband's Irish grandmother for her complicity in this act, but his ancestry was sufficient to open the door and his training began. And, much to his annoyance, the training continued and continued, in spite of the growing Nazi threat. So, when his twentieth birthday finally arrived, Jonjo expected to be sent out on the next ship but this momentous day was met with no such urgency.

Indeed, it was a full month after Jonjo had taken it upon himself to tell the sergeant that he was now twenty before anything happened and they were told to prepare to leave Wellington Barracks in London. He was informed by his new acquaintances, with some certainty, that they would shortly be joining the 1st Battalion in Norway. But, in the days that followed, he realised that gossip and rumour were the favourite pastimes of the British Tommy. The following morning, the 2nd Battalion were shipped out to somewhere called Old Dean Camp, but the relocation failed to signal a call to action. Jonjo was moving to Surrey rather than France. And any thoughts of combat were completely dismissed when large numbers of the men were granted leave for Whitsun and many of those from Ireland decided to return home for the break. Jonjo had certainly not expected to get holidays in the army, not with a war to fight. The departure of many of his colleagues did not dishearten Jonjo for, in truth, he had made very few new acquaintances.

Following his experience at school, Jonjo had expected the army to provide him with many new and greater friendships than he had known in his childhood, but it failed to be so. At school, John Joseph Thompson was an intelligent, popular and well-read young man. When teams were selected for street games or football, Jonjo was always the first to be chosen by his classmates.

His popularity with his peers was replicated by his elders. His parents had brought him up to be respectful to neighbours and he often ran errands for the older residents of the terraced street where he lived. He would collect food for old Mrs Podolski's cats at the local pet shop and often popped round to the corner store if somebody had ran out of tea or sugar. He was a studious boy, to an extent that set him apart from his contemporaries. But now, since joining the army, he suddenly lost the elevated status he had enjoyed as a boy. Whether it was this or simply the harrowing experience of war, Jonjo never engaged with his fellow Irish Guards as he had done with his school friends.

The reality of war and its objective or purpose drove him to take his responsibilities in an adult and determined manner. His character was one created by the books he had read, not by any actual experiences. He lived in a world of literature and poetry. His companions in the Guards were, in the main, less well read and, as books were his great love, he had less in common with them. He convinced himself that his colleagues considered him well off or from a good background, by which they meant wealthy. Nothing could be further from the truth, for he lived in a tiny terraced house with an outside toilet and no garden. But he had no inclination to tell them the truth. His knowledge of good writers and poets gave him a larger vocabulary than most foot soldiers and, from this, others concluded that he must have been privately educated, which was absurd. And so, except for a few individuals, he became isolated from the other men, which simply drove him deeper into books and the cycle of separation burgeoned. So, when many of the guardsmen were sent home for Whitsun, he didn't feel especially lonely because he had not really made any new friends.

For those left behind, training continued as normal, but in different surroundings. It was no coincidence that they would be performing their first night exercises in the unfamiliar landscape of the Surrey countryside. Jonjo missed that clue. So far he hadn't even loaded a live round of ammunition, so he didn't anticipate this being his final rehearsal for the real thing.

He tried to sleep during the day but the experience was alien to him. So, by the time they were six hours into the night exercise, weariness and exhaustion began to overtake him and he was glad to hear the sound of the sergeant's whistle. Jonjo was almost asleep as they marched back to barracks but he was woken from his standing stupor by a screaming guardsman as they marched past the orderly room. The man ran from the wooden building shouting at everyone to pack up and prepare to move out. The sudden burst of activity overpowered his tiredness and he gathered his gear together. The next hour was filled with even more rumours than usual. German parachutists had landed in Kent, German bombers were over the channel and, although none of these were true, it was clear that training was over.

Without a moment's rest after the night manoeuvres, the battalion left Surrey and moved off towards Kent and, when they finally set up camp, Jonjo couldn't believe where he was. He had spent so many summers on the Beltring Hop Farm near Paddock Wood, where he had picked hops with his parents, it felt incredible to be back there now in such altered circumstances. It was more than twenty-four hours since he had last slept and when he finally laid his head down in a tent set among the oast houses and wooden sheds of the hop farm, his mind was too active to rest. Apparently there was no truth in the many rumours that had circulated during the day, but these had now been replaced by another one. And the number and diversity of the purveyors of this particular rumour suggested it was true.

In the early hours of the morning, having fallen into a brief but deep sleep, Jonjo was awakened by the call to parade. He had to think about where he was. It took a few moments to realise he was no longer in Wellington Barracks or Old Dean Camp. It was as if he had fallen asleep on holiday with his parents at the hop farm and woken years later as a man. He recognised the smell and the faint sounds of the countryside over the noise of hundreds of soldiers rousing themselves from their beds. Orders had been received overnight and these were about to be communicated to the men, most of whom had slept for less than two hours. A lieutenant handed a document to a sergeant who read it aloud to the gathered troops, who were now fully dressed and paraded in the dawning light.

"Instructions received from the War Office to the Brigade Commander. You will command a composite battalion of the brigade; this battalion will embark at Dover for Holland tomorrow afternoon." He paused, looking at his watch, before correcting himself. "Or, rather, this afternoon."

"All that time we've waited for the bloody call to arms," mumbled the guardsman next to Jonjo as they were dismissed. "And half the buggers have pissed off back to Ireland."

It was true, thought Jonjo. Many of the older soldiers were cynical critics of their officers but, on this occasion, it appeared to be warranted. A depleted force, kept awake for thirty-six hours and with just one practice session with live ammunition, were being marched towards the railway station and the trains that would take them off to Dover. There they would travel to mainland Europe, which could, as far as anyone knew, be occupied by vast numbers of German troops with air support. Jonjo had spent much of his youth around men who had served in the Great War. Not many of them believed there was anything great about it. Millions had died, even more died of influenza soon after the war and, of those who survived, there was little reason for cheer. So it was not surprising that they turned their resentment on their officers. Most thought they could have done a better job. Many considered the war ill-conceived but kept their counsel or it might seem their colleagues had died in vain. So it was not unexpected to see the residue of doubt, distrust and sarcasm that so many of Jonjo's contemporaries had been brought up with. The more sophisticated training methods that Jonjo experienced changed the hearts of many in this respect. The Irish Guards, like the other guards regiments, were seen as the elite; they had a reputation to live up to and there was pride in the ranks. The peer pressure of the more enthusiastic young men, who were proud to wear the uniform, eventually overwhelmed the pessimism and misanthropy of the sceptics. And, by the time they reached this point of their training, comments like the one mumbled in the ranks on parade were infrequent and largely scorned by the men. In the end, it was just a question of numbers. By design or good fortune the young enthusiasts outnumbered the older cynics and, in the end, they found their voice and overpowered the disparagement that threatened to undermine their purpose. Nobody wanted to be part of something considered futile or unworthy. This was a different war to the one fought by their fathers. The intention and rationale of this war was more transparent, more palpable. It wasn't founded on the nationalistic fervour of the last war but on the sincere belief in a right and just cause.

It was not until he was sitting on the train, half asleep and half awake, that fear began to creep into Jonjo's mind. There had been no time for it previously, but the possibility of death crept closer to him until it rested on his shoulders like a yoke. He tried to ignore it and convinced himself that it was not possible to have courage without fear. If someone performed a brave act but felt no fear, then how could it be courage? Courage is only possible when there is something to lose. Jonjo was twenty years old and had been born two years after the Great War ended. He had witnessed the injuries of war, as they lingered and littered his childhood with agonising memories of how such afflictions might have been suffered. But death was an infrequent visitor in such times and, even then, apart from young Andrew Martin, it had appeared only on the periphery of his life. Death's sting had yet to be felt and yet it seemed so close to him now, sitting in the railway carriage as it trudged slowly towards the port.

The short train journey to Dover should have presented an opportunity to sleep but the guardsmen sitting next to him had managed to buy a newspaper as they moved through the station to the train. Neville Chamberlain had resigned and Lord Halifax had rejected the office of prime minister. Overnight Winston

Churchill had taken up the post and was already, it seemed, directing the war. The men took no convincing that it was his appointment that had summoned them into action so suddenly after so many had been given leave for Whitsun. In truth, it was no more than poor communication that had caused the telegram from the War Office suspending all leave to arrive too late to prevent the men leaving the camp.

Overnight on 10 May the Government of the Netherlands requested urgent assistance from the British Government. German forces had landed on the coast near The Hague and large numbers of parachutists had been seen in the surrounding area. The only available troops were the 2nd Battalion of the Irish Guards and many of them had already been given leave.

Two battalions of the Irish and Welsh Guards were cobbled together in the absence of those sent home on Whitsun leave and given the code name Harpoon Force by the War Office. According to common rumour, the men were being sent to rescue the Queen of the Belgians.

In Dover Harbour stood two steamers, whose captains were anxious to leave in order to arrive at the Hook of Holland before dawn. The Germans were bombing Belgian and Dutch ports and they could easily be waiting for them. So an arrival in darkness was preferable if casualties were to be minimised.

It was a rough sea crossing and the men spent a miserable night being sick or speculating about the mission. That speculation grew when an officer told them that they had been honoured with a code name. What could Harpoon Force mean, they wondered. There had been talk of extending the British Expeditionary Force and so it was presumed by many that they might be making their way to the Maginot Line to support the French and Belgians.

A grey dawn broke on one side of the SS *Canterbury* and the men stirred from their restless slumber. As their families at home slept soundly in their beds on that Whitsunday night, the troops sighted the Dutch coastline, not knowing whether the Germans occupied the port or not. A cheer went up as one of their number saw a British destroyer in the harbour and marines standing on the quay. For Jonjo and many of the others who were still being seasick it was joy enough to have reached dry land. As they unloaded the stores and disembarked, a single German bomber appeared from the southeast, despatched its bombs randomly and left. Many feared it to be a foreshadowing of what was to follow.

When the men finally paraded on the quay, Jonjo was able to examine the landscape. The Hook of Holland turned out to be a small port set on a flat terrain that spread for miles. If the Germans did decide to bomb this place, there was nowhere to take cover, apart from the ditches that ran alongside the narrow country roads, and the brigade would be sitting ducks. Jonjo watched the single German bomber disappear into the distant sky but his young mind could not conjure up what he was about to witness over the next forty-eight hours.

Anyone with a rifle helped form a perimeter around the quay and there the guardsmen stood for two hours waiting for a German attack. In the distance the dawning grey sky was turned red. Rotterdam, they were told, was burning. As the morning mist cleared, the little village they had travelled so far to defend appeared around them. Small streets of houses and shops, just like any they would find at home, awoke to an unwelcomed day and among the buildings a sign stood out above the sparse rooftops identifying the Hotel Amerika. Between the village and an unseen but obviously advancing German army stood Jonjo and six hundred and fifty fellow Irish and Welsh guardsmen. Only one of them wondered about the strange spelling of America. Around noon, a fleet of black cars with motorcycle outriders drew up and, after a discussion with a sergeant, it passed along the road to the quay. Anti-aircraft guns were erected and the men took up positions in ditches and anywhere else that provided some protection. There they remained, a few feet apart from each other, looking into the distance across the unbroken plain ahead of them. Six hours after the previous cars had passed the checkpoint, another convoy of cars arrived, following the same route.

As nightfall approached, the rumbling sound of distant aircraft could be heard in the darkness above them. One of the more experienced men recognised it as the sound of German bombers. The relative silence that accompanied the day suddenly changed as the groan of German aircraft engines grew louder, a prelude to the sound of machine-gun fire and exploding bombs that produced a cacophony of noise so loud that it drowned out the screams of the dying and injured. Jonjo took cover in a ditch close to an anti-aircraft gun position manned by a lance sergeant he recognised. What followed was, for most, their first experience of this kind. Some guardsmen froze in the face of death, but not many. Others saw it as an opportunity to display supreme heroism. Most simply followed to the letter everything they had been taught in their training at Wellington Barracks and Camberley. They didn't think of death, for there was little time for thinking at all, other than to defend your life and the lives of those around you. This was a time to do, not think, and the men did it to their best ability. There was no cover for the large anti-aircraft gun alongside Jonjo and it soon became a target set against the flat terrain. The lance sergeant manning the gun post next to Jonjo fired an unremitting stream of shells into the sky, aiming at a sound rather than anything he could see. But it was all to no avail. Jonjo was suddenly conscious that the monotonous banging sound next to him had stopped. It took a few seconds to realise that the anti-tank gun had fallen silent and the lance sergeant was slumped backwards, badly wounded by machine-gun fire from the air. He pulled the man down on the floor and called for the medics. He was still trying to remember how the gun worked when a more experienced soldier pushed him out of the way and began firing shells into the sky. Scenes of bravery were all around him. A lance corporal manning another such gun replaced it six times after the tripod was hit by successive shells. He just kept standing it upright again and continued firing until, on the seventh occasion, the gun itself was hit and destroyed. What happened to the lance corporal was difficult to see through the smoke but nobody left their post. As futile as it seemed, the men of the Irish and Welsh Guards continued firing their rifles through the smoke at the invisible aircraft until, eventually, the noise of the machine guns stopped and the time between the sound of bombs exploding increased and was eventually replaced by the drone of aircraft engines departing. Only then did Jonjo become aware of the groaning, crying and screaming that had continued throughout, unheard, silenced by the deafening sounds of war.

It was difficult to assess the damage inflicted on the village as smoke and dust filled the air and everyone was too busy to consider structural devastation, such was the injury and death that surrounded them.

Jonjo helped a medical sergeant and several orderlies as they attended to the wounded, carrying them back to the destroyer that still waited in the harbour. Twenty-three wounded and seven bodies were taken on board. It was a miracle there weren't more because there had been nowhere to shelter from the relentless attack. There was nowhere to rest either and rumours continued to spread among the men. Some said that the Harpoon Force would continue to The Hague, others said that Rotterdam was in flames, and a guardsman who shared a cigarette with Jonjo said he had seen the Queen of the Belgians and her entourage go onto one of the destroyers and she was now on her way to Blighty.

Another night air raid was expected but the experienced soldiers said it wouldn't come until daylight. Why would Jerry drop bombs in the dark when they had such a clear target to aim at? They were right and, after the men had eaten some breakfast at around half past nine, even more aircraft arrived from the eastern sky, heavily laden with bombs. Having lost all the anti-aircraft guns, defences were weakened and, to a great extent, the enemy aircraft could deliver their bombs and machine-gun fire with greater accuracy, causing severe damage and loss of life. Four more guardsmen died and many were injured, along with countless civilians. For two hours after the raid, men, women and children walked or ran around the village and quay, calling out for loved ones who they feared lost or injured. It was difficult to describe such a scene as anything but chaotic and yet as hundreds, if not thousands, were added to their number as refugees poured into the village from Rotterdam, there was a strange calmness. The rumours of the city's destruction were true and the horror that Jonjo witnessed was even worse than his first twenty-four hours in the Netherlands. The column of bedraggled and wounded people approached from the southeast, pushing prams and wheel carts containing their belongings and seriously wounded relatives who couldn't walk. In some cases, the prams contained the bodies of dead children that parents could not bear to leave behind and were now being carried from the war-torn city towards the hope of freedom.

The village, or what could be seen of it through the dust, was largely rubble and debris, although many buildings remained intact. The Hotel Amerika and the house next to it had disappeared. And, as the German aircraft left, presumably to rearm, the destroyer HMS *Malcolm* put into the harbour and, to the relief of everyone, the evacuation began.

On the dockside, as the medics treated the injured, the chaplain was comforting the bereaved families. As Jonjo passed him, carrying a fallen colleague on a stretcher, he paused, wondering which of the two groups to leave him with. The chaplain spoke of a confused kaleidoscope of horrors. It expressed, greater than anything Jonjo could conceive, the full hideousness of events. And yet, it was difficult to imagine that any spiritual succour was delivered that Whitsun. Humanity, mercy and clemency were set aside by mankind, buried under the rubble.

There was no equipment or large guns to be loaded onto the ship for the return journey as everything had been destroyed, such was the effectiveness of the air raid. The stores had been hit, as had the reserve ammunition. On the dock, trucks were on fire and wireless instruments lay destroyed alongside the injured and dying.

When everyone else had boarded the ships, the Irish Guards were called forward in half-platoon units. As they marched down the jetty to the waiting ships, it was as if they were parading in the forecourt of Buckingham Palace and there were men aboard HMS *Malcolm* and HMS *Whitshed* who wept at the sight. Once aboard, Jonjo slumped next to a naval officer working at a makeshift desk. It was his duty to record events, as best he could. '*It was deliberate and calculated murder,*' he wrote. '*By no stretch of imagination could the pitiful crowd have been mistaken for armed troops.*'

Jonjo wished he, too, could write down his thoughts but he was too exhausted and his eyes shut on a day he would wish to forget.

They embarked in Dover forty-eight hours after they had left and, as they arrived, Welsh guardsmen flanked the roadside and cheered loudly.

When Jonjo collapsed onto his bed back at Old Dean Camp it was difficult not to imagine that this had all been an appalling, yet realistic, nightmare. He shook with relief that it was over and he had returned physically unharmed. But in six days' time, that nightmare was to begin all over again.

4

Thursday 21 May 2015 — Evestown

When I met him at the funeral directors the following morning, I had almost forgotten about Tonka's plan to visit France. It was shortly after nine o'clock and he had already collected the death certificate from the hospital and was waiting patiently outside the undertaker's office for me to arrive. The reception area contained four comfortable seats and a small coffee table and we were led from there into a room, similarly understated and minimally furnished in cream and teak. The undertaker examined his diary. Reassuringly, it was a traditional desk diary rather than a computer. The elderly and conservatively dressed man removed the top from his fountain pen and proposed that the funeral should take place the following Tuesday. This was much sooner than either of us had expected and I got the impression that there was a vacant slot to fill. Quite how such a vacancy might come about distracted my attention for a few moments. It was difficult to imagine that there had been a cancellation.

While I was musing over this possibility, Tonka was objecting to the man's suggestion, saying that his father was undergoing an operation on his foot on that day and would probably not be released from hospital until next Friday at the earliest. The man tried to hide his disappointment at the delay and a lost opportunity to fill the vacant slot, but flicked meditatively through the pages of the diary. As he turned each page he murmured dejectedly and shook his head. There appeared to be no availability for at least another week and he eventually arrived at a blank page. He smiled, looked up and said there were quite a few options for dates more than ten days ahead. Tonka nodded in agreement and suggested they made a telephone call to Father McNally. The undertaker duly obliged and Tonka got his own way. It was agreed to lay Grandad to rest in two weeks' time on Thursday 4 June at Evestown Cemetery after a requiem mass at St Vincent's Church.

While I was thinking about how the delay would enable Joe to recover from his operation, Tonka was thinking about other arrangements that the deferment might accommodate. And, as we drove back to his house, his next question baffled me.

"Are you sure you can spare the time?" my best friend asked incongruously and I couldn't think what he could be referring to. At first, I thought he was suggesting that I might consider missing the funeral, but I knew he couldn't mean that. The last detailed conversation I remember having with him was about a business proposition that provided freelance investigative journalism services to the press. However, before I could seek clarification, he began delivering his plan for the trip to Boulogne.

"We can travel over on Saturday, then return home on Monday morning and be back in time to take Dad to the hospital the next day. I'm not sure whether there are any events or functions after the service on Sunday, so we could come back straight afterwards if you prefer to do that. But we need to book tickets for the Channel Tunnel car train in advance, so we just need to decide what days we want to travel."

As he rattled off his suggested itinerary, I sat wondering whether there were any reasons why I could not agree. I didn't mind the fact that he assumed I had no objections to his plans. Indeed, he may have believed that the original suggestion came from me, rather than Ludo. In any case, I had already made my mind up to keep my diary free for the next week or so, in order to look after Tonka, so certain was I that he would need my support at this difficult time. We had both loved Grandad, but he wasn't actually my grandfather and I couldn't truly appreciate how affected Tonka might be by his loss.

"I don't mind, whatever you prefer," I answered. "We can take my car if you like."

Even before I had dropped him back at his home, Tonka had begun the search for a hotel on his iPhone. He found one in the old town of Outreau, where the battle had been fought. It meant we wouldn't have to drive while we were staying there, which suggested a large amount of alcohol was likely to be consumed.

"Do you know anyone who is attending the service?" I asked.

"No, there was an event five years ago, but I was away on active service at the time and I don't think Grandad attended."

Later that day, when Tonka had shared his plans with his partner, Gabriella contacted Ludo and accepted her invitation to stay with her, so they could share a car while we were away. Little Giacomo wanted to come with us and we had to think of numerous very good reasons why he couldn't before he eventually conceded the point.

~~~~~

The arrangements for Grandad's funeral service, including his favourite hymns, had all been finalised when I called round to see Tonka the following day. I could see from the documentation littering the coffee table that the arrangements for our trip to Boulogne were now at an advanced stage. Ann deposited me in the living room and went off to make a pot of tea. It was a room with which I was familiar. Photographs stood in frames around the cluttered room and the chairs were functional rather than fashionable. The couch and armchairs were for comfort not show in this house. I slumped down onto the couch and looked around the room.

There was no sign of Tonka but he had printed off details of our travel booking and hotel accommodation and I was giving this a cursory examination when his mother returned to the room carrying a tray of tea with sufficient biscuits to feed a small African nation. Ann told me her son was upstairs and she called to him to let him know I had arrived. I sat for a few minutes reading about the hotel before he walked in carrying another stack of paperwork. I cleared the table of one pile of documentation and he dropped another bundle in the space I had left.

"We're only going for two days," I said, assuming he had printed off even more information about the trip. He ignored my comment and began moving the paperwork around the table.

"I was going through Grandad's personal effects in his bedroom. I don't suppose we'll find a will, but then again, he didn't have anything to leave anyway."

A collection of photographs, a small and rather grubby holy medal that was missing its chain, together with birth certificates, a marriage certificate and other memorabilia littered the table. I remembered Tonka telling me stories of his SAS service and how they frequently needed to collect personal documentation from enemy camps after a successful attack, along with DNA samples from their fallen foe, in order to identify those who had been killed and recover important documents and artefacts for intelligence information. Owing to US influence, this had become standard practice during the Iraq War and was adopted in all subsequent conflicts. The US Defence Intelligence Agency had actually developed and famously used a set of playing cards to identify the most wanted members on the enemy side since the Civil War, but most people associated it with the capture of Bin Laden and other members of Al-Qaeda. In the modern era the collection of DNA samples was the acceptable proof that a notable member of the enemy force had been killed and the process became public in the Iraq conflict.

So, from his great experience in such matters, I was confident that if there had been a will, Tonka would have found it. He was highly trained in retrieving precisely what was needed and, for this reason, I was interested in what Tonka had considered worthy of examination from his grandad's bedroom.

"Why did you pick up this old book?" I asked, holding up a ragged copy of *Barrack Room Ballads* by Rudyard Kipling.

"Well, firstly," he replied, "there weren't many books."

"That's a surprise. I would have thought he'd have hundreds."

"There were a few but it's only a small bedroom and, more importantly, this was the only one with an inscription inside the cover."

I opened the cover and, written neatly in fountain pen, it read: *'Best wishes from Mr and Mrs Martin – Christmas 1934'*.

"Who are Mr and Mrs Martin?" I asked.

He shrugged. "Mum and Dad will probably know."

There were four old black and white photographs in the collection of documents. One was of Ivy and Grandad's wedding. He had been a young man when the picture was taken but he looked older than his years. It showed just how much weight he had lost as a prisoner of war. His uniform hung loosely about him, his eyes shadowed and his cheeks sunken. His complexion was sallow and gaunt and his smile looked laboured. Ivy stood proudly next to him, smiling and keeping a firm grip on her new husband's arm.

In her other hand she held a small posy of flowers. Her own effortless smile and bright eyes suggested it was the happiest day of her life and her buoyant appearance stood in stark contrast to the haggard and pinched features surrounding her husband's strained and lethargic posture. It was difficult to recognise the jovial old man who cultivated our fertile minds with wondrous tales of heroic enterprise.

It was easy to see now, in retrospect, who had been responsible for his salvation. Ivy adored Jonjo Thompson and her joy at marrying her childhood love was easily apparent in the photo. It was she who would take him from his depths of despair and banish all those dark thoughts of what had taken place over the past five years. And he had wanted to forget. He had wanted to dispel the events that lay so forcefully across his shoulders as if they had never taken place, or become as one of his fanciful stories, an invention of a world turned mad.

The second photograph was of Grandad in his uniform, but he was younger still in this one and to help us someone had written a date on the back — *'April 1940'*. One assumed he had just signed up or perhaps returned home on leave. The third photograph was of a scruffy football team in formal pose. Six men stood at the back and five knelt in front with an old brown lace-up football in the arms of one of them. Grandad could easily be identified as one of those standing up. A wooden board beside them simply said 'Stalag XXV'. It hadn't occurred to me that prisoners of war might play football but then life goes on, even one where the individual is denied liberty. "Dad was a survivor," Joe had said. And I suppose that is how survival is achieved, through a stubborn detachment, taking each day as a separate challenge; never counting the days or recounting the lost memories. How difficult it must have been to address an undefined confinement. Even criminals know when they will be released but this must have been dreadful, not knowing when, or if, you would ever see your family again.

Tonka folded his grandparents' birth certificates, both of which were copies, together with their marriage certificate and placed them with Grandad's death certificate in an envelope. As he did so, I picked up the last of the photos. This showed an attractive and smartly dressed woman alongside a teenage boy, both standing upright, with the Eiffel Tower in the distance behind them. The woman rested her right hand on his shoulder as if she was a proud mother. By comparing this with the photo taken in 1940, I could see it was Grandad as a teenager, a few years before. However, the woman alongside him was certainly not his mother. Grandad was as tall as the woman, even though she was wearing high-heeled shoes.

"Who's this with your grandad?"

Tonka took the photo from me and examined it carefully. Just like me he turned it over to see if the reverse contained any clues. There was nothing to help.

"Is it a relative of your grandad?" I repeated.

"No. I've seen lots of photos of the few relations he had and I don't recall this woman. Nor do I remember him ever mentioning a trip to Paris."

"Well," I answered, "it's difficult to tell with your grandad. He made up so many tales that it is possible some were real."

"Oh yeah, which one?" replied Tonka. "The one where he was a pirate or the one where he cleaned up the Wild West?"

It was the first time that Tonka had laughed since his beloved grandfather had died and he became conscious of this when his father limped into the room and slumped into his armchair. I moved a chair in his direction so he could rest his foot on it.

"Do you know this woman, Joe?" I asked him.

He scrutinised it close up and then far away. "Never seen this before," he replied. "No, I don't know her." He sounded a little disappointed, as if he should be familiar with everyone his father knew.

Tonka stopped what he was doing. "It might help," he said, thinking aloud. "The photo fell out of this book when I picked it up." He held up the book of Kipling poems.

"Well then," I suggested, "perhaps she is the Mrs Martin who gave him this book."

"But what would Grandad be doing in Paris with a Mrs Martin, whoever she is?" asked Tonka in a slow, thoughtful tone, but directing the question to his dad.

"It's all before my time. But I don't remember a Mrs Martin or a trip to Paris. I'm sure my dad would have told me if he had, 'cause he loved telling stories."

Clearly that last statement wasn't true, for here was a photograph of Grandad in Paris and he obviously hadn't told Joe.

Ann walked into the room carrying a fresh pot of tea and we put the puzzle to her. After a pause for consideration, she explained that Ivy and Grandad's family homes had been bombed in the Blitz, which is why they had moved to the Evestown area. That would have been in 1940, when Grandad was a prisoner of war. When he was a teenager, he lived in the east end of London, so Mrs Martin would have lived there. She might have been his godmother or a friend of Ivy's."

It was a good guess because the absence of close relations and the need, in those days, to find two Catholic godparents would have limited the choice.

"But why would the woman take him on holiday to Paris?" Tonka asked. "That was a pretty exotic place in the 1930s."

"And not cheap either," Joe chipped in.

"Would anyone down the Legion know?" asked Tonka.

"Not likely," answered Joe. "I don't think there is anyone still living round here who were victims of the Blitz."

"It's a pity Ivy isn't still with us," said Ann. "She knew who everyone was."

Tonka's grandmother, Ivy Thompson nee Frampton, passed away nearly five years ago, just nine months after Tonka's Aunt Vera had died of cancer. Old Mrs Thompson could never come to terms with the loss of her only daughter and everyone said she willed herself to death. There was nothing that Tonka's mum and dad could do but, fortunately, they both retired last year and saw Grandad several times each week until, eventually he moved into their spare bedroom six months ago. Tonka and I used to joke with Grandad about getting married again but he never did of course.

Tonka gathered up the photographs in the hope that he may meet someone who had known Grandad at the service in Boulogne on Sunday. He also picked up the grubby holy medal that had no chain. It looked like the Miraculous Medal issued to all children attending a Catholic primary school in the 1950s or 1960s. I took the medal from him and examined it, rubbing it against my clothing to see if I could make out the depiction. It was oval shaped and showed the head and shoulders of a holy man on one side. He carried a staff and was obviously a saint as a halo hovered over his head. The name of the saint was embossed above the figure but the encrusted dirt made it impossible to make out. It was a short name, certainly not long enough to be Saint Christopher, as I had first expected it to be. There was nothing on the other side.

"Now, Dad," said Tonka in a reassuring tone, "Jack and I will be back in time to take you to the hospital on Tuesday. We're on the lunchtime train back from France, so we'll be home on Monday evening."

"Never mind that," said Joe. "Just make sure you join us at the Legion tomorrow night to give Dad a good send off."

Tonka looked at me and I assured him that I would be there.

"I know there's not much time," he said as he saw me to the door. "But I'd really like to find out some information about what the Irish Guards were doing in Boulogne when Grandad was captured. He hardly mentioned anything about his army service, apart from a few titbits about his time as a prisoner of war and it would be good to know the background before we go on Sunday."

I suggested that, with his military background, Tonka was probably best placed to get this information. But he assured me how difficult it can be to retrieve, especially after seventy-five years.

"I'm not sure where to start," I replied. Tonka just looked at me, as if I was the most resourceful man he knew. So I asked what his grandad had told him about his experiences just prior to being captured.

"Very little," he answered. "He joined the Irish Guards and they were sent on a ship to rescue the Queen of the Belgians. When they got back to England, they realised she had forgotten her crown jewels and they were sent back to retrieve them. That's when he was taken prisoner."

"Well, there you are then," I replied, telling him that this sounded incredibly plausible, considering it came from one of the world's greatest storytellers. He wasn't impressed and, with less than forty-eight hours before we left for France, I surrendered and promised to find out what I could about Grandad's black op.

5

Wednesday 22 May 1940 — Boulogne

The sea crossing wasn't as rough as the previous one to the Hook. It gave Jonjo time to put everything in perspective; well, perhaps not everything, but the important things, those matters of life and death. He recalled Violet Martin stubbing her cigarette out in the ashtray and telling him that one error of judgement could be forgiven, before adding, "but anyone making the same mistake twice deserves anything that befalls them." There was a certain apocalyptic resonance to the words. Just like last week, the 2nd Battalion had just completed night manoeuvres when they were summoned into combat. Just like last week, the ships were not large enough to take all their equipment. And, just like last week, the men were exhausted, ill-equipped and had little information about what they might find on their arrival at Boulogne. This had all the hallmarks of making the same mistake twice; Violet Martin would not be sympathetic of the outcome.

How many mistakes can one make before one proves fatal? Jonjo was not blessed with nine lives like one of Mrs Podolski's cats.

The boat slowed up and everyone knew they were about to disembark on another foreign field. Jonjo had let Andrew Martin down on that fateful journey to school. He didn't atone for that mistake last week. Apart from firing aimlessly into the sky and carrying a few stretchers to the harbour, he had contributed little. He recalled one of the last schoolbooks he had read for history homework. Leonidas and three hundred Spartans had held off 300,000 Persians at a narrow pass near Thermopylae. The Spartans had applied a selfless tactic that took their enemy by surprise. None of them feared dying and their sole purpose was to ensure that their colleague standing next to them lived. Each one was charged to protect the man to his left and ignore his own safety. They did it willingly, believing that to die in battle was the greatest honour that could be bestowed upon them.

The Persians attacked men who were not even looking at them but were slain by the man at their victim's side. Time and again the Persians attacked the narrow pass and for days it was defended by the Spartans. Eventually force of numbers won the day but, although the battle was lost, the war was eventually won by the bravery of the three hundred and 20,000 Persians were killed at Thermopylae. Jonjo was determined to equal their bravery, to redeem himself from the haunting memory of Andrew Martin. He, too, he resolved, would sacrifice himself for his fellow man when the time came.

Shouting came from up on deck; the men were stirring, putting their backpacks on, checking their rifles. "Do we need our capes?" one voice called. "Too bloody right," another shouted above the grinding of the ship's engine. The men below felt the hull collide gently with the wooden pier. And, in that moment, Jonjo collected his equipment, put aside childish thoughts and became a man.

The unseasonal heatwave that had accompanied the battalion's departure from Dover the previous afternoon was replaced by a torrential downpour that drenched the hordes of civilians who had crammed themselves on to the quayside as the SS *Queen of the*

Channel berthed at Boulogne. It was dawn and the long queue of guardsmen stretched from the deck, down the stairs and into the bowels of the ship. As he waited his turn to disembark, Jonjo noticed that the others in the queue were donning the oilskin capes that had been issued to them for gas attacks. He looked questioningly at the man in front as he unfurled his cape and was told that they would serve their purpose just as well in the rain.

A combination of the pouring rain and an inestimable number of would-be evacuees made disembarking difficult and it was five hours before the soldiers had clambered through the throng of people and over their belongings and joined some Belgian troops in a large shed on the dockside. It seemed strange to Jonjo that they should be arriving when so many people wanted to leave. He looked heavenwards and the rain appeared as though it may stop, but the men were reluctant to put their capes back in their packs until they had dried out a little. They were glad they didn't because there was no time to rest and the men of the 2nd Battalion were told to take up positions in the small village that overlooked the port.

"There's nothing worse than the rain, is there?" a strong Irish brogue commented as the soldier pulled the hood of the cape over his head.

"You obviously wasn't at the Hook last week, mate," said Jonjo, but his voice was overpowered by a sudden rush of heavy rain, which didn't ease until the men had marched up the steep hill through the village of Outreau and began to take up positions to defend the small town.

Captain 'Axe' Egan and two sergeants made their way through the throng of inhabitants who were still heading in the opposite direction, carrying what items of personal property they could manage. There was no sign of any Germans, so it wasn't clear why so many refugees were streaming away. Rumour was enough, it seemed, to cause such panic. The captain gave a thumbs-up to a jeep carrying a lieutenant and three armed soldiers as it drove past, accompanied by two motor cyclists and headed off towards the village of Nesles where the enemy was reported to be. Axe instructed his sergeants to spread the men out in a semicircle to defend the village.

Most of the men were sheltered in doorways and by the time the sun escaped from behind the black clouds that occupied a grey sky, it was early afternoon. Axe organised three small groups to conduct a recognisance of the area. Sergeant Donovan went with two guardsmen towards the southwest and Sergeant Randall took two more to the east. Axe himself grabbed the two soldiers nearest to him and decided to climb a steep hill to the south of the town in order to get a bird's eye view of the surrounding area. The three men made their way through a wood towards the top of the hill. Once they had reached the peak they could see above the copse they had just passed through and were provided with a relatively good view of the surrounding area. But the drizzling rain reduced visibility and the captain decided to shelter under the trees for a short time as the clouds seemed to be clearing at last.

He looked into the faces of the two men as they sat against a large oak and lit up cigarettes. He had seen both of them before but couldn't remember speaking to them.

"What are your names?" he asked and the Irishman answered first.

"O'Reilly, Sir. Eamon O'Reilly."

The other one recognised the voice of the Irishman who had spoken to him when leaving the shed. Jonjo waited, unsure whether O'Reilly intended to add anything to his introduction. But he didn't.

"2720093 Guardsman Thompson, 2nd Battalion Irish Guards, Sir."

"What's your first name, Thompson?"

"John Joseph, Sir, but my folks call me Jonjo."

The captain picked the loose tobacco from his lips. "Welcome to the war, lads. Have you seen any action yet?"

O'Reilly shook his head.

"Last week, Sir, Hook of Holland," Jonjo answered.

Axe looked into his eyes, hoping to see some evidence of how the soldier responded to the experience. But the young man's face remained expressionless.

"What do you think?" he asked eventually.

"I saw some terrible things, Sir."

"Nightmares?"

"I don't actually remember sleeping since then, Sir. So no, Sir, no nightmares." He paused. "I saw some extraordinary bravery too though, Sir, incredible courage, Sir."

"They won't be the last," answered Egan as he stubbed his cigarette out.

Egan had been at the Hook the previous week and, as their current location was two hundred miles west of there, he really didn't expect to engage any Germans for at least a couple of days. He wanted to reassure the two men but decided they didn't need to know. Moreover, they needed to stay alert.

The rain began to ease, so they got up to continue their walk up the hill. In the distance, Axe thought he could hear the motor cyclists returning to the town, so presumably they had found nothing of interest in Nesles. As they came out of the copse of trees, he looked at his watch. It was two o'clock and the rain had indeed stopped. The sky began to clear and they made their way to the highest point he could find on his map. As they did so, they had their backs to the town and needed to get farther up the hill to see over the tops of the trees that had just protected them from the rain. When they eventually arrived at the summit, the men were suddenly startled by a booming sound in the distance below them. O'Reilly thought it was thunder, but Axe recognised the worrying sound of German light-infantry guns. From the direction of the shelling, it was clear that the enemy now occupied the area at the foot of the hill they had just climbed. In the time it had taken them to climb the hill, German artillery had taken up a position and in the distance he could see heavier field guns and tanks beginning to move towards the town in support of the smaller weapons already in place.

Through his field binoculars the captain could now see the jeep and outriders that had returned from Nesles. They were all alive but the vehicle was riddled with bullet holes.

Taking out his notebook, Axe quickly drew a sketch of the German positions. His first thought was to get back to the village, so he told the two men to follow him back down the hill. When they got to the other side of the trees, they were stunned by the size of the enemy force that was now in position below them. Quite how none of the recognisance groups had detected them was a mystery. They had all been lured into a false sense of security, not realising how far west the German front line had moved in the past week. It seemed the local inhabitants had been right to evacuate the village.

Hiding in the small wood and with only two men, Egan had to decide what to do next. They had three rifles and two revolvers between them and, through his field binoculars, he could now see even more tanks rolling into support positions just outside Outreau. The 2nd Battalion had been divided into four companies. Number one company appeared to be isolated on the edge of the town and was coming under heavy fire. Egan decided to remain on the high ground and assess the situation. The hours ticked away and the position of the position of the British troops below worsened.

Axe and the two men would almost certainly be captured if they attempted to return to the town. With an excellent view of proceedings, perhaps he could find some way through the enemy lines. He studied the sketch he had made and hoped his troops had taken up their final positions before the shelling began. It was just beginning to get dark and aircraft began bombing and machine gunning the British forces defending the village.

As the light failed, the sound of the two British anti-tank guns fell silent and Egan concluded that they had probably been taken out by the German shelling or aircraft support. With only rifles against tanks and heavy cannon, the company of Irish Guards defending the section of the town near the reservoir were sustaining heavy casualties, and through the gloom Axe and the two guardsmen witnessed the awful consequences of leaving most of the heavy armour back on the dockside at Dover.

As the light failed and darkness prevailed, an eerie silence fell across the land. Apart from the occasional round, shelling stopped for a couple of hours and it seemed almost as if the battle might be deferred until daylight. But, at ten o'clock, through the fading light Axe could see that the forward platoon of number one company had been outflanked on the lower road. Only a few men escaped the enemy manoeuvre but it was, at least, the final activity of the night.

The three men were kept awake by sporadic gunfire and the occasional cannon fire but it was relatively quiet until dawn. Egan regretted his indecision, but he wasn't sure which part of that indecision he regretted most. Should he have taken advantage of his position to kill as many Germans as he could? Or perhaps he should have used the darkness to escape eastwards in an attempt to fulfil his mission. It was too late now; the sun was rising fast on the eastern skyline and men in both camps were stirring, preparing for what might be their last day on earth.

There was a good view of the high ground near the reservoir on the edge of town and the company defending this sector was now coming under increasing fire as number one company suffered heavy losses and became depleted. Even without the benefit of binoculars, O'Reilly and Thompson could see the precarious position their comrades were in. Jonjo wondered why it was taking the captain so long to make a decision and issue instructions.

"Sir," he ventured after a while, "Sir, it's getting light now, we could take out twenty or thirty of them before they realise where the shots are coming from."

Egan looked at him but didn't reply. He was thinking about using what was left of the darkness to escape eastwards in an attempt to continue his mission but, as there was still a chance that the situation might be reversed, he decided to sit out what was left of the night on the hilltop. Perhaps British aircraft support would arrive at daylight. That could create a breach in the German attack for them to slip through.

"Sir," asked Jonjo again a few minutes later. "Do you want me to start shooting the Germans, Sir?" The captain didn't reply. Jonjo looked at the assault on number four company near the reservoir and looked back at Egan for an order.

"I'm not afraid, Sir," Jonjo added.

"Not afraid?" Axe replied. "Well you bloody should be, Guardsman, that's a German panzer division down there and if we don't get air cover soon we're in big trouble."

"So do you want me to take some of them out, Sir?"

"No," Axe answered firmly.

"Are *you* afraid, Sir?" Jonjo asked, tentatively.

"Afraid? Me? Look, soldier, I don't fear death, I fear only failure."

Jonjo was still waiting for the answer to his earlier question. He was checking out his rifle and put a box of shells on the ground next to the tree. Axe looked at him and shook his head.

"You're thinking in too narrow terms, Guardsman. You're thinking too much about the outcome of the battle." He paused and looked into the murk that surrounded them. "We have an opportunity to affect the outcome of the war, Thompson. And that might mean us not affecting the outcome of this battle. Now let me think for a moment and put those bullets back in your pocket." He hesitated before adding a postscript. "Have you actually ever shot anyone, Thompson, because this isn't knocking down ducks at the fair, you know."

"I don't know, Sir. I fired off a lot of shots at the Hook last week but they were mainly at aircraft. I don't suppose I hit anyone."

Axe told him to shut up and rest, while he decided what to do next.

The shelling continued into daybreak and, when the sun came up, the captain expected to see a town littered with British dead. Instead, in the distance, through the poor light of dawn he could see the guardsmen still in position around the town, defending the main road. On the edge of the village a garage near the railway line was being used as a makeshift hospital. A bright morning sun appeared from behind the cloud and with it came a forceful attack by the panzer division. By midday it was clear that the object of the officers on the ground was now simply to get as many of the British Expeditionary Force back to the port and out on the waiting ships, except that there would be no 'simply' about it. In the absence of any air support the soldiers had become like the refugees they had come to protect. Throughout the day, Egan watched developments, hoping for a British air attack to reverse the obvious outcome of events. But none came and Egan knew he would soon need to make a decision.

The three men made their way back up to the top of the hill. From here they could see that Outreau was completely cut off. Axe had hoped that it might be possible to breach the line and send Thompson and O'Reilly back into the village to fetch Sergeants Donovan and Randall, but he couldn't see a way through the enemy lines that now surrounded the town. So he weighed up his options and concluded he had only two. He could do as Jonjo had suggested and effectively abandon the mission by attacking the enemy line from their current advantageous position. He thought, for a moment, about his great grandfather who had served with Lord Cardigan in the British Light Cavalry at the

Battle of Balaclava. He had died in the Charge of the Light Brigade and Axe saw the opportunity to emulate him. But what good would that serve? Alternatively, he could ignore the battle that was raging around him and continue his mission either alone, or with the two raw recruits he had available.

Egan took a cigarette out and lit it. The two men knew he wanted a few moments to consider the situation and so remained silent. After five minutes elapsed he chose the latter of his two options and, much to the surprise of O'Reilly and Jonjo, he told them they were going to make their way to another small wood on the other side of the hilltop and wait for nightfall. They paused at the top of the hill to watch the final resistance of their colleagues in what was now a fierce battle.

Just before they began their journey down the other side of the hill, they looked back down the slope to see their colleagues retreating back towards the harbour area of the town. Small groups continued to defend the town and only number four company remained, as a unit, across the southern end of Outreau. It was becoming clear that they were to defend their position until what remained of the other three units of Irish and Welsh Guards had evacuated Boulogne on the British ships that were waiting just outside the harbour. Number four company did their job well and, apart from some tank shelling and sniper fire from an upstairs window in a side street, the evacuees' journey was made relatively safe. Once the remainder of the other three companies arrived on the quayside, the roads were blocked with vehicles and barrels, and these positions were defended by what was left of the soldiers in number four company with rifles and what automatic weapons they had.

Suddenly, in the dim light of dusk, Axe and the two guardsmen heard the rumbling sound of aircraft. It was almost seven o'clock when more than one hundred enemy aircraft appeared in the eastern sky. The men looked eagerly into the western night sky, where lighter aircraft could be heard. Then, from out of the clouds, around twenty Spitfires appeared and the strangest tactical battle commenced. The object for the British flyers was not to take out the bombers, but to drive them so high in the sky that they were unable to drop any bombs with any real hope of hitting the dockside or the two British destroyers that approached the quay. HMS *Verity* was the first to enter the inner harbour and, as it did so, it came under extremely heavy fire. It was hit and set alight amid ships by the first salvo and it was clearly the enemy's intention to sink her in the narrowest part of the harbour in order to block the way for any other ships wanting to evacuate the retreating Irish and Welsh Guards. The action that the commander of the *Verity* then took must have astounded the waiting evacuees, just as it did the three men standing at the summit of the hill.

With no thought for his own safety, the *Verity* went astern at full speed, while firing with every gun at the enemy. Ignoring the obvious fact that the quicker he steamed out to sea, the faster the flames spread through his ship, the captain inflicted as much damage on the German front line as was possible, before clearing the path for the other destroyer to enter the harbour and evacuate the waiting troops. The noise generated by the close proximity of the destroyer's guns and the enemy's heavy artillery was deafening for the three men on the hill and they could not imagine how it must have been for the men on the quay. Egan waited on the brow of the hill to see the ships clear the harbour with all the British troops they could take. Only the men of number four company remained and, when the end came for them, retreat was not possible, for they were too close to the enemy lines and would certainly have been killed if they had attempted to escape. As darkness hid the wrecked landscape of war, the remaining members of the Irish Guards surrendered and the two destroyers sailed back into the channel, taking their colleagues to safety. As they did so, Axe Egan took Jonjo and Eamon down the hillside, in the opposite direction, towards another small wood that would shelter them from the view of the German forces now occupying Outreau.

In his mind, Axe repeated what he had said to Jonjo and convinced himself that the mission must come first. The battle may have been lost, but he still had a chance to affect the outcome of the war. Complete the task, unquestioningly. Six hundred and fifty men had brought him to this point. God only knows how many had failed to return home. Number four company must have been captured and dozens must have died. The three of them might well have reduced that number if Axe had chosen to attack the enemy front line as Jonjo had suggested. But would it have affected the outcome of the battle? Egan convinced himself otherwise. They would have been captured or killed and the outcome would have been the same. He wondered what had happened to Donovan and Randall and wished that he had them with him now. Perhaps they would be sent back to complete the mission, unaware that Axe was still out there. After all, High Command HQ couldn't possibly know that Axe Egan was still in play.

The Harpoon Force, thought Egan. A harpoon was something that was sent out to bring something back. That was too much of a clue. They had brought back the Dutch Government from the Hook of Holland, along with Queen Wilhelmina, who had turned up only after Churchill had convinced her that Zeeland could not be defended against the Germans. Axe reflected on the irony of it. They had told the men they were going to Belgium to rescue the Queen of the Belgians, who had been dead for five years and they had ended up rescuing the Queen of the Netherlands. The truth just reinforced the story they leaked to the men about the Boulogne trip. Going back to retrieve the Belgian crown jewels was again, in his mind, too close to the truth.

6

Friday 22 May 2015 — Evestown

Tonka never had any difficulty sleeping; anywhere, anytime, anyplace. It was a talent that came in very handy in his chosen profession, because I'm sure he had to bed down in some very difficult locations. On lurching ships and big old aircraft that were noisier than a Keith Moon drum solo. He was the opposite of me, someone for whom insomnia was part of the genetic makeup. Tonka was always asleep before me when I stayed over at his house, comatose in seconds. Whereas I lay there for hours wondering about the strange story I had just been told. The Crimson Pirate, his weird cat and even stranger parrot were certainly not going to sleep, so neither could I. But Grandad certainly empathised with my problem.

"You see," he had said one night, "people like you and me, our minds are just so occupied that it's difficult to actually stop thinking. When I was small," he continued, "my mum used to tell people that I thought about things too much. And it was true, I did. But she said it as if it was an illness, not something to be proud of. Because it is, you know. Being able to think about things is a great gift; a privilege."

He had then proceeded to provide suggestions on how to get to sleep. Visualise a blank page, he suggested, but there was still too much to think about. Visualise a black page, pitch darkness, he advised, but that proved unsuccessful. Take yourself on a journey, in your mind, walk to the station, get on a train and, in your mind, go on a holiday to the seaside. But that just led to adventures, I told him.

"Yes," he replied in a resigned tone, "that's what happens to me, too."

It was on that same night, I'm sure, that he had almost managed to convince me that I had a small man in my brain, who worked only when I was asleep, and it was his job to file away all the stuff I had thought about during the day. All the information I learned at school, the knowledge I gained and all the experiences I had during the day needed to be recorded and filed away every night. But the little man in my brain couldn't do it while I was awake and the more I disturbed him by waking up, the less he could do and the more jumbled all the stuff in my head got.

If the thought of having a little man in my head wasn't enough to distract me from my shuteye, then reaffirming my belief that I had too much information in my head certainly did. But, the thought did make some sense.

"Do you know when you wake up in the morning and there's a dream hanging around in your head?" he asked one night.

"Yes," I replied, relieved that I wasn't the only one who seemed to swim out of strange dreams into the morning light on most mornings. Dreams didn't melt instantly on my waking but lingered like fragments of people, places and experiences that needed to be joined together in order to make any sense of my thoughts.

"And you know how they don't seem to make any sense at all?"

"Yes, yes."

"Well that's because the man in your head hasn't had time to finish his night's work and all the files have got jumbled up. That wasn't your dream, that was everything that happened to you since you last slept, all jumbled up because he didn't have time to file it in its right place."

It didn't help, of course. Bedtime for me was more a night vigil, interrupted by intermittent periods of sleep. However, his ramblings came back to me on many occasions, mainly as I lay awake wondering about that little man in my head dropping all the files on the floor of my brain and mixing them up. And so it was that morning. Finally falling asleep to such distant recollections lent itself to a deranged and preposterous dream.

My sleepy eyes opened to the alliterative screeching of a large green parrot that was perched on the shoulder of the pirate skipper. "Awound the howizon came the Cwimson Piwate," it squawked and, as it did so, a three-legged cat named Dolores ran around the captain's feet, with its peg leg clicking on the deck as she did.

"Cut your cackling, Oscar," bawled his owner and my night-time imaginings sailed off across their own distant ocean.

Now, I thought, contrary to what Grandad had told me all those years ago, that certainly wasn't stuff that I had done but something he had told me, in one of his outlandish tales of buried treasure.

I suppose the more curious and preposterous a story is, the greater the achievement of the teller, if a storyteller is able to suspend belief as dreams do; if they can coerce and compel the listener to give the story life in spite of its lack of integrity then success belongs to the singer not the song. I lay there and recalled asking Grandad how Dolores was supposed to catch mice and rats if she was clip-clopping around the deck giving them ample warning of her presence.

But, instead of falling on the floor laughing at the fact that I could possibly try to place some credibility on his piece of fiction, he had engaged with me on the weaknesses in it. In truth, he probably thought I really did have too much 'stuff' in my head if the only shortcoming of his three-legged cat story was how its peg leg might affect its career as a mouser. And yet he never showed it.

"Good point," he replied, "but it wasn't the only flaw in the wooden appendage," he answered. "Her peg leg used to get stuck in the wet sand when they went to bury the treasure too."

I had to agree but it didn't help me get to sleep that night. It merely prompted me to consider all the handicaps that might beleaguer a three-legged cat.

For his part, Grandad seemed to like challenges to his imaginings because he was able to think on his feet and he enjoyed using that ability, if only to bolster the legitimacy of his wondrously beguiling tales.

Moreover, one should consider all storytellers liars, I suppose, and Grandad was a credible and persuasive one, but as I left the illusory world of dreams and awakened slowly into the daylight of the real one, I wasn't convinced he had been lying about the actual events of his life. He had told Tonka that he was sent with the Irish Guards on a mission to rescue the Queen of the Belgians and then, a week later, was sent back to collect the crown jewels that she had forgotten. Grandad hadn't elaborated on this story; he could easily have transformed this simple and, in his mind, factual series of events, into one of his most incredible stories. But he hadn't. And the reason for this was that he implicitly believed what he had been told by his commanding officer, just as we believed every fanciful tale he had ever told us.

One thing was certain in my mind. Grandad had never lied about the real events in his life, he only fabricated stories from fiction or ancient history. He never told contemporary stories. And that is why I was so surprised when I read the information on the screen of my laptop when I sat in the house alone after Ludo had taken Giacomo to school. Astrid, wife of King Leopold III and Queen of the Belgians, was born in 1905 and died in a motoring accident in Switzerland in August 1935, five years before Jonjo Thompson and his fellow Irish Guards had supposedly rescued her from the advancing Nazi hoards. I checked it of course. I checked it several times, so convinced was I that it must be incorrect. Astrid was the last Queen of the Belgians, there was no Queen of the Belgians in 1940 so, whatever Jonjo was doing, he wasn't rescuing *her*. Either he didn't know the truth of the mission or he had lied; not the lie of a storyteller or even that of the vainglorious egotist, but a blatant and uncharacteristic lie. I spent the rest of the day wondering whether to tell Tonka or to wait and see if I stumbled upon any other information about his grandad's short military career.

~~~~~

The British Legion building was designed with all the artistic merits of a bus garage or at best a parish hall, except there was no church attached to it. It was sandwiched between the local mini-cab firm and a Chinese restaurant, on the western outskirts of Evestown, not far from where I lived at Beadsman's Cross. It consisted of an immoderately lit rectangular room with a bar running along half the length of one wall and a small kitchen and toilets at the far end from the entrance. The deceptively large interior was disguised by the tiny frontage of a building that expanded behind the taxi firm and restaurant. A long glass mirror ran the length of the bar and a Union Jack was draped at one end. The wall opposite the entrance was filled with a larger-than-life picture of the queen. The remaining walls, where windows did not prevent it, were filled with pictures of Churchill, Montgomery and other wartime leaders and memorabilia, regimental badges and emblems.

The SAS emblem had been placed by Tonka next to the regimental badge and motto of Grandad's Irish Guards. *'Quis Separabit'* — who will separate us. Well, the Germans certainly separated them in May 1940 when Grandad was captured.

Tonka, Gabriella, Joe and Ann were already there when Ludo and I arrived. On the adjacent table sat old Tom Anderson, Mrs Griffiths and Ivy O'Brien. Mr Greaves and my mother's old neighbour Mrs Joiner, who was looking increasingly like Yoda's older sister, sat close by.

Ludo slid in next to Gabriella at the table and blamed the babysitter for our late arrival. I remained silent about the fact that the babysitter had arrived twenty minutes before she had finished putting on her make-up. Tonka joined me at the bar to get drinks for everyone. My observant friend had a photographic memory and was able to recall what each person was drinking, including any preference for slimline or normal tonic, or any requirement for ice or a slice of lemon. It wasn't a party trick, just a necessity of his former profession.

A conversation about the late and already legendary Jonjo Thompson had begun when we returned to the table. Some of his old friends, none of whom were still alive, used to call him Longhop and the discussion was on how this nickname had come about. Nobody knew because Grandad was the last of that generation. Tom Anderson informed us that it was a type of bowl in cricket, like an off-spin or leg-break, so Grandad had probably played cricket, he suggested. Everyone agreed that Ivy would know if she was still here, which sent Ann off on a tangent about how her husband's parents were childhood sweethearts and she took us through everything she had been told about the courtship of her parents-in-law.

"Joe's sister, Vera, was named after Vera Lynn," she said, suggesting that her in-laws had courted to her songs. She seemed to have forgotten that Vera Lynn peaked during the war and Grandad was away for five years at that time. Ann rambled on, bringing us up-to-date after dwelling on how much Grandad had missed Ivy and Vera. I changed the subject in order to save everyone from Ann's tearjerker of a romantic story. I showed them the photographs of Jonjo with the mysterious older woman, but nobody at the Legion recognised her or had heard of Mr and Mrs Martin. Most simply confirmed that Grandad's parents and Ivy's family had moved to Evestown in the war, when the east end of London was bombed, so they had not been living here at the time the photograph was taken. Mrs Griffiths thought Grandad would have been about thirteen or fourteen years old when she looked at the picture and wondered if the other person was a teacher on a school trip.

"A school trip," choked Ann on her gin and tonic. "They couldn't even afford shoes in those days, let alone school trips to Paris. And, in any case, if she had been a teacher it probably wouldn't be signed 'Mr and Mrs', would it? I reckoned they were his godparents."

Joe reminded everyone that kids had left school at fourteen in those days, so it certainly wouldn't be a school trip.

It was difficult to hold any sort of personal discussion as people were shouting across the table and the opportunity to talk to Tonka about my business proposition never presented itself. I consoled myself with the fact that we would be together for a few days and I would have ample opportunity to persuade him to join me in the investigative journalism project. As the evening wore on, we returned to the same aspects of Grandad's life—Ivy, the war and whether the nickname of Longhop had anything to do with cricket. In the end Tonka was driven to searching for it on Google and found that it was, indeed, a very poor delivery in cricket.

Just before last orders were called a familiar face entered the bar. It was my old boss from Woolly Fold Manor, Lieutenant Colonel Elton.

"Can we talk, Jack?" asked Elton as he sauntered past our table to a vacant one in a corner with a restricted view of the empty stage. It sounded less like a question and more like an instruction. "Mine's a malt," he added.

"What on earth are you doing here?" I exclaimed ungenerously.

"Why, Jack, I'm a former officer of Her Majesty's Armed Forces, so I think I have earned the right to drink at the British Legion."

I purchased the required drink and sat on the spare chair next to him before apologising for my rudeness. But I knew Colonel Elton was a shrewd old guy who didn't turn up anywhere by chance. I'd had first-hand knowledge of his guile and cunning when I worked with him about five years ago. Elton was too busy to rely on an opportunist meeting, so I was sure he'd got one of his underlings to bug my telephone or track me down. He was an intelligence officer, employed by the government to seek out ways to manipulate the weather. His small team was based at Woolly Fold Manor and my role had been to ensure that nobody ever discovered the truth about that place. Whenever the press began to suspect that the recent extreme weather or climate change was the result of anything other than global warming, my job was to deflect their attention towards something else of public interest. It occurred to me as I placed the glass in front of him that I may have left the job, but I had signed the Official Secrets Act and there was no expiry date to that undertaking.

There was no doubt in my mind that the secret base in Woolly Fold Wood was still operative. This was a long-term project made eternal by the need to ensure that nobody ever succeeded and gained control of nature's power. I was just as convinced that Elton held at least one more role for the government and it wasn't to review the levels of service at British Legion clubs. No, his presence here was no coincidence.

The colonel was of medium height, slim with narrow eyes and a well-trimmed moustache. He was old enough to have served in the Korean War and young enough to hold down a responsible position in what might be broadly referred to as British intelligence. I knew enough about him to be sure he was neither CI5 nor MI5. He was part of that small group of people with links to both organisations, as well as Chatham House and selected senior civil servants at the Ministry of Defence. He would be kept well away from the Secretary of State for Defence and probably only a single member of the permanent staff there was aware of his various and secretive roles.

"I hear you may be available for some private work in the field of investigation," he said, sipping at his whisky.

"Investigative journalism," I explained. "Not the furtive cold war espionage you specialise in."

"You misjudge me, Jack."

"That's because I don't make it my business to scrape up all the information and scandal I can about you, the way you do about other people. Anyway, your business is a little too dangerous for me."

"Jack, Jack, you know I would never put you in danger."

"I had a gun held to my head," I said, reminding him how my previous employment with him had ended.

"That was of your own making, young man. Nothing to do with me."

"Anyway," I countered, "I'm resting at the moment. I have some personal business to attend to."

He told me he was very sorry to hear about the death of Tonka's grandfather and was aware of my visit to Boulogne for the seventy-fifth anniversary event. I didn't even bother to ask him how he knew all this stuff about me because it would simply provide confirmation that his information was correct.

"If anyone can get to the bottom of it, you can, Jack."

"Get to the bottom of what?" I asked. But he said we should just wait to see how it panned out.

"I'm here if you need me, Jack. Always happy to help."

"Well, maybe you can," I suggested. "Tonka has been trying to discover the nature of his grandad's mission when he was captured. But he doesn't seem to be able to find anything out.

"You know the British Government, Jack. That mission was a failure so you may never find out what its true purpose was. History is in the hands of the victor, Jack, and we're happy it is so." I went to get up but he hadn't finished speaking.

"I can tell you something about his first mission if you want," he said calmly and smiled. "Let's call it a free introductory offer."

I sat down, concerned that he had somehow anticipated the events of this evening. Why on earth would he have prepared precisely the information I was going to ask for?

"John Joseph Thompson's active service lasted only thirteen days in 1940, Jack. Those thirteen days began on 11 May when the 2nd Battalion of the Irish Guards was sent to the Hook of Holland to bring the Dutch Government back to Britain. The Germans were already bombing Rotterdam and Queen Wilhelmina was hoping to defend her country from one of the islands in Zeeland, but she met up with the 2nd Battalion at the Hook and Churchill convinced her to return with them to England."

"That sort of fits," I replied. But I didn't want to be in the colonel's debt, so thought twice about taking the enquiry any further. He stood up, swigged back the malt whisky and spoke one last sentence before leaving.

"I'm here if you need me, Jack. Then perhaps we can meet up when you're back. Shame to waste your undoubted talent, especially when it's backed up by one of the toughest individuals the SAS has produced. Goodnight, Jack."

He paused as I told him I wasn't planning to open a detective agency, but an investigative news agency.

"Yes, yes, it's actually just using your brain, Jack, and you are surprisingly quite good at that. Anyway, we can talk about it when you get back from France."

He'd stirred my interest and pressed all the right buttons, now he just wanted to go, leaving more questions than answers, as he always did.

I wanted to ask him how he knew about our trip to Boulogne but stopped myself from boosting his self-esteem. So I had to invent something to put him down.

"Anyway," I said, "I knew most of that stuff. It's the second mission I was trying to find out about. The one that led to Tonka's grandad being incarcerated in Stalag XXV for five years."

It wasn't the most disparaging comment but, strangely, it had the right effect. The colonel's expression changed and he sat back down.

"Tonka's grandad was captured in May 1940," said Elton and the statement sounded like a question, as if he was confused.

"Yes, at the Battle of Boulogne."

"Are you sure?"

Now I was confused. The colonel appeared to know more about this matter than I did and yet here he was confirming the most basic of information.

"Yes, he was captured at the Battle of Boulogne, defending the town of Outreau. And the battle was in May 1940. As far as I know, his company was sent to hold off the German advance while the other three companies made their escape at the harbour."

He nodded to confirm that what I said was correct, but something was still troubling the colonel.

"Did he move camps?"

"Camps?" I asked.

"Prisoner-of-war camp. Did he move?"

"No, I'm pretty sure he only spoke about his time at Stalag XXV," I replied as I got up and walked over to Tonka. The colonel was deep in thought when I returned a minute later with one of the photographs. It showed a ragged football team with a wooden sign saying 'Stalag XXV'.

Something about that photo and about my last comment affected the colonel. Something that didn't fit with the research he had conducted on Tonka's grandad. But he wasn't going to tell me what it was. Instead he changed the subject and said he wasn't even sure there was ever a central record for missing personnel in 1940. At that time, the British had no idea how far the Germans had advanced and so declaring soldiers missing might have seemed a little premature.

I knew about the colonel's job on the weather modification team but I was sure our conversation had nothing to do with that work. So it seemed the old army man was multitasking, as I suspected. But why was he so interested in Grandad's mission and why was he disturbed about the date of Grandad's capture or where he spent the war? So, I asked him, not expecting him to reveal anything. I was right.

"Well let's just say I'm interested enough to give you some assistance, provided you keep me informed of developments."

"What developments? We're just going to a reunion, a celebration of the seventy-fifth anniversary of the Battle of Boulogne."

"Yes, Jack, now you and Tonka go off and play. Have a good time in France and let me know if you come across anything in the meantime. Do you have the same mobile number?"

"What, you mean you don't know?"

"Jack , I just pay attention to what is going on around me, a bit like you do. That doesn't make me a bad person and I don't have any particular interest in you. I certainly don't keep a record of your mobile numbers."

As the mini cab drove away from the British Legion club, Tonka asked me what the colonel wanted and why I had shown him one of his grandad's photographs. I told him I didn't know, which was true, but shared with him my concerns about Elton's motives. I wanted time to think about this myself, so I changed the subject.

"Do you remember how your grandad used to read books to us like *Brer Rabbit* and *Treasure Island* and we insisted he told us one of his own stories instead?" I asked Tonka. "Something he made up."

He nodded and gazed at the floor as he recalled those childhood nights when I had slept over at the Thompson's house.

"And do you recall," I asked, "how he used to include himself in the adventure?"

He did remember of course. Those memories were cast forever in our minds. How Grandad had fought in the American Civil War and rode on the posse to capture the Clanton gang. His good friend Wyatt Earp killed them in a gunfight a few days later when Grandad was off fighting red Indians, otherwise he would have been there for sure, alongside Doc Holliday and the Earp brothers.

As the cab approached the first stop to drop our friends off, Tonka and I both sat in silence for a few minutes revisiting those days of our youth. I remember asking Grandad if he had fought in the Crimean War, when we had been studying it at school. He'd hesitated, I suppose, wondering what I knew of that particular part of history. Once he realised I knew very little, he'd taken off on one of his fantastic journeys. But there was something different on that occasion. That time, it wasn't Grandad who'd stood alongside Lord Cardigan at the Battle of Balaclava, but someone he'd referred to as a friend, or rather his friend's grandad, if I recall correctly. Someone called Egan took the glory that day, perhaps because all those who'd charged the enemy guns were killed and it might have proved difficult to explain his presence at our bedside in those circumstances. This had never presented an obstacle in the past and, even on those occasions, neither Tonka nor I could ever bring ourselves to question his authority on such matters, nor did we wish to interrupt the thrilling tale of heroism and chivalry.

The character of Egan had made guest appearances in many of Grandad's stories. He was Axe Egan, the captain of the Jolly Roger, which Grandad served on as first mate and he was Captain Egan of the Seventh Cavalry when Grandad scouted for him in Nevada and Utah. Later Grandad and Egan rode the purple sage sierras together and fought the evil Deacon Tull and his gang of outlaws. Of all the outlaws who rode the west, the Dalton gang, the Clantons and McCrorys, none was deadlier on the draw than the evil Deacon Tull.

"Why did you ask about Grandad's appearance in his own stories?" Tonka asked as he and Gabriella got out of the car.

"I don't know, Tonka," I said forlornly. "But somewhere in all those stories there are elements of the truth. I just wish I could separate the fact and fiction."

Grandad's stories were, indeed, littered with true facts, such as his throwaway comment that all spiral staircases in castles turn clockwise going up the stairs, in order that the knights defending the castle could use their sword in their right hand. Those attacking and trying to proceed up the stairs would need to fight left-handed in order to make progress. Such truisms could be verified and so provided validation to Grandad's stories. He wove truth and fiction so well that it was difficult for a child to distinguish between the two. If I was to uncover the truth of Grandad's service in the war, I would need to unpick that fine stitching to reveal the real events that had produced such an engaging man.

7

Thursday 23 May 1940 – Outreau

The indecipherable sound of the mistral scuttled through the branches of the tree above his head, laden with cryptic prophecies of things to come. Does everything have a purpose in life, Jonjo wondered. Father Cullen certainly thought so, and said so when he finally went to the confessional box after the death of Andrew Martin.

"God's purpose needs to be fulfilled. You cling on to your own mortality too tightly, John. Death isn't the end."

It had certainly seemed like the end when he'd stood over Andrew's lifeless body lying half on the pavement and half in the road as the car driver ran back towards them. Does everything have a purpose? Apparently so, and surely so if everything is pre-ordained, as Father Cullen suggested. One event cannot happen unless something else happens before it. Each event in life's complex tapestry cannot be realised through its own volition. Simply to enable Jonjo to be standing under this tree today, Andrew had to die. That didn't make sense. How can God know what Jonjo would do next; he didn't even know that himself.

The captain had instructed them to stop and keep silent. A sound had been heard in the copse ahead. It could have been the enemy but it wasn't, it was a small roe deer that scampered away as the squally wind buffeted the leaves above.

Moving as quickly but as quietly as they could, the three men made their way down the other side of the hill and rested in a clearing just below its highest point on the eastern edge of a heavily canopied forest. Egan took out a pair of binoculars and began to survey the surrounding area. There were a few small clumps of trees on the hillside they would need to travel down but these provided little cover. Beyond this, as the valley below levelled out, fields of wheat and barley grew alongside each other, separated by blackthorn hedge that might provide a method of concealment as the three soldiers moved towards another forest that occupied the hillside on the other side of the gorge. The captain unfolded a map, looked at a compass and plotted his path, mentally calculating how long it would take them to reach the security of that wood.

"There's nothing worse than being lost," commented O'Reilly quietly to his fellow guardsman. But he was overheard by Egan.

"We're not lost," snarled the captain. "And there are many things worse than being lost."

"Like being lost behind enemy lines," mumbled Jonjo to himself.

But Egan had good hearing. "There aren't any lines at the moment, Guardsman. Lines of attack and defence are yet to be defined."

Five minutes elapsed as Egan put away the compass and map, then took a swig from his water canteen and thought about his next move.

"We're eighty miles from the Belgian border," he said eventually. "But the first stage is to get to the wooded area at the top of that hill." He pointed in an easterly direction and neither Jonjo nor O'Reilly deemed it sensible to ask why they were heading east instead of north to one of the channel ports. In spite of the captain's insistence that the battle lines were still to be defined, Jonjo was convinced that Egan had already concluded it was impossible to make their escape through the German front line that was now firmly established around Boulogne.

Travelling only during the hours of darkness, Egan calculated that it would take them three days to reach the border. Jonjo had visited Belgium only a couple of weeks ago, or so he thought, and it hadn't been occupied by the Germans at that time, so making their way to one of the Belgian ports made sense to him. Hitler might send squadrons of bombers to take out a battalion but the Fuehrer surely wouldn't bother for just three men unless, of course, they really were looking to steal the crown jewels.

Egan looked at the two guardsmen and lamented the need to abandon his original plan. In training he had been taught to turn adversity into advantage but he couldn't see how this was possible with two such raw recruits. The plan was to take Sergeants Donovan and Randall, an interpreter and a small company of men to recover a valuable cache of diamonds held in Amsterdam. Last week's eventful mission to the Hook of Holland saw a successful rescue by the Harpoon Force. It may have cost the lives of eleven soldiers from the 2nd Battalion of the Irish Guards, but Queen Wilhelmina and members of the Netherlands Government were returned unharmed to Britain. Of course, Jonjo still believed it was the Queen of the Belgians and her entourage, which served only to reinforce the rumours that he had been told.

One Dutch Government official had brought with him information about the country's largest hoard of diamonds, which had been moved to a secret location in Amsterdam in case they were captured when making their escape to England. As it turned out, that was a poor decision because if Rotterdam had fallen, Amsterdam must now be occupied by German forces. Egan was charged with recovering those diamonds and, in case rumours of the mission were detected by the Germans, the guardsmen attached to his unit were told they were recovering the crown jewels that the Queen of the Belgians had left behind. It was almost true, but as the queen had died in 1935 any Nazi interrogator would conclude the captured soldier knew nothing of the mission's true objective.

Any hopes of returning to Holland by the same route that had proved successful the previous week were dashed when the Luftwaffe began bombing the coastal ports of Belgium and Holland. Most of the guardsmen at the Hook weren't even aware that the refugees who appeared on the quayside as they were leaving were evacuating the bombed and overrun city of Rotterdam. The harbour was secured by the Germans as soon as the Royal Navy destroyers left it. So Egan's mission to recover the Gemini diamond collection was wrapped up in the advance of a larger British Expeditionary Force to Boulogne in the hope that he could then make quick headway to the Low Countries. But such progress relied heavily on the Maginot Line being held. It was clear from the reception at Boulogne that the Germans had advanced through or around the French and Belgian line of defence that had been set up along the border between those countries. The bombing of the ports indicated that the Germans had probably taken a force around the Maginot Line and through Belgium, so it was possible that some parts of that line were still held. Egan knew that the fortress of Maubeuge, near Maulde, was one of the strongest points in that defensive line and that town was about eighty miles from the position he now found himself in.

Without his two best men, Egan had to make do with two inexperienced guardsmen. One of the backup plans discussed before they left England was to make contact with the commander of Maubeuge, Captain Schwengler, so Egan decided to make his way there and recruit a more effective unit of men to make the onward journey to Amsterdam.

It was a dark night and just a sliver of moon shone above a thick layer of cloud. The three men avoided the minor roads and tracks that crossed the valley and made their way along the inside of the hedgerows that surrounded the fields thereabout. Gradually, in a zigzag movement, they found themselves at the foot of the hill they had been looking at when they began their dash. They now needed to get to the woodland at the top of the hill and find themselves somewhere to hide before the sun rose.

Nestled between the fields that occupied the valley stood a farmhouse. As they reached the rough stone wall that surrounded it, they peeped over and could see only a faint light from inside the small building. There was still some activity. Farmers worked long days at this time of the year and whoever lived there was probably eating their supper before settling down for the night. On a clothes line outside the door hung some ragged looking shirts, socks and long johns, drying in the light warm winds. For a moment the captain considered knocking on the door and simply asking for some food. They hadn't eaten since they had left England and although he had limited provisions in his kit, he wanted to conserve these. He decided against taking that risk and told the others that they needed to move on up the hill and hope they could catch something to eat up there.

"What about the clothes?" asked Jonjo. "Shall we take them?" He paused while the captain considered his suggestion. Jonjo grabbed his tunic. "We're sitting ducks in these uniforms, Sir."

"No," said Egan forcefully and he quietly and patiently explained the consequences of being captured out of uniform. "We can be shot as spies," he said. "At the moment, we must concentrate on not getting caught. If we fail, we'll simply spend the rest of the war in a prison. But, at least we'll be alive." Axe was intent on fulfilling his mission. Even if captured, he was resolved to escape and continue with his assignment. "Never give in," Churchill had said, "never, never, never". Egan didn't need telling twice.

In the dark it was possible to see light on the hillside, but there wasn't any. It was not too cold and the captain knew that the

Germans would avoid making camp fires, so they still needed to proceed with caution. Fortunately, they were now far enough behind enemy lines to be out of the range of the guns on the British ships in the harbour and the Germans would not expect any British soldiers to be this far inland. Most of the Germans had moved to the front line, so the large wooded hillside was 'sans Hun' as the captain said with some relief and using the only French word he knew. Apart from Sergeants Donovan and Randall, Egan had been allocated a trained interpreter and could choose six of the most experienced soldiers available for the mission. Instead, he was accompanied by two recruits whose only combat experience amounted to just two weeks' active service. "Played one, lost one," he mumbled to himself, taking solace in the fact that 2nd Battalion had acquitted itself bravely in the action.

"Sir," asked Jonjo when they stopped for a brief rest. "How did the Germans reach Boulogne? What happened to the Maginot Line?"

But before the captain could respond, O'Reilly offered his own answer. "Built by Frenchmen, that's why. They should have brought in a team of proper Irish navvies for the job."

Egan ignored him and explained that the Germans must have gone around the defensive line and the bombing of the Dutch and Belgian coastline was an essential part of that plan.

Through the dense canopy of the forest the first signs of a new day could be seen. The captain knew he had to find somewhere to hide during the daylight hours. He had to act quickly, so avoided his first instinct to delegate the next task and simply told the two soldiers to follow him. Eventually, close to a large tree, deep inside the wood, he found what he was looking for. It was a hole about ten inches across.

"Dig into that hole and make it big enough for us to get into," he whispered to them.

"What's in there?" asked Jonjo.

Egan was shocked that a guardsman should question his authority, but O'Reilly intervened.

"It's only a badger sett."

"What if there's a badger in there?" asked Jonjo.

"There won't be any badgers in there," said the Irishman with some assurance. "If they were in there they would cover the hole behind them. They're very tidy animals, are badgers."

But, by this time, Jonjo had seen the captain's face and he was already digging away at the hole.

As he walked around collecting twigs and branches, Egan told them to leave the front of the hole as small as possible. He then laid his collection of timber and shrubbery close to the hole.

"There's nothing worse than being buried underground," said O'Reilly sagely.

"I'm not sure I want to be buried alive, Sir," said Jonjo, without stopping his digging.

"Would you prefer to be shot, then?" asked Egan.

Jonjo wasn't sure whether he meant shot by the Germans or by his own captain, but it was enough to convince the young man to stop questioning who was in command.

They finished digging the hole about thirty minutes before sunrise and Egan explained to them that they would need to stay in the hole until dusk. He pulled a large bar of chocolate from his kitbag, broke it into three pieces and told the others to make the most of it because he wasn't sure when they would eat again.

"It's all we're going to get before tomorrow night, so don't eat it all at once. Sleep as best you can. Now, once we get inside this hole, no talking and no sounds of any kind." Egan wasn't sure they would be eating at all tomorrow night and he hoped that at least one of his colleagues knew something about living off the land. The atmosphere was hot and oppressive underground and it was difficult to remain silent. There was so much to think about, particularly for the captain. The absence of rest over the last week eventually caused them all to sleep, although it took regular kicks to stop O'Reilly from snoring.

The sun set slowly and impatience nearly got the better of Jonjo, but he remained compliant to the officer's instructions after waking. Eventually it was as dark outside the hole as it was inside. It was cooler too and Egan suggested they moved quietly, listening out for streams or rivers. He told them it was important to take on as much water as possible and to fill the water cans at every opportunity.

That night they made good ground, walking through fields of high maize that provided cover. In the early hours of the morning, just before sunrise, they looked for another wood or forest and Egan told them to find some food. To the delight of the others, O'Reilly announced that he used to be a poacher back in Ireland and he turned out to be a good one. He knew where local poachers and gamekeepers would set their traps and brought back a rabbit, which he picked the fur from with his stubby fingers and began preparing a fire to cook it on.

"What do you think you are doing?" asked Egan, when he looked up from his map.

O'Reilly assured him that he was just as good a cook as he was a hunter and the rabbit was big enough for all three of them.

"There'll be no fire here," Egan replied. "Are you mad? Are you trying to attract the Germans?"

"What are we supposed to do with the rabbit then?" asked Jonjo.

"Eat it, of course."

"What, raw?"

"Yes, of course," replied Egan, who could see the look of horror on Jonjo's face.

"By the end of this war, Thompson, raw rabbit will be as a feast to you."

Jonjo managed to eat one very chewy raw rabbit leg and Egan managed not much more. O'Reilly, however, enjoyed the rest and gnawed on the bones too.

"It's an Irish thing," Egan assured Jonjo as he looked at the Irishman in disgust.

"Have you got any chocolate left?" asked the young cockney boy.

They buried any evidence and didn't stay where they had eaten, but continued their journey deeper into the wood in case any signs were found. They covered a good distance that night and began making their camp a little late. By the time they had dug their way into another badger sett, the sun was bright. As if crafted by the gifted genius Michelangelo himself, huge white and charcoal boulder-like clouds loitered against a pale blue sky and created white mountains that sat against the skyline on the eastern horizon. Only the canopy of the forest sheltered them from a hot day.

"The nights are getting shorter at this time of year," said Egan. "We need to cover more ground."

"I suggest we dump Eamon then, Sir, we can make better ground without him."

"He's the only one managing to find food at the moment, so he stays."

O'Reilly was beginning to get on Jonjo's nerves with his inane comments. And, when they slept, Jonjo and the captain had to keep waking up to keep the Irishman's snoring at bay.

"In a few weeks it will be the longest day," continued Egan, who was more concerned about it being the shortest night too, giving them less travelling time. He had avoided telling the other two about the objective of the mission, or that there was a tight timescale for completing it. The best intelligence they had indicated that the Germans could be in Paris by the middle of June and that was only a little more than two weeks away. A large British Expeditionary Force was on its way to support the French and Belgians but, if Boulogne was any indication, this would not be enough to stop Paris falling. Egan had no interest in Paris, of course, but if the capital was occupied, then it was likely the seaports would be too.

"I thought all the days were the same size," said O'Reilly. "Do some have less than twenty-four hours, then?"

Egan ignored him, but it didn't stop him talking.

"'Cause that would explain why I feel so tired some mornings."

"O'Reilly, shut your gabbing and walk a bit faster," the captain ordered.

By the end of the third night, they had managed to evade detection and were now close to the Belgian border. They ate what they could catch and occasionally found duck eggs in nests alongside the small rivers and streams where they filled their water cans. Using the fields of growing crops, they extended their walk into the early daylight hours, keeping close to hedgerows and taking cover when they heard any sounds. But there didn't appear to be much activity and they certainly hadn't seen any Germans on their travels. Then, in the distance they could hear what sounded like thunder. There had been no rain since their arrival in France, although it was hot enough for a storm.

As they headed east, the captain halted occasionally to remove his binoculars and examine the horizon. As dawn approached they reached a small wood and Egan said he could see the fortress at Maulde in the distance. It soon became apparent that it wasn't thunder they could hear, but the 75mm guns at the fort of Maubeuge. It seemed the Germans were being held at this point by the French and Belgian defences. Quite how the Germans had managed to arrive in Boulogne without capturing the fort or the town of Maulde concerned Egan a little. He also knew he couldn't simply walk up to the fortress and knock on the door, so he decided to make camp, eat what they could find and try to move towards the building that night.

It was a still day and as the three men rested themselves in the middle of a field of maize and waited for dusk the silence was interrupted at regular intervals by the booming noise of the guns. The shade provided an opportunity to rest and Jonjo lay there gazing at a blue sky occasionally broken by fluffy white clouds. He remembered going to Paris with the Martins and wondered how far he was now from that city. Metaphorically speaking, he was a long way from that day in Paris. He had grown to manhood and survived intense battles at the Hook of Holland and at Outreau. He had seen colleagues die, experienced sleep deprivation, hunger and fear — a type of fear he had never thought possible. And yet here he was, deep inside enemy territory, on a mission that seemed to have no relevance to the war that raged around them.

Occasionally the distant sound of shelling stopped and an uneasy silence prevailed. These were rare moments of peace, although the anxious feelings in their stomachs never rested. At around mid-morning, before the sun had reached its highest point, an extended moment of stillness overpowered the clamour of war and a church bell could be heard summoning the faithful to mass. Jonjo closed his eyes and returned to another world, in another time. As a child, he would make every excuse for not attending mass on Sunday but, right now, he would give anything for the opportunity to be sitting alongside his family and friends in the parish church at home.

He managed to sleep that afternoon and, shortly after a large red sun had set behind them, the men gathered their few belongings and began to move off. Just then, there was a large flash of light in the sky ahead of them and a second later a deafening blast shook the ground beneath their feet. Egan realised that yet another opportunity had been missed. A series of smaller explosions followed, but what sounded like the ammunition block being hit by a German shell was actually Captain Schwengler sabotaging and evacuating the fort. Either way, the help he had expected to get at the fort disappeared in an instant. Egan shook his head and realised that yet another alternative plan needed to be implemented. If the fort had fallen, then the town would follow soon so, scanning his ragged maps, he found a small village called Touberge that was situated close to a dense forest that he could see to the north. He decided to head towards the town in the hope that he might meet and perhaps enlist the support of some of Schwengler's men in getting him to Amsterdam.

Moving across the countryside and avoiding the roads meant they rarely saw any road signs to assist their journey. Unlike back in Britain, such signs had been left in place by the French, but they were of little use to the captain. A map and a compass would need to suffice as they traced their way across fields in the direction of the village, which sat on the border between France and Belgium.

It was getting light when they reached a dense forest so, sheltered by the trees and keeping a look out for German troops, they made good progress towards their next destination of Touberge. Eventually, as the trees began to thin out, they saw the lights of the village in the distance. They hadn't seen any evidence of the enemy but it did not make sense simply to walk out of the forest in daylight.

As they approached what appeared to be the edge of the forest, a long, shallow stream ran across their path. Egan was reluctant to cross it but there appeared to be no way round it or any bridges or fords. They knelt at the muddy bank and filled their water cans, as they had done at every watering hole they came across.

"Look," Egan said to them firmly. "I'm going to walk across this brook and unfortunately I will leave rather distinctive footprints. Now, we're not going to be able to cover these up without attracting attention to them, so this is what we are going to do." He waited until he had their full attention. "You two follow me across, stepping exactly into my footprints, okay?"

They nodded. "At least if they are discovered by Jerry, they will think there is only one of us."

So, they did as they had been instructed and all three arrived safely on the other side. Egan looked back at the muddy imprints and sighed. They had managed to tidy the bank of the stream where they had filled their water cans, but any attempt to cover the footprints across the shallow brook would create even greater suspicion. Through the trees, the captain could see that the sun was now fully risen and he got the sense that they were close to the edge of the wood. So, following his instructions, they all went off to find another badger sett to accommodate them until sunset. They decided that during the night they would each take it in turns to conduct reconnaissance of the area. If they were caught, the footprints at the edge of the forest would confirm the soldier was simply a straggler who, by some miracle, had reached the Belgian border. If it was Thompson or O'Reilly they would know nothing of the mission and if it was Egan, he would never reveal their true purpose or objective.

So, when darkness fell, Egan was the first to leave the hideout to reconnoitre the area outside the wood. As he skirted the forest, he scribbled a roughly drawn map. From the trees that skirted a small road, he could see some buildings. The area was occupied by German forces and officers had set up their headquarters at a chateau just outside the village. Through the shadows he could hear them talking, eating and drinking the excellent stock of French wines. The junior officers were barracked under canvas in a field by the road leading to Lille, with senior officers billeted in the main house. Moving quietly west from that point led the captain to the village. About one hundred metres from where he hid, German soldiers were walking into town for the evening to enjoy a beer. They seemed relaxed and clearly didn't suspect in the least that British soldiers might be in the area. After all, they were camped more than one hundred miles from Boulogne, where the British advance had been pushed back. Small units of infantry were despatched occasionally to inspect the woodland and hillside around the town but these excursions provided no more than an opportunity for a cigarette. It reminded Egan of how negligent he had been at Outreau. He realised now that the Germans had already occupied the high ground around that village before the Harpoon Force had arrived. He dismissed such negative thoughts; what was done was done, it couldn't be changed.

Occasionally some soldiers passed close to where the other two British soldiers were bedded down but could not see anything suspicious in the dark. To the east of the village there were large barns that local farmers used to store grain. These were rested aboveground on wooden plinths. It was dark enough for Egan to make his way from the forest to the nearest of the barns. He crawled from the forest to a hedgerow that ran alongside a narrow country lane and then scrambled his way to the first of the barns. The gap underneath the wooden structure was insufficient to crawl through but, by digging a hole under the edge of the barn, the space below became much larger and it was certainly enough to hide three men. They would simply need to refill the hole at the edge of the barn to cover their presence there.

Egan returned to the badger sett where he had left the others and told them to gather everything up.

"We're moving to a new location and we have a couple of hours to do it."

He led the men back towards the grain barn, avoiding the rarely used footpaths and stopped occasionally to listen for the sound of any guards. After digging a small trench they clambered under the barn and pushed the earth back up to conceal the entrance hole. Egan was pleased with his night's work, although for the two soldiers this was nothing like the training they had received for night manoeuvres.

The new home was more spacious than the dens they had grown used to on their travels. For the first time there was sufficient room for Egan to propose an armoury check. The two guardsmen had a rifle and about fifty rounds of ammunition each, whereas the captain had two hand guns, around twenty bullets and a large sheaf knife. After the inspection, he ordered the two men to sleep while he stayed awake in case of visitors. Although this proved unnecessary, he was able to prod O'Reilly whenever he began snoring. It would soon be daylight and the local area would be swarming with Germans.

Captain Egan was sure the Germans would move out of the village after resting for a couple of days and continue their journey west towards the front line. Time was running out for him but, by waiting, he could gather provisions and begin the final stage of the journey to Amsterdam. However, the next day passed and then the next and he began to realise that the Germans were creating a staging post at the village. They were not going anywhere and he was running out of options. The decision now was whether he should move off through Belgium and Holland alone, or with the two men, in order to complete the mission.

The formalities between the officer and his men were gradually dismantled over those two days. Guardsman O'Reilly became Eamon and Guardsman Thompson explained how his names of John Joseph were corrupted to produce Jonjo. Finally, on the second night, the captain explained how he came to be known as 'Axe' to many of his men. A, X and E were simply his initials and Anthony Xavier Egan told them his family had served in the army for generations. There was little room for conventionality in the narrow gap below the barn and so, almost without noticing, the captain became Axe to the two men and the officer made no objection.

"My great grandfather served under Lord Cardigan with the British Light Cavalry at the Battle of Balaclava," said Egan proudly, adding that his grandfather and father had followed suit. "My father served in the Irish Guards and I always wanted to follow him."

O'Reilly nodded sagely as he listened to the sincere reminiscing of his captain. "Of course, I'm a career soldier too," he declared.

"Your father served before you, did he?"

"Erm, no," answered Eamon, "but I'm not a conscript, I volunteered."

"But you're hardly a career soldier, O'Reilly," answered Egan as he rolled a cigarette. "I hate these things," he continued, referring to the cigarette as he lit it. I wish I could have my good old pipe, but Jerry would smell it a mile away."

"My uncle served in the Great War," said O'Reilly, still trying to convince the other two that he had some hereditary background in the army.

"That doesn't make him a career soldier either," replied Egan, hoping to end the conversation.

"My uncle," said O'Reilly, musing over his subject, "was the first casualty of the Great War."

"Really?" asked the captain, suddenly gaining interest. "That's remarkable. What regiment did he serve in?"

"First Wiltshire Rifles, Sir. They landed at Normandy in the early days of the war and he was ordered to set up camp. He saw some old wooden crates and thought they would make a good fire. Unfortunately, his mates hadn't emptied all the ammunition out of them and he blew his fecking leg off."

"Jesus," said Jonjo a little too loudly, "you tell some bloody awful stories, Eamon. Are there any more at home like you?"

"None in England but I've got hundreds of cousins back in Ireland."

On the third night, after three days under the floor of the barn, Egan realised that the Germans were not going to move on towards the western front and concluded it was they who would need to move out of the village. They had eaten little and had left their hideout only to fill the water bottles and gather what food they could. Tomorrow would be the last day of May, he thought, and he had wasted three days waiting for safe passage. So, as soon as darkness fell outside the barn, he took them into the woods and climbed the hill so that they could get a view of the route for the next stage for the journey. There was still a half moon but he couldn't wait any longer. Anyway, it was pitch darkness in the thick forest and they could barely see where they were walking. They needed to get to the eastern side of the hill and Egan gave the others their instructions. By working individually, if one was caught, the Germans would probably think he was alone. They were not far from the small river crossing where the captain had got them to tread in the same footsteps to convince the Germans that there was only one of them should that situation arise. O'Reilly's task was to locate a badger sett on this side of the hill and dig it out for them to use. This would enable them to continue their journey the following night without having to pass by the village and the German troops. Jonjo's task was to get some food. In the meantime, Axe moved to the far side of the forest to see what the fields leading northeast had in them.

Axe was the first to complete his task. From that edge of the forest he saw some fields of wheat down the hill, which would not provide very good cover. However, beyond these, there were extensive fields of maize. Although it was only the early days of summer, the maize looked sufficiently high to provide the cover they needed in order to travel during dusk.

Jonjo found a poacher's trap with a hare in it. He sat at the foot of a large tree and began to pluck the fur from the creature as he waited for the agreed signal. There was little bird call in the forest that night and eventually he heard Eamon's rather poor imitation of an owl and moved off towards it. In the meantime, Axe had memorised the route away from the forest and was heading back towards where he had left the other two. He stopped occasionally to listen for the sound of an owl. It was extremely dark and he could barely see the forest floor as he walked slowly through the trees. Suddenly, there was a loud clanging of metal and an animal trap clamped shut around his ankle. The rusty blades that should have snapped the neck of a rabbit or hare had embedded themselves into his calf, just above the ankle. In the darkness, he reached down and was trying to remove the trap when a rifle barrel appeared in his face.

8

Saturday 23 May 2015 — M25, Kent

As we drove towards the Channel Tunnel, I apologised to Tonka for my overly sensationalised meanderings on the way home the previous night, assuring him that Colonel Elton had that effect on people. He was an old-school, cold-war intelligence officer who couldn't resist jabbing his finger at a situation to see if it produced anything of interest. I'm sure Tonka was even less convinced of Elton's innocent questioning than I was and we both sat in silence for a while wondering what possible interest the old man could have in our trip to Boulogne. As the monotony of the motorway and the self-sameness of the landscape began to produce a hypnotic state I decided to wait for another clue before speculating further. If there was a purpose in his conspicuous visit to the club, then he would turn up again, like the proverbial bad penny. Trying to interpret the colonel's comments in order to understand his ulterior motive was a waste of energy, so best to wait until he took another step into my life. So I chose to adopt the tactics of the counter attack and wait for his next move.

Despite my best intentions, after twenty minutes I broke the monotonous drone of the car engine to assure Tonka that the colonel was only interested in enlisting our help on some future project connected to his unsavoury work. That was my conclusion from the evidence already to hand. The cover of two investigative journalists probably suited his needs although, in truth, I couldn't help recalling what Elton had said early on in our conversation. "If anyone can get to the bottom of it, you can, Jack." There wasn't anything to get to the bottom of, I assured myself. But the colonel's words suggested this assumption was incorrect. What possible interest could Elton have in our trip to France?

Having too long to think about anything was not always a good thing but it seemed sensible that, whatever Elton was interested in, it had something to do with Tonka's grandad, or at least the mission he had been on when he was captured. I tried to recall anything the late John Joseph Thompson had ever said about the war, but it was very little. All I recalled were those incredible tales of adventure and none of those, as far as I could remember, were set in the Second World War. With nothing else to go on, after ten minutes, I became convinced that a clue might be found among those bedtime stories. After all, this was all I knew about the man and this trip was about him. And, despite the connection, Elton's interest could not be about Grandad's military career because he spent almost the entire war in a prisoner-of-war camp. So I began separating the fact from the fiction in those late-night tales. Firstly I eliminated the locations and events of every story because it was clear that Grandad could only have read about these, not actually been involved in them. I then considered Grandad's particular contribution to each story in case there was some relevance there. And then I set about eliminating the other characters. Obviously the three-legged cat called Dolores, for whom he made a peg-leg while serving on the Jolly Roger, was completely fictitious and couldn't even be a characterisation of a real person. And the parrot named Oscar, who spoke with a speech impediment because his previous owner had one, seemed just as unlikely. Deacon Tull, the Crimson Pirate and Blackbeard were presumably characters from movies he had seen, or books he had read, so there didn't appear to be any significance there.

It occurred to me that Tonka and I had been at secondary school before we'd realised all the stories he'd told were lies, fantasies of his vivid imagination and I was just beginning to dismiss the whole theory of some connection when we pulled up at passport control before boarding the Channel Tunnel train. The uniformed guard looked at our passports and then handed them back to us along with a large envelope which, at first, Tonka thought contained the tickets.

"This was left here this morning for you," the guard said and I noticed it had a government seal on it.

As Tonka drove towards a long queue of cars in front of us, I tore open the envelope to find a cardboard folder with documents divided into two sections. The first section was headed: *'Report on the Operations of 2nd Battalion Irish Guards in the Boulogne Area from Tuesday 21 May 1940 to Thursday 23 May 1940'*. It consisted of extemporaneous notes written at the time, presumably by a junior officer assigned to complete a record of the events. It began from the time an order had been received to move from battalion headquarters on the morning of 21 May 1940 and ended when they had returned to Tweseldown Camp at half past six in the morning, three days later. The first of four appendices provided the names of the officers involved and the second appendix showed the numbers of other ranks. Thirty-three officers were accompanied by six hundred and seventy-nine guardsmen. The third appendix was headed: *'Lessons Drawn from the Experiences of the Battalion'*. And the fourth appendix contained the number of casualties. Two were killed in action, one died from his wounds, thirteen were known to be wounded, eleven were believed to be in hospital and one hundred and seventy-four were missing.

Grandad was, presumably, one of that one hundred and seventy-four. There was a note to say that the number of dead had been amended following information received subsequent to this report being written.

Tonka looked at me and recognised the expression of anxiety.

"What the hell is all this?" I asked as I sat there feeling and presumably looking like someone who was being stalked.

"Perhaps he's just trying to be helpful."

The comment was intended to dispel my fears but I'm sure he shared my suspicion that we were being shadowed.

"What is it he wants, Tonka?"

"Don't let him rile you, Jack," he answered. "Be patient and wait for him to reveal himself. If you're that sure he has an ulterior motive, he has to come out of the shadows to make his move."

We decided to leave the report until we could read it together on the train.

"Do you know what?" I said after putting all the documents back in their folder as we waited to drive into the carriage.

"What?" asked Tonka.

"I can't imagine your grandad killing someone, you know, shooting them. Even in a battle situation, it's difficult to visualise him doing it. He didn't seem capable."

"You'd be surprised, Jack. Self-preservation, the need to follow instructions or simply peer pressure. Very few people wouldn't do it in a kill-or-be-killed situation."

"What was it like the first time you did it?" I asked.

"I can't even remember when the first time was, Jack. Half the time you don't even know if you've killed someone. I'm pretty certain it would have been like that at Boulogne for Grandad. The target is rarely an individual but rather a barricade and what is behind it."

Once on the train, Tonka and I divided the report into two parts and began reading it. Strangely, neither of us even mentioned who had sent the report to us. There was no covering letter or note and nothing to say where it had come from. That in itself was worrying because we both assumed, quite rightly it seems, that the colonel had sent it. In fact, it wasn't until the train pulled into Calais that Tonka handed the paperwork back to me and asked whether the colonel had mentioned this report last night. I tried to recall exactly what was said, believing the exact words might be important.

"I told the colonel we were interested in knowing what the aim of your grandad's mission had been when he was captured in Boulogne," I replied. "He seemed to be just as interested as we were, which concerned me a little. He also knew quite a lot about events back in 1940, too." I admitted to feeling very uneasy about the meeting.

"Why, what did he say?"

"He knew we were going to Boulogne. He knew about the service on Sunday; he knew your grandad had been captured and, most worryingly, he had certainly swotted up on the matter before he walked into the Legion club. He knew I was going to be at the club that night, Tonka. He planned everything that happened and he has some ulterior motive."

"So, how did the conversation finish? Did he say he was sending you these documents?"

"No. He just said he was sufficiently interested in our trip to give me some assistance, provided I kept him informed of developments."

"What developments?" Tonka asked. "We're only going to a service of remembrance for those who served at the Battle of Boulogne."

I had to admit that I had no idea. Tonka thought I was suffering from paranoia and suggested that Colonel Elton had simply learned of our trip through one of his military contacts and had responded when I'd told him we were interested in learning a little more about the Battle of Boulogne. Tonka always saw the simplest solution to puzzles and I had to admit that my own reasoning took on all the incredulity of one of Grandad's bedtime stories.

It was only a short drive to Boulogne, but it gave me time to underline any points of interest in the report.

The battalion was given very short notice of the mission. A large number of Irish Guards had been given leave as it was the Whitsun holiday weekend, so the battalion numbers were depleted. Those remaining had just finished night manoeuvres when new orders arrived from the War Office so, by the time they arrived at Dover, they hadn't slept for thirty-six hours. Some Welsh Guards, whose battalion was also reduced, were added to make up the unit and the ship provided for the cross-channel journey turned out to be too small. As a consequence, much of the artillery was left on the quay and, apart from two anti-tank guns, the limited armoury they took consisted mainly of rifles.

The preparations couldn't have been much worse. A depleted force, without sleep for thirty-six hours and cobbled together for the first time, were sent to defend France armed only with rifles, not knowing if the enemy was already dug in or not.

Fortunately the enemy was not dug in, as reconnaissance of the surrounding area established. However, that cursory reconnaissance was flawed and, shortly after the Irish Guards had taken up a position around the village of Outreau, they came under heavy fire from a German panzer division with air support.

The report of events provided to us by the colonel was written in an improvised and dispassionate hand. Its detached terminology only made the record more emotive and palpable. It described events as they occurred, with personal references only to the officers. The worst of the battle took place after sundown. Relentless shelling of the Guards' position continued through the night. With no heavy guns, mortar or air support the battalion did well to hold a line across a two-mile-wide front that defended the village.

One important piece of information that Tonka and I were missing was which company his grandad had been assigned to. However, the records showed that almost all the members of number four company were captured by the Germans at the end of the battle, because that company had been given the task of holding off the enemy, while the other three companies made their escape via the harbour area. It was not unreasonable to assume, therefore, that Grandad had been a member of number four company.

I skipped through the report looking for references to number four company. It was recorded that, soon after shelling recommenced on the second morning, number four company was forced to withdraw from the southern outskirts of Outreau village. A later report read: *'At this stage, I did not yet realise that number one and number four companies had already been reduced to almost microscopic numbers'*. The record showed that, of one hundred and seven men of number four company who landed in Boulogne, only nineteen returned. The report written as daylight returned to the scene on the second morning continued: *'I think I had expected to see corpses everywhere, but the only person in sight was a lieutenant standing behind a wall with a revolver in his hand. The noise of rifles and machine guns soon showed that there were really hundreds of men all around me, but our own men and the Germans were all hidden'*.

Slipped in among the report I found a separate sheet of paper, which transpired to be a report from a naval officer serving on HMS *Whitshed*, which had been sent to Boulogne to assist the evacuation. *'The machine-gun fire sounded very close and as the destroyer, going into action, cleared a long shed on the quay, the captain suddenly saw what was going on. A section of Irish Guards were engaging with rifle fire an enemy machine-gun post established in a warehouse, as coolly and methodically as if they had been on the practice ranges. "Tell the foremost guns to open fire," the captain yelled. The guns swung round and with a crash two 4.7 HE shells tore into the building and blew it to the skies. Meanwhile the German infantry now*

103

passed ahead of their tanks and infiltrated closer and closer to the quays, the fine discipline of the Guards earned the awed open-mouthed respect of all. Watching them in perfect order, moving exactly together, engaging target after target as though on parade ground drill, it was difficult to realise that this was the grim reality of battle. They were truly magnificent and no sailor who saw them could ever forget the feeling of pride he experienced.'

I continued reading the report. As the evacuation continued, twenty large German aircraft had begun bombing the harbour when nine British fighter planes swept out of the sky and tore into them. The joy of the guards on the ground was short-lived as they saw sixty Stuka dive bombers sweep in and peel off to dive. As their bombs dropped, German infantry poured down the streets of Outreau towards the harbour. *'The din was appalling,'* the report read. *'To the deafening roar of guns was added the scream of falling bombs, the snarl of crashing planes and the angry hornet noise of dive bombers. Huge fountains of mud and water rose alongside the destroyers in the harbour, drenching everybody at the guns.'*

Number four company had been left to hold off the German advance while the other three companies escaped. The last report of that group was that they *'were now so close to the enemy lines that retreat was impossible'*. Those words resonated in my head. I read it two or three times. It was so succinctly put, written in the heat of battle, yet it dispassionately expressed the unenviable choice they made. If they had turned their backs they would have been shot, so they chose capture. It is difficult to imagine Grandad surrendering and I'm not sure he would have done so if he had known the agony that was to follow. In his bedtime stories, he had shot it out with the Dalton gang and Deacon Tull but the real thing had proved too difficult.

As we drove along the dual carriageway towards Boulogne, Tonka was concentrating on looking for signs to Outreau, so I turned to the document headed *'Lessons Drawn from the Experiences of the Battalion'*. Just as Tonka turned into a side street and drew up outside the hotel, I quickly read one last paragraph. *'Circumstances force the battalion and the anti-tank guns attached to it to move into position by daylight. There is little doubt that the latter part of the occupation was observed by the enemy from the ridge that overlooked Outreau. Thus, from the beginning, the Germans must have been well aware of the general line occupied by us and probably also of the exact positions in which at least some of the anti-tank guns had been placed.'*

"Anything interesting?" Tonka asked as we got out of the car.

I puffed my cheeks out, wondering how to begin to describe what I had read. "You need to read it yourself, Tonka. However, there are a couple of references to the name of the mission or perhaps the code name for the battalion on this operation."

"What was it?"

"The Harpoon Force."

Once we had unpacked I sent a text home to let Ludo and Gabriella know we had arrived safely. We sat outside the hotel in the fading sunlight and chatted about the documents. Tonka told me that nowadays the British Army used a computer to produce the names of operations. These were selected at random and bore no resemblance to the object of the mission. Years ago, in the war, operational names were chosen by human beings at the War Office and there was always the danger that they would, subliminally, reflect the intentions of the project. The harpoon, suggested Tonka, was a weapon fired with the intention of bringing something back, like a fish.

"So, perhaps if Grandad really did rescue a queen on the first mission, albeit by chance rather than design, perhaps he was genuinely going back for her crown jewels on the second one," suggested Tonka.

"It's a long way to go across country. Why wouldn't we have parachuted someone into the Netherlands?" I asked.

"Rotterdam had just been bombed and the Irish Guards were chased out of the Hook of Holland by advancing German troops."

Tonka shook his head and I paused, desperately wanting to change the subject, very aware that I was in danger of allowing my paranoia to spoil Tonka's trip to his grandad's old battleground. But I couldn't help myself.

"Why," I asked, "do you think Elton is so interested in the Harpoon Force then?"

"You're doing it again, Jack. Don't cloud your mind with a load of supposition."

"The colonel looked very surprised when I showed him the photograph of the football team."

"Perhaps he was surprised that prisoners of war played football. I don't suppose they did in Malaya, where Elton served."

"No, it was something to do with the camp. The sign saying 'Stalag XXV' is what took his attention."

It had been a long day and, after a few drinks, we were just thinking about turning in when my mobile telephone rang. I didn't recognise the number but certainly recognised the voice. It was Colonel Elton and as he spoke I wondered whether he was standing close by, watching our every move.

"We received the paperwork," I said, anticipating the intention of his call.

"Yes, I know that, Jack. I always make sure a job is closed out properly. That isn't what I am calling you about."

I tried to interrupt but he simply continued unabated. "Stalag XXV was not built until June 1940 and didn't take in any prisoners until the end of that month. All those captured at Boulogne were sent to Stalag XXII. I just thought that information might be useful. Good luck."

The phone went dead. I wanted to ask what the significance of this statement was, but he knew I could work it out for myself. Having just spoken about Stalag XXV, my fears that Colonel Elton was loitering nearby hardened.

"Do you see what I mean?" I said, a little too loudly, to Tonka. "Here we are discussing the photo of Stalag XXV and Elton phones with guidance about that very subject. It's like we're being bugged."

Tonka shook his head and we started to make our way up to the bedrooms.

"*You* would know, wouldn't you, Tonka?"

"Know what?" he asked.

"Well, you were in the SAS. You could tell if we were being bugged, couldn't you?"

"Jack, stop it. You'll be looking under the car for bombs next and that's when I'll slap you."

9

Tuesday 28 May 1940 — Foret Isole

With the long barrel of an old rifle only a few inches from his nose, Egan tried to stop screaming, but the pain was so great he almost wanted to be put out of his misery. Indeed, if he had been a horse that is exactly what would have happened. In the shadowy darkness of the forest it was difficult to make out whether the rifle was being held by a German soldier or not.

To his relief, the voice spoke French rather than German, although he didn't understand what had been said.

"British soldier," he answered, pronouncing each syllable individually.

"Oui, soldat Britannique," repeated the Frenchman, pointing his rifle at the uniform Axe was wearing.

Axe wasn't sure if the man was annoyed at the fact that he was a British soldier or if he had just stated the obvious. Either way, it wasn't the most important issue at the moment. The elderly man was dressed more like a gamekeeper than a poacher. He knelt down and opened the trap. Axe eased his leg out and suppressed a scream of agony as the tips of the blades came out of his flesh.

The gamekeeper handed him a scarf to wrap around the wound. In the silence of the night, they heard movement in the trees behind them and the man raised his rifle in preparation. Eamon and Jonjo halted as they came into sight and saw the gun pointing at them. They had heard the clang and at least one of them had thought it might be another meal. Instead they were faced with an armed stranger and a very seriously injured captain.

"Attendre ici," the man said and left, disappearing into the darkness as he walked back in the direction of the village.

"Can you move?" Jonjo asked the captain as soon as the man had gone.

"You'd have to carry me, but we wouldn't get far." He paused. "The die is cast, boys," he added. "If he comes back with Jerry, then it's all over."

"Who is he?" Eamon asked.

"Well, he's French and I'd guess he was the local gamekeeper for the tenants at the chateau. But, whoever he is, I think we're in his hands. You two could make a run for it, but I'm not sure where you would go." He explained that now the fort had fallen, the area would be swamped with Germans heading across France to the channel ports.

The three men sat on the ground and prepared themselves for whatever fate had decided for them. Fifteen minutes later, through the darkness, the gamekeeper returned with another man in his late fifties. There was an immediate language problem because neither of the men spoke English and Captain Egan didn't speak French. From what Axe could make out, the other man was possibly the town mayor and his name was Henri Poirier. It soon became clear that the three soldiers could not understand anything they were saying, so the captain decided to interrupt.

"Is this the village of Touberge?" He pointed towards the village. "Touberge?"

"Touberge?" Poirier replied indignantly. "Ce n'est pas Touberge."

The man looked as if he had been delivered a terrible insult.

"Touberge?" he repeated, as if it was a very stupid suggestion to make. "C'est Cache Moyen. Notre village est plus de important que Touberge."

The two Frenchmen discussed the insult between themselves. Considerable rivalry existed between the two local villages since Touberge had been awarded the Croix de Guerre in recognition of its bravery in the Great War. The gamekeeper insisted that they should allow them to go to Touberge if that was what the British soldiers wanted, but the mayor disagreed, saying this could be their opportunity to secure an even greater award themselves. He corrected himself.

"Pour la village."

"Indifférence ce n'est pas suffit, mon ami."

"Mais c'est censé être en dange," the gamekeeper replied anxiously.

For the pride of the village, he added, before turning to the three men and lecturing them on the merits of Cache Moyen, as if they were themselves judges in a best-kept village competition.

"Il est Cache Moyenaise qui recevoir le Croix de Guerre, ou peut-être L'Ordre de la Libération, ou même Le Legion d'honneur."

The captain did not understand and shrugged his shoulders. The mayor decided to continue speaking in French, which was all he knew, but he now started to speak more slowly and began adding some description with his hands.

"Cinq cents metres," Poirier said pointing towards the village.

"Five hundred metres," the captain replied, in explanation to his colleagues. "We are five hundred metres from the village."

"We knew that," mumbled Jonjo.

"Oui. A la direction."

"In that direction."

Jonjo was not impressed but the mayor smiled at the limited progress they were making.

"Est la village."

"Is the village." The captain put the three parts of the sentence together. "Five hundred metres in that direction is the village."

"Oui, bon."

"Ma fille, Elodie," Poirier continued, splaying his arms to indicate he was wearing a dress.

"Your woman, Elodie," the captain replied, to the wonderment of O'Reilly, who was easily impressed by the captain's grasp of the French language.

"Elodie, servirons, être présen, manger," each word was accompanied by a hand gesture and Axe continued playing this strange game of charades.

"Elodie will bring food," he said, almost too loudly.

"Par le cimetière, arrièr, adjacent," Poirier added pointing towards a small cemetery that lay at the edge of the forest close to the inn that Poirier owned. "A vingt trois heures demain," he added pointing to his watch. Egan shrugged at the last piece of information, so the mayor indicated twenty-three with his fingers. It was well after midnight, so the captain knew the man must mean tomorrow night at eleven o'clock.

Axe turned to his colleagues. "A woman, his wife or mother I think, will bring food and leave it at the cemetery at eleven o'clock tomorrow night. Her name or the password, I'm not sure which, is Elodie." He hesitated. "I think that is what he said."

Poirier then bandaged the captain's leg and the two soldiers carried him back to the barn to discuss a plan. They decided to abandon the idea of moving to the badger sett that Eamon had dug, as the injury sustained by Axe meant he was unable to climb into the hole.

"We're not at Toubeuge," Axe said, looking at the map with a torch. "We seem to be near a village called Cache Moyen in the Foret Isole, which I think means isolated or lonely forest."

After a brief discussion about their situation, the captain wanted time to think. They remained silent for most of the following day as it was difficult to determine how close the German troops might be. They were unlikely to be searching the area because they couldn't possibly know that the three soldiers were around. At worst they may have seen the footprints at the stream and searched the local area.

Blood continued to slowly ooze through the bandage during the day but they had no medical supplies to treat it with. Using the sheaf knife, Jonjo cut the tail of his shirt off and cut this into strips, before tying it around the reddening bandage. He then cut the tops of his socks and pulled these up over the Captain's leg to hold the bandage in place. He then put his hands against the bottom of Egan's foot and asked quietly if he could push against it. He winced as he did so and whispered that he couldn't put any weight on it.

"I don't think there are any bones broken," said Jonjo in a hushed tone. "It should heal up in a couple of days."

"A couple of days will be too late," replied the captain and Jonjo wanted to ask why. He didn't, knowing that Egan would tell him what the plan was when the time was right. It didn't look as though the time was right now.

The afternoon was spent quietly speculating about what food they might receive from the man's wife that night. They hadn't eaten real food for a few days, if you discounted duck eggs and raw rabbit.

"They eat snails over here," mumbled Eamon.

"Don't tell me that after all this time I've got to eat a slug," whispered Jonjo.

"Shut up, lads. It'll probably be a nice chunk of French cheese and a bottle of Margaux."

Neither of the other two knew what Margaux was, but didn't like to admit it.

They slept at intervals and, at a little after ten thirty that evening, Jonjo pulled some earth away from where they had covered up the entrance to their hiding place under the barn. He pushed his head out into the darkness and tried not to disturb the gorse, bramble and nettle that surrounded it and provided extra cover for the hideout. He waited for a few seconds. Being underground all day, his eyes were accustomed to the darkness, but he wanted to listen for any movement or sounds. Once he was satisfied that they were alone in the field he scrambled out and pushed the foliage back over the hole under the barn. He then crawled across the short distance to the edge of the forest, paying particular attention to where he was treading in order to avoid any animal traps. He then made his way slowly through the wood to the wall of the cemetery. With a small jump his hands grabbed the top of the wall and he pulled himself up.

The graveyard was quiet but, in the distance beyond the church, he could hear some stifled noise from the inn. He lifted himself onto the top of the wall and dropped down the other side as quietly as he could. In the corner there was a wild thyme bush that butted up against a whitethorn hedge that stretched down to the road in front of the church. It made a good hiding place and he crouched down waiting for the arrival of the old woman.

The clock on the church tower chimed eleven times and Jonjo heard the sound of footsteps coming along the gravel path that led through the churchyard to the small cemetery. Through the shadows he could see what looked like a girl or young woman, but certainly not someone who could be the Frenchman's wife or mother. As she drew nearer, he could see she was carrying a basket containing flowers. She approached a grave that stood against the back wall and placed the flowers on it before kneeling down to place them in a dirty stone vase that stood there.

She seemed to be taking undue time to complete her task and Jonjo wondered if the woman he was due to meet had been deterred by this other visitor. After lying still all day long and then crouching for ten minutes, he was beginning to get cramp. He stifled a groan and listened as the young woman began to pray, or at least speak to the grave in front of her. At first he took little notice of her words until he realised she was speaking in English. Quite why a French girl was speaking to her dead mother in English baffled Jonjo for a moment but then he realised that this must be his contact after all. He stepped out from behind the whitethorn hedge and tried not to startle her.

"Elodie?"

"Yes," she replied. "Where have you been?" She spoke good but broken English.

"I was expecting someone older," he answered as he approached and a shadowy outline turned into an actual person. The woman was slightly younger than Jonjo. Her slim figure was covered in a shabby dress with a pinafore and her olive skin made her eyes seem almost as bright as the smile she produced in response to his answer. That look on her face told him that she was expecting someone older too and, in spite of his unshaven face, tousled hair and filthy uniform, there was a certain attraction that the expression on her face could not disguise. He stood still, holding three dirty brown and dented canteens used for drinking water. From her basket, she removed a bag of food and handed it to him.

"There's a tap over there that you can fill your water bottles from," she said, pointing to a dark place at the back of the graveyard.

"I'm Jonjo," he said, but she wasn't sure she wanted to know anything about him. His life was in danger and his being here put other lives in danger too.

She repeated his name softly in a way he had never heard it spoken before. It sounded like 'Jzonjzo' as she struggled to pronounce the first and fourth letter.

He repeated his name, but this time mimicking her accent. She smiled.

"Wait here," she said as she walked towards a shabby old wooden shed that stood against the wall of the graveyard. She opened the door quietly and reached inside to where her father had left a hessian sack containing some old clothes. Jonjo kept looking around for signs of anyone else but the night was still, even the birdsong had stopped.

"Here are some clothes that my father thought might be useful."

Jonjo remembered what the captain had told him on that first night spent in the woods outside Boulogne and wondered if she knew the consequences of him being captured out of uniform.

"Your father is very kind," he said in an attempt to continue the conversation. He hadn't been in the company of a young woman for months and never one as beautiful as Elodie. He wanted to ask her if she would like a cigarette because he certainly needed one. But he knew that any light might alert others of their presence in the graveyard. "You're very kind, too," he added.

"What are you doing here?" she asked.

"I can't say."

His cautionary response made him sound more interesting than the more correct answer of, 'I don't know.' 'I can't say,' had a suggestion of intrigue, whereas, 'I don't know,' simply made him sound like an idiot who was lost behind enemy lines.

The reality of the truth did not occur to her, but in an instance she was captivated by the fascinating and, in her young mind, clearly audaciously courageous young man.

"It's best you don't know," he added, reinforcing his enigmatic status with the impressionable girl.

She sighed. "How long will you be here?"

"We can't go anywhere until the captain is able to walk again."

She smiled because she had assumed she would never see Jonjo again after this night and this thought made her feel sad. Self-conscious of her own smile, she blushed and tried to look away, but she couldn't take her eyes from the young paramour. Her attempt to conceal her feelings had the opposite affect and Jonjo knew immediately that they shared an immediate and identical attachment to each other. And, in that instance, Jonjo became lost in that smile. He gazed at her sublime beauty and a thousand questions entered his head. He wanted to ask her so many things, tell her so much. And, for her part, she too wanted to know everything about this beguiling young man. But, instead, they stood in silence for a few moments, neither knowing what to say. Jonjo felt a strange affinity with her. Just as his mother had accused him of thinking too deeply of worldly matters, so Elodie appeared to him in the same character. The expression on her young face was ever questioning, as if the world could never provide sufficient answers to all the unresolved issues that occupied her mind. As if the mystery of life bewitched her very being. She thought too much and too long about the world, dwelt too long in its gaze and was absorbed by its mysteries, just as he was. Living in a tiny village, the world made little sense to her and even now, surrounded by invading German soldiers, she felt like a spectator, an observer of the world's upheavals. She had no involvement in it or, at least, not until this moment. The arrival of Jonjo changed all that and suddenly that quizzical look began to dissolve and was extinguished by a smile. It took but a moment in time and it lit up the world and beguiled the young man who stood before her. From that moment on, the broadest smiles, those created in an instant like this one, would be saved for Jonjo. The questions that had overpowered the smile remained unanswered but lived a new life in a world inhabited by Jonjo. Now, those answers could wait for another day.

"Will you come back tomorrow night?" she asked.

"Eleven o'clock?"

"Yes," she answered as she reluctantly walked away. She so wanted him to kiss her. Her mundane life had been transformed by this engaging and mysterious young man. Her life had become an adventure and she slept little that night, thinking only of meeting him again the following day.

Once the water bottles had been filled he threw them and the bag of clothes over the wall. He followed them over and swiftly returned through the forest to the hideout under the barn, carrying these and the bag of food like a thief in the night. He checked the surrounding area and pushed the large bag of clothes ahead of him, before clambering into the narrow space available below the barn.

"What have you got?" asked the captain.

"It's some clothes and, here," he said showing them the smaller bag, "I have some cheese, ham and some sort of cake."

"Can she speak good English?" asked the captain. "The woman you made contact with," he added.

"Yes, pretty good."

"What did fille mean then?" the captain asked. "Is it mother or wife?"

"Well a filly is a girl horse," replied Eamon, "so fille must mean woman."

"Yes," replied Axe quietly, "but was she his wife or his mother?"

"I'm not sure," answered Jonjo. "It was dark." He paused. "I'll find out tomorrow."

But the captain had other ideas and gave an instruction that Eamon should meet the woman the following night. It was important he felt, that they both got some exercise. Jonjo raised every objection he could to dissuade the captain from replacing him with O'Reilly. It was important to develop a relationship with their contact, he suggested. He knew the way; there was a high wall that was difficult to climb; he knew where the water tap was. But the captain reminded him of his constant questioning of his authority and told Jonjo to share out the food.

After a hot day under the barn and considerable, but quiet, discussion on the matter, it was agreed that Eamon would change into the clothes that they had been given by the inn keeper. In the end, Axe thought he should respect the individual's choice in this matter. He didn't want to prejudice anything that might befall the man who was risking his life to get some food.

Just before eleven o'clock the following evening, Eamon set off through the forest and walked cautiously towards the cemetery. Jonjo had told him about the choice of hiding places and, in the absence of the old woman's presence, Eamon decided to wait in the ramshackle shed from which Elodie had retrieved the bag of clothes. It contained some tools, including a spade that O'Reilly thought would be useful to them. He thought about taking it but decided not to steal from the people who were helping them. On the other side of the stone wall that the shed stood against, he heard the sound of passing German soldiers. He couldn't understand what they were saying, of course, but recognised the guttural tone of the language. For a moment he regretted not taking the revolver that the captain had offered him. He looked around and picked up the old spade to defend himself with if they entered the graveyard, but the sound of their footsteps gradually disappeared into the distance. A few moments passed and a young woman walked up the gravel path past the church and approached the back wall of the graveyard. The shed door stood ajar and Eamon could see her placing some flowers on a grave. Then, looking towards the bush that Jonjo had appeared from the previous night, she called in a subdued voice.

"Jzonjzo, Jzonjzo."

"Did your mother send you?" asked a strangely melodic voice behind her.

She stood up quickly and took three steps backwards. A dishevelled and dirty man in clothes she half recognised was standing in front of her holding up a spade. She dropped the small bag she was holding and moved farther away.

"It's okay," Eamon said. "I'm Jonjo's mate. The captain sent me tonight. My name is Eamon."

"Is Jzonjzo okay?" she asked in a worried voice.

"Aw, he's marvellous fine," replied Eamon, noticing her disappointment and sensing she had a soft spot for his handsome friend. "Is this the food?" he asked, picking up the bag with one hand, while holding on to the shovel with the other. He couldn't resist examining the contents of the bag.

"Aw great," he said, "some more of that fine cake."

As she stood there wondering what to say or do next, the two German soldiers who Eamon had heard passing by the wall, appeared at the end of the path that ran alongside the church. They stood still for a moment and removed the rifles that hung over their shoulders. But, seeing what appeared to be two villagers, they just walked slowly towards them.

"Do you speak French?" Elodie asked Eamon quietly as the two men got nearer.

"No."

"German?"

"No."

"Anything, other than English?" she asked as the two soldiers got slowly nearer.

"Gaelic," he replied. "I speak fluent Gaelic."

"Well," she said, with a sense of urgency in her voice. "Whatever they say, just answer in Gaelic, whatever Gaelic is. I shall tell them I have lost an earring and you are helping me search for it."

The taller of the two German soldiers looked them both up and down and, speaking a little French, asked them who they were. Elodie explained that she was the innkeeper's daughter and the other soldier confirmed he had seen her working at the inn with her father, Monsieur Poirier.

Neither of the soldiers recognised O'Reilly, so they asked him who he was. But he simply shrugged his shoulders and mumbled something to Elodie. They asked him to speak up but, even when he did, neither of the Germans understood the language he was speaking. They knew it wasn't French or English and it certainly wasn't German. Sensing the suspicion this created, Elodie intervened.

"This is Patrice, the village gravedigger," she said confidently. "He is Wallonian."

"Why is he not speaking French?" asked the soldier.

"There are many languages spoken in this area," explained Elodie. "French, of course, Dutch, some German," she added, which pleased them. "But there are many other minor languages and dialects too that are spoken hereabouts. We are close to the border and our constitution protects the country's freedom of language. It states that languages spoken in this country are optional. It is our right, our tradition to speak one of the many dialects that have been spoken here for generations."

She was worried that she was talking too much, perhaps explaining in too much detail, but the soldiers appeared agitated, so she reinforced her vindication of her friend's garbled response.

"People also speak Flemish around here," she said. "And Brabantian, Limburghish, Walloon, Picard, Champenois, Lorrain and, of course, the Jews speak Yiddish. And, even with the Flemish there is East Flemish and West Flemish."

She waited but the soldiers continued to look at Eamon suspiciously.

"Patrice," she said pointing to her friend and told them again that he was the village gravedigger, empathising his role in the community and making a digging movement at the ground so that Eamon might understand what she was saying too. Patrice, she explained was from Wallonia and spoke in the Walloon dialect, or a mixture of Champenois and Walloon, she added, in case one of them happened to speak Walloon. Worried that her explanation was a little too boisterous, she stopped talking for a moment, hoping the two soldiers would turn away.

The smaller of the two soldiers suggested that they ought to search them. The other replied, agreeing, but only if he could search the girl. They both laughed and chose not to risk being reported to the commandant. The taller soldier was concerned about how little the man spoke and instructed Elodie to tell him to explain himself. Working at the inn, she had learned a little English and German but much less of the many dialects spoken in the region. She tried to remember some Walloon and made suitable hand gestures for O'Reilly to say something in his defence. Fortunately he grasped what was required and spoke up in perfect Gaelic.

"Is minic a ghjeibhean beal oscailt diog dunta!"

"Look," she said pointing to the spade. "Creuser, tombe, umgraben männlich, gravedigger."

The soldier seemed to understand her explanation and asked what they were doing in the graveyard at this time of night.

She paused and smiled confidently. Then, speaking firmly and looking him directly in the eyes, she tried to come up with a convincing reason for her attendance there, but she could think of nothing better than her original idea. He wasn't entirely persuaded by her explanation that she had lost an earring in the cemetery when she brought some flowers to her mother's grave earlier. She had returned to ask Patrice to look out for it.

The soldier was quick enough to notice that Elodie did not wear earrings and pointed to her ears. Eamon was wondering why the soldier was pointing at the young woman's ear and thought he was threatening to shoot her in the head. He raised the spade slightly off the ground and Elodie sensed his confusion. She placed her arm around his shoulders, both in assurance and to prevent him from attacking the soldiers.

The smaller of the two soldiers asked why he had not seen Patrice in the village before and Elodie explained that he had been visiting his mother in Wallonia for the past few days. She turned away from the soldiers, grabbed him firmly by his arm and led him off to give her father news of his mother's recovery from tuberculosis.

"Has your mother fully recovered from the tuberculosis?" she said loudly to Eamon, placing a strong emphasis on the name of the disease.

The two soldiers took several steps backwards as they recognised the contagious illness she was referring to. The taller of the two Germans muttered something under his breath and left with his colleague, reaching the gate before the young woman and shabbily dressed man.

Had the two German soldiers found O'Reilly alone in the graveyard, he would now be under arrest or dead. Elodie's quick thinking had saved his life, although Eamon was not aware of the significant role she had played in rescuing him from a dangerous situation. They paused for a few moments in the cemetery until the two soldiers had left. She took his arm and looked about her wondering what to do.

"You can't go back to the hideout," she told him once they were alone. "You must now remain in the village and continue your pretence of being the village gravedigger. I will speak with the priest and ask him to verify your identity."

"I must get back to the captain," answered Eamon.

"The Germans will only wonder where you have gone and it won't be long before they work out that you are not the local gravedigger."

"But where shall I stay?" he asked.

"We'll find somewhere but, in the meantime, you can sleep in that shed," she said, pointing towards the tiny wooden building that Eamon had taken refuge in before she arrived.

"Could you spare some bedding?" he asked politely.

She led him out of the graveyard to begin his new life as a Wallonian gravedigger. "By the way, what was it you said to the German soldiers?"

"Just an old saying from my homeland," he said. "An open mouth often catches a closed fist."

Elodie took Eamon to her father and he agreed that she had made the right decision. He gave the Irishman some bedclothes and told him to make a bed for himself in the shed. He said he would speak with the priest in the morning and decide what course of action to take next.

~~~~~

When O'Reilly failed to return to the hideout, the captain had to decide whether they needed to move camps. It was easy to conclude that Eamon had been captured. There was no doubt about that, otherwise why would he not have returned. The question was whether O'Reilly would disclose the location of their hideout. How long would it take, Egan wondered, for Eamon to tell the Germans of both their existence and their whereabouts? His first problem was to stop the stream of speculation from Jonjo, who was worrying about how he might move the captain in his current condition. Two hours before sunrise they decided to wait one more hour and then move to a new hideout. Once the Germans were alerted, they would search under all the barns, then the badger setts, and they were both convinced that Eamon would break down fairly quickly under questioning.

They hadn't hidden in hedgerows yet and the captain had noted one a short distance away. Convinced that the ditch it stood in would be dry, he told Jonjo to go and check, outside before deciding how he might struggle to the place himself.

Jonjo was gone for just a few minutes before returning to say that the area was clear. With only an hour before sunrise, Jonjo decided to carry the captain over his shoulder, then return to the barn to retrieve the rifles and other equipment.

There had been little rain and so they were able to build a shelter in the trench that the hedge stood in. It proved a good spot to hide and their only problem was the absence of any food. With too few alternatives available, Jonjo convinced Egan to let him visit the cemetery the following night. They had to find out what had happened to O'Reilly and decide what their next move should be. Egan was resigned to the fact that he would not be able to make the long journey to Amsterdam himself, or at least not until he had received medical treatment on his leg. That was not going to happen soon and it would take months to recover by resting it alone.

As they sat in the ditch through the long day, waiting for the sun to go down, Egan wondered whether he needed to tell Jonjo about the mission. The sound of the church bells earlier in the day had reminded him that it was now Sunday 2 June. Even for a fit man, it was still a three-day journey to Amsterdam and he wasn't a fit man. If the Germans had not seized the diamonds already, there was certainly not much time left to stop them from doing so. It could not possibly wait until his leg had healed and, now that O'Reilly had been captured, sending Thompson was the only viable option. Any further delay in making a decision would jeopardise the mission and endanger their lives. He sighed and concluded that the chances of success were now so slim that anything was worth trying. He spent the next twenty minutes considering his approach to Jonjo. At first he thought he should allow the young guardsman some discretion. But, reflecting on Jonjo's history of questioning his orders, he decided against such a liberal approach. His decision was to give him an order and leave him no choice in the matter.

As it began to get dark, Egan pushed, pulled and slid himself along the ground until he was lying next to Jonjo. He spoke as quietly but as firmly as possible. He began by explaining that, along with Queen Wilhelmina and members of the Dutch Government, two other men were rescued at the Hook of Holland. They were two Jewish brothers named Ephrem and Mendel Fleischmann and they were the directors and owners of the House of Fleischman Diamond Company in Amsterdam. A large stock of diamonds had been recovered back to Britain with members of the Dutch parliament when the 2nd Battalion returned from the Hook of Holland. But the Fleischmann brothers did not bring their valuable collection of diamonds with them. Hearing about the destruction of Rotterdam and fearing capture they left their most valuable gems in a secret location in Amsterdam and were prepared to disclose their whereabouts only if they were granted certain concessions by the British Government. Once the brothers were safe in Britain, the terms were agreed and Captain Egan had been given the job of recovering the hoard of diamonds, among which was the priceless and legendry Gemini diamond. At over 3,000 carats, this was the most valuable diamond ever found and it was so large that special tools were being manufactured so that it could be cut by the talented Fleischmann brothers.

Jonjo listened intently to the story, remembering all the rumours that had been spread before that operation began. What he hadn't yet considered was why Egan was telling him all this. But, once the captain was convinced he had taken it all in, he delivered his instruction.

"You are going to go to Amsterdam to get those diamonds, Thompson, and then make your way back to England. You will succeed by any means possible." He paused. "Do you know what I mean by that, Jonjo? By any means possible."

Jonjo nodded, he understood the significance of what the captain was saying, but he had no idea how he would get to Amsterdam and he was more interested in how he could possibly make his way back home.

"How do I get back to England?"

"I can't be sure what your best escape plan is, Thompson. This is a fast-changing situation. We have been out of touch with HQ for ten days now, so I don't know which ports are held by the Germans and which are still held by us or our allies. We may have been driven out of Boulogne but hopefully, the British Expeditionary Force is still present at one or two other French ports. Directly north of here is the city of Lille and north of that are the ports of Ostend and Dunkerque. The intention of the British Expeditionary Force was to consolidate their defensive position west of Dunkerque. When you have the diamonds in your possession, I suggest you head for that port. You need to move quickly if you are to have any hope of getting there in time to get home. Make contact with any British troops and tell them you are the only surviving member of the Harpoon Force. With any luck, they can get you back home."

Jonjo winced at his words. Why would he be the only surviving member of the team? It was a question he didn't want to ask. In the days that Jonjo had been with Captain Egan he had learned not to question his authority. So, although the mission appeared hopeless and the captain's instructions were far beyond his capabilities, Jonjo was unable to say as much.

"And if the ports are occupied, where do I turn?"

"If all else fails, I suggest you try to make contact with the Communist Party of the Netherlands, the CPN are a bunch of communist resistance fighters. But that's a last resort, Thompson."

"Did you even have an escape plan?"

"Yes," answered Egan, reluctantly.

"Well, what was it?"

"We needed to get to Dunkerque by 4 June."

"The day after tomorrow?"

Egan nodded and reassured him that it was still possible to complete the mission and get home with the diamonds. He told him to go to the cemetery at eleven o'clock that night and, if he made contact with anyone, to take what food he was given and set off to Amsterdam. As he was speaking, he handed Jonjo a compass, a map and a revolver. He told him to open the map and began marking some important points on it.

"The Germans entered Amsterdam across the Berlage Bridge, so the south of the city is probably heavily fortified. The north has been bombed and, in the east, the Dutch have been pushed back to the Afsluitdijk Causeway, which means they have probably secured positions across the northwest of the city. It will be difficult to get through but the west is mainly farmland." He marked the suggested access points to the city and Jonjo asked what some existing markings indicated on the map.

"They are the Dutch airfields at Ypenburg, Ockenburg and Waalhaven. As far as we know, they have all been bombed and are probably now occupied by the Germans. Now," he added as he remembered something else, "if you hear that the British have parachuted in to a position near the Maas River or taken the bridge at Dordrecht, ignore it. Don't go near those places, we leaked some misinformation."

Jonjo wondered if he stood any chance of remembering half of what the captain had stored in his head.

"I'll keep the rifles and the other handgun," Egan said. "Contact the Jewish brothers' uncle in Amsterdam. His name is Fleischmann, too. When you meet him, you need to say that 'Mutt and Jeff are okay'. Apparently that's what the uncle calls his nephews. He will then give you the diamonds." He paused and stopped Jonjo from speaking. He wanted to make sure he understood the instructions. "Who have you got to contact?"

"Mr Fleischmann."

"What have you got to say to him?"

"Mutt and Jeff are okay."

"Good, don't forget it. Now memorise this address and under no circumstances write it down. It is situated in a suburb of Amsterdam called Spaarndammer. The address is 14 Elleburgen, near the timber docks. Can you remember all that?"

"I'm not sure."

"Well, you must. Amsterdam; Spaarndammer, 14 Elleburgen. Okay?"

"I'll try," sighed Jonjo. "I'm pretty good at remembering poetry, so I'll try to put it into verse if I can think of anything to rhyme with bloody Elleburgen." He checked he had everything he needed.

"What about the uncle?" asked Jonjo.

"What about him?"

"What do I do with him?"

"He's staying in the Netherlands; his choice. Just worry about yourself and getting those diamonds back to Blighty."

The captain was reluctant to instruct Jonjo to change into civilian clothes but the young guardsman knew he stood no chance of reaching Amsterdam in a British uniform, so he put them on and prepared to leave the hideout. Jonjo looked out through the gorse and branches and saw only darkness.

"What are you going to do, Sir?" he said, turning round to look at Egan.

"I'll wait 'til my leg heals up and then make my way back home, too."

Jonjo thought that scenario was even less likely than his rescue of the diamonds.

Egan held out his hand. "I'll see you back at Wellington Barracks, Guardsman Thompson. Good luck."

"I'll do my best, Sir. I'm just not sure it's going to be good enough." He paused. "I think I probably need some inspirational words if you can manage any," he added, as he thought about climbing out from under the barn.

"I'm not very good with that sort of stuff," Egan apologised. "I'm more leading from the front, I suppose."

Jonjo nodded his agreement, but doubted that the captain believed he could get home himself.

"That's okay, Sir, I can remember some from Mr Churchill. He said that courage was the greatest gift because it was this gift that guaranteed all others."

"I think that's true, Thompson. So hang on to that one then," replied the captain. "Along with that bloody address in Amsterdam."

They both laughed and Jonjo clambered out of the hole, convinced he would never see Axe Egan again.

10

Sunday 24 May 2015 — Outreau

When I awoke to the sound of church bells the following morning, it felt like I had been asleep for only a couple of hours. I had struggled to get to sleep thinking about the colonel's telephone call. If John Joseph Thompson had been captured at Boulogne on 23 May 1940, then why was he not sent to a prisoner-of-war camp until four or five weeks later? The obvious conclusion was that he had been interrogated. After all, it was the early stages of the war and gathering intelligence would have been of paramount importance. Grandad was among the earliest soldiers captured in the war so, naturally, they would have questioned him over a long period. The question was, why Grandad and not the other soldiers who were captured with him? They were all sent to other camps weeks beforehand, but he wasn't. Dozens of possibilities went through my head as I stood under the shower, but none of them made any sense.

As I got dressed the feeble conclusion I'd reached started to make sense, until I thought about who was being placed in the first stalags to be built. One would assume it would be Poles or perhaps Belgians or Dutch, but a return call to Elton suggested otherwise. Annoyingly, he'd anticipated my call. "Thought you might ask that," he said irritatingly. "No, I told you, Jack, with the exception of Tonka's grandad, everyone from Boulogne was sent to Stalag XXII."

"Do you know why?" I asked, convinced the colonel was holding some information back.

"Of course not, Jack, I didn't know he'd been sent to Stalag XXV until you showed me the photograph."

"Why Grandad?" I asked Tonka over breakfast.

He couldn't answer, of course, but even he had to admit that it was suspicious. My friend rarely asked me for anything, so I was persuaded to keep my counsel when he suggested that we should park this matter up while we attended the function, fulfilled the purpose of the journey and remembered his grandad. He spoke from the heart and I apologised for ruining the trip with my fears and speculation. Determined to ensure my friend enjoyed this special day, I filed the issue away and looked skywards, trying to clear my mind. Some charcoal grey clouds drifted away and a reluctant sun crept above the hills that looked down on the town.

We followed the signs to the town centre of Outreau, which was, in fact, not the centre but a square situated at the top of a steep hill, above the main residential area. The small terraced houses, balanced close to the roadside, resembled a coal mining town in Wales or Yorkshire. The narrow main street up the hill appeared just as it must have done to the 2nd Battalion of the Irish Guards when they had arrived to defend this small community from the advancing German army.

The area at the top of the hill was pedestrianised for the day so that the town might pay its lasting respects to the fallen and injured and to those few who still lived and remembered the Battle of Boulogne.

An enterprising man might have considered building a cafe or bar halfway up the hill, but he hadn't, so Tonka and I needed to march to the top before we could take a much-needed drink. The strenuous walk took nothing out of my friend. He had climbed the severest of terrains in Somalia, Iraq and Afghanistan under the weight of a full pack and in temperatures much hotter or colder than today. And on none of those occasions had he been able to pause, as we did, at the top of the hill, to quench our thirst with a cold beer.

It was a little early for alcohol but there was about an hour to kill before the service was due to start and we had seen most of the small town during our short walk before dinner the previous evening. There were several posters giving details of the event but we didn't meet any other attendees on our travels. I don't think it had occurred to us that most of them might be in the church, which stood on the other side of a small flower garden, adjacent to the town memorial. The square had been cordoned off for the morning by temporary barriers. A disabled section in front of the memorial was flanked by areas for local councillors, officials, serving military personnel and relatives of those who had fought in this particular battle.

It was a warm Sunday in May once the clouds cleared and as we sat there people began to gather around. The church bells rang out and a few moments later the congregation left the church to take up their positions for the ceremony. As we finished our beer, the passengers from the coaches parked nearby began their walk across the square to the designated area. Tonka and I followed on behind them and waited for the town mayor and other dignitaries to arrive.

A military band that occupied a temporary stage nearby began playing. The French flag, the Union Jack and the European Union flag wistfully fluttered in the light breeze, alongside another, which I did not recognise. It was not German of course but, more likely, the colours of the local town or region.

When all were gathered the town mayor, dressed in a red cloak, a three-cornered hat and a chain of office, stepped forward sedately and placed a large wreath at the foot of the memorial obelisk. He turned, walked back to a small plinth, tapped the microphone and addressed the crowd, speaking slowly in French. In deference to the many British visitors, his words were translated by a small elderly man with moustache and glasses, who was elegantly dressed in a formal black frock coat.

The mayor spoke of honour and unbounded courage by the men of the Irish and Welsh Guards, who fought for two days against an enemy of greater strength, number and armoury. They fought, he said, not just for the people of Outreau, but to protect the civilised world against tyranny and, although the battle was not won on that day, victory in the war was built on such courage and such endeavour. The will of the righteous, he added almost in tears, would always prevail. He paused before asking whether victory through superior fire power was a victory to be proud of. He spoke emotionally and it was difficult for the interpreter to translate with the same passion, but he tried.

"Seventy-five years ago today, honour and great bravery ensured that peace through the will of man, rather than superior fire power, is a peace much more worthy of the lives of the men who died here that day."

The mayor's throat was becoming dry and he paused for one last moment before speaking in English, declaring, "They who are remembered never die." He finished with what sounded like a battle cry: "Let us remember them this day."

A cheer rose from the crowd, applause broke out and the band struck up a rousing tune. The local councillors and officials congratulated him on his rousing speech and members of the organising committee began shaking hands and kissing each other on the cheeks.

When the ceremony ended, most of the attendees remained in the square and the sound of their chatter drowned out the distant hum of traffic at the foot of the hill. Some people renewed old acquaintances, others forged new ones. There didn't appear to be anyone who had fought at the battle, so it seemed to us that

Grandad may have been the last surviving member of the conflict that took place in this small town seventy-five years ago. Others assured us that this could not be so because they were aware of those who were simply too elderly or poorly to travel. The only possibilities among the attendees were two elderly men in wheelchairs and Tonka approached them to see if they had known his grandfather. They were locals and so he conversed with them in French. They had lived in Outreau all their lives and recalled their childhood memories of that day, but neither of them could remember any individual soldier.

Tonka continued his mild interrogation of anyone who was likely to know anything about the day in general or his grandad in particular. As he did so, I copied his action, but there were not many locals who spoke English and my oral French was poor. So I concentrated on the British visitors, although they seemed to be dispersing much quicker than the locals, who were happy to stand in the sunshine and discuss that famous day in the town's history.

Soon there were two main clusters of people; the locals chatting idly in the main square and the British who were now gathered around three coaches parked on the far side of the square. Some people walked between the two groups, saying goodbye and promising to visit again. And some laid flowers at the foot of the obelisk. Eventually, the departing coaches pulled away and Tonka ended his quest to find out something about his grandad's participation in the battle. We ended up on the far side of the square, out of sight of the coaches, where the lunchtime sun streamed down through the flagpoles. Tonka was talking to a Welsh couple who were the descendents of a guardsman killed in the battle. They had attended the same ceremony five years ago and had returned in order to remember their grandfather. They now intended to drive to a military cemetery close by to lay flowers on his grave. I joined this conversation just as an old Irishman walked up and introduced himself as Brendan. He was alone and seemed desperate to join the discussion, so the four of us told him our names and he repeated each one so he would remember them.

"Isn't this a glorious day," he declared boldly when the discussion paused. His accent was as distinctly Irish as the couple's was Welsh. "And to think they said it might rain," he added. "It's a pity they don't let the astrologers forecast the weather, they seem to be better at such matters than the meteornologists."

We all wanted to correct his mispronunciation of meteorologists, but politeness prevented us.

"To be sure, it's nice to have such fine weather on what is, after all, a very sad day. Did you all lose someone at the battle that took place here?"

"We lost our grandad," replied the couple in Welsh harmony.

"My grandad was taken prisoner here," added Tonka.

"Aw, we only need one who got away and we'd have the full set," the Irishman laughed.

"What happened to your grandad?" I asked him.

"He died back in Ballygarrow years ago."

"And he served in the army?"

"He did so for sure, I think."

"And he fought here at Boulogne?"

"Aw no. My grandfather was an Irish Republican. He fought against the British in the troubles."

We all looked a little confused by his reply and I asked him what he was doing here.

"'Twas my uncle who fought in the battle here. Served in the Irish Guards, did my uncle."

"And what happened to him?"

His jolly demeanour changed at my question. "Killed in action," he replied sadly.

"Was he buried nearby?" the Welsh lady asked politely.

"No, we never found out where he was buried. My mammy calls him the unknown warrior."

"Oh dear," replied the Welsh lady. "That is sad."

"No grave to visit," her husband added solemnly and the Irishman shook his head again.

"My mother, his sister, is still alive, thank God, back in the old country. She'll be pleased to hear about the service here today."

There was a long sad pause, as if we were holding a minute's silence in his memory when, suddenly, Brendan perked up and patted me on the shoulder with his large rough hand, before asking, "What time do the coaches leave?"

Tonka and I looked at each other, as did the Welsh couple.

"What coaches?" I asked.

"The ones we came here on."

All four of us declared we had not travelled by coach. "We drove here."

"Were you not on the coach with me?" he asked with a tone of desperation creeping into his voice.

"Afraid not," I replied and stepped back so I could see across the square, past the building that was blocking our view. "The coaches have gone," I declared timidly.

The old man took a few steps forward and looked in the same direction as me.

"Now that can't be right," he stuttered with misplaced optimism. "It didn't say anything about missing a coach in my horoscope this morning."

Tonka took control of the situation and suggested that we retired to the cafe across the square to consider how we could repatriate Brendan with his fellow passengers. As we walked across the now empty square, the Welsh couple returned to their car to begin their long journey back to the Valleys. I took the opportunity to reassure the Irishman that his coach would return for him as soon as they realised they were one passenger short.

"And how will they know that?" he asked.

"Well, they'll count the passengers, won't they," I assured him.

"Aw, they already did that before I came over to chat with you lads."

Tonka looked less confident about any prompt repatriation but tried to offer some consolation. "Let's sit down here, have a beer or a coffee and, if the coach hasn't returned by then, Jack and I will take you back to Calais and find your coach."

Brendan looked a little confused and asked why the coach would be going to Calais.

"To go home, of course."

"But the holiday has only just started," he replied.

"What holiday?"

"The tour of the battlefields of France and Belgium."

Now, by this time, even the very patient Tonka Thompson was becoming agitated.

"So, where were you going next?" I asked.

"Aw, now I know that because I was paying attention to the lovely young lady courier, I was." He hesitated and we waited for his next piece of information. "It was a beautiful French town on the border with Belgium." But he couldn't recall the name of that town. We implored him to remember something about it, but his only recollection was that it had won an award.

"Best-kept village?" Tonka asked sarcastically.

"Aw no, something much more important than that. A proper award, a great honour. The 'groin de girl' or something similar."

The waiter placed the coffee cups on the table and corrected him politely. "Croix de Guerre."

Tonka recognised the name and asked the waiter if he knew of a village near Belgium that had won the honour.

"Of course," he replied. "It is the town that most of the coach trips visit after Outreau. It is the town of Touberge, close to the Foret Isole."

We were pleased to see a sign of recognition on Brendan's face.

"And how far is it?"

"About two hours drive. But they stay overnight there so you don't need to rush."

Tonka and I had both been drinking and, as we had rooms booked at the hotel in Outreau that night, we suggested to Brendan that he checked in too and we would set off early in the morning to meet up with the coach before it left Touberge.

And so it was agreed, although it became apparent when the waiter returned that Brendan had left his wallet on the coach, along with the rest of his belongings. I insisted that he shouldn't worry about the money although, to be fair, he didn't look the slightest bit concerned about having his expenses paid by a couple of strangers.

"Well," said Brendan a little more cheerfully. "If we're not going until morning, let's have a drink."

"What would you like?" I asked.

"Aw, I don't drink much," he answered. "To be sure, I haven't had a drink since New Year when a Scottish pal of mine took me to a mahogmanay party."

"Hogmanay," Tonka corrected him, but the old man wasn't listening.

"Have you got any whiskey from the old country?" he asked the waiter as he passed by. "From Ireland," he explained.

"We have Bushmills."

"And is it pot stilled?"

"I don't think so, Sir."

"Aw, okay," he replied a little disappointedly, "I'll have a large one." He turned to face us. "I'll pay you boys back when I'm reunited with my wallet."

That afternoon, Brendan made up for his long period of abstinence by devouring nearly half a bottle of Irish whiskey and that evening, when we took him out for a meal, he seemed none the worse for it.

Brendan was a short, stocky man of sixty-five, with thick-rimmed glasses, which he switched at intervals in order to read menus. He was slightly balding but what hair he had was as white as snow. He had large hands, disproportionate to the rest of his body and he spoke with a broad Irish lilt.

We agreed to meet very early the next morning, in order to ensure we reached the coach party before they left Touberge. It was too early for breakfast and the sun had not yet taken the chill from the square outside the hotel. Brendan looked decidedly shabby as he stood in the dawning light. He had no change of clothes and it would have been foolish to offer anything of ours as we were both twice his height and half his breadth. However, he was on time and was standing outside in a shaft of early morning sunlight as we came out of the building. His cheerful disposition had not been diminished by his circumstances.

"The top of the morning to you, boys. I found an English newspaper," he said with a smile. "In the reception, it was." Tonka and I nodded. "It's yesterday's newspaper but I like to keep up with my horoscope and I haven't seen one since we left England. Mustn't miss it, actually. My mammy bought me one of them little computer thingies, like a lap dog."

Tonka interrupted, "laptop."

"No, I think it was smaller than that. An I pet."

"It's an iPad," came Tonka's impatient correction. But Brendan ignored him.

"You'd be amazed at what this thing can do," he said, adding ruefully, "if ever we get it back from the coach. I can subscribe to the newspaper and check my horoscope online. Now, how ingenuous is that?"

"Ingenious," mumbled Tonka as he stowed our luggage in the boot and opened the rear door for our guest.

"It certainly is, my friend," noted Brendan. "Anyway, let's see what it says."

He made himself comfortable, strapped himself in and flicked through the pages to locate that day's horoscope.

"Are you sure you don't want me to drive?" I asked Tonka.

He looked at Brendan, anticipated a bromidic and largely mispronounced conversation, and shook his head. Our passenger wanted our full attention, so waited until we were comfortably on our way before continuing his recital of his daily horoscope.

"'Cosmic activity in your opposite sign warns that you'll only reach your goals if you enlist the aid of those who share your aims and ambitions. In other words, you can't do it alone.' Now isn't that remarkable, boys? Spot on. Do you see it? I've had to enlist your help to get back to the coach party. Quite remarkable, do you not agree?"

We both agreed, but with less enthusiasm than Brendan.

He was thick-skinned but even he must have been conscious of the fact that Tonka did not, surprisingly, want to participate in this enthralling conversation. On the other hand, he probably already knew me well enough to realise I was too polite to tell him to shut up, so he asked me what my star sign was.

"Gemini," I answered, reluctantly.

"Ah, here we are. Let's see what the stars have for you, Jack. 'You will be in inspired form this week. Wherever you go and whatever you do, you will find a way to succeed. Best of all you will have the kind of fun that others can enjoy with you. Even if you find yourself among total strangers, you will get along as if you are long-lost friends.'" Brendan stared at us with an exultant look in his eye. "Is that not incredible, lads?"

"Truly remarkable," I said, unconvincingly.

Brendan desperately wanted to ask Tonka what his star sign was but decided to wait for a suitable moment. As we left the town and picked up the dual carriageway, two of us in the car were desperate to arrive in Touberge before the coach left. Brendan, on the other hand, appeared indifferent to his predicament and, incapable of keeping silent for even a few minutes, he began telling us about his late uncle and then went on to his living relatives. His mother, Brenda Donnelly, still lived back in Ireland. Her brother had served in the Irish Guards during the Second World War and fought at the Battle of Boulogne. He'd joined the British forces in 1940 and never returned. It was difficult to get information about British servicemen back in Ireland. Brendan explained that there was no military pension for Irishmen who had served the British during the war and, under the Starvation Order passed by Eamon de Valera, any Irishman who fought with the British was barred from most kinds of work and did not receive demob benefits either. They were persona non grata in Ireland, or 'person and gratzie', as Brendan called it. It was impossible to find out anything about his uncle back in Ireland and it was dangerous to even ask.

"The last my mother heard from my uncle was that he'd joined the Irish Guards. And after the war, when we made enquiries, we were told he was killed in action."

"It was very brave of him to sign up," said Tonka earnestly. "Giving everything up and going to fight a war when his country wanted him to step aside."

"If you can't feel the heat, get into the kitchen."

"No, Brendan. If you can't stand the heat, get out of the kitchen."

He looked bewildered. "Why would anyone want to get out of a warm kitchen? It was the only room that wasn't freezing in our house back in Cork."

"Do you know," said Tonka, choosing to ignore the ramblings of our passenger in the back seat. "I think I know why my grandad's mates called him Longhop. I don't think it was anything to do with cricket or the way he bowled. He went on two missions and came back five years later from the second one. So I reckon his real nickname was 'Long op', not 'Longhop.'"

I could see his logic. Long operation seemed to make more sense than Longhop.

"You could be right," I said and wanted to pursue a sensible conversation, but Tonka was trying to concentrate on driving along the wrong side of the road while being bombarded by inanities from Brendan, so I remained quiet. Eventually my patience was rewarded and we found a sign to Lille.

"We need to bypass Lille," I reminded Tonka. "And pick up a sign to Touberge. Then we pick up a road that skirts the forest."

Tonka looked at me and smiled. He had already checked the map before we left and memorised it.

"This is very charitable of you two boys," declared Brendan. "You've fed and watered me and now you are going out of your way to return me to the coach party. I was lucky indeed to meet the pair of you."

I assured him that we were pleased to help. By leaving the hotel early we were in good time to get back to Calais for our return train that afternoon.

"Do you know what your friend's star sign is?" he asked me quietly, not wanting to disturb the driver.

"I'm afraid not," I replied.

"Do you happen to know his birthday, then?"

"I leave birthdays and anniversaries to my wife," I lied, convinced that he would be reciting Tonka's horoscope if I told him the date.

"Oh, and what's your wife's star sign then?"

He was the time-honoured dog with a bone and seemed unable or unwilling to stop pestering me until I had revealed the names of relatives or friends who were born under each sign of the zodiac.

"Have you got the weather in there for the rest of your holiday?" I asked in a desperate attempt to deflect his attention.

"Aw, I don't listen to that rubbish, Jack. That's a load of baloney. Who could possibly know what the weather is going to be?"

11

Sunday 2 June 1940 — Cache Moyen, Foret Isole

In the hushed night, only the incoherent utterings of the Boreas and Zephyrus winds could be heard as their whispers brushed the branches above him. The discourse of the dark, intelligible only to the aged oak, the repository of antiquities.

The ark of memories, recalled Jonjo, as he crept through the canopied forest remembering stories from his childhood. He listened as each tree creaked and groaned under its obligation to remember all the secrets entrusted to it by the celestial winds. As he approached that nebulous place where forest met the first trace of human habitation, the sound of the whispering wind was overpowered by something louder, something more ethological, humanoid and yet less compassionate in its domesticity. The presence of an unseen village was discernible only by the opaque and incomprehensible babbling of a hundred voices chattering outside the inn.

Beyond the wall against which Jonjo rested his back as he sat listening to the chatter on the far side of the graveyard and the church, Henri Poirier and his daughter cleared the empty glasses from the tables as German soldiers relaxed on a warm night, drinking beer, laughing and feeling less vulnerable than others close by. The landlord was unsure how practical or enforceable his closing time of half past ten was now they were an occupied nation. But, in spite of the uncertainty of such turbulent times, convention continued to afford a certain visceral deference to the Sabbath and the soldiers finished their drinks and slowly began heading back to their camp on the edge of town.

The soldiers were unlikely to wander into the woods, although there was a possibility that one might choose to relieve himself against the wall of the graveyard. So Jonjo decided to drop over the wall and hide himself in the shed that stood, half concealed by ivy and unchecked wisteria, on the far side of the holy ground. The boisterous conversations of the departing revellers gradually faded, the night grew still and Jonjo began wondering whether Elodie had stopped visiting the graveyard since the capture of O'Reilly. He knew he should leave in order to make the most of the remaining hours of darkness, but he could not stop thinking about the possibility of meeting the young French woman one last time. He was looking around the shed to see if there was anything that might prove useful on his journey when, suddenly, the door swung open and Jonjo fumbled for his revolver. When he saw it was Guardsman Eamon O'Reilly standing in front of him, a thousand scenarios passed through his mind. The worst of these were dispensed with as he realised the Irishman was alone and not accompanied by a troop of German soldiers.

"What are you doing here?" he asked but, before Eamon could answer, he fired a second question. "Why didn't you come back to the hideout?" and then a third, "where have you been?"

Eventually Jonjo stopped asking questions and provided his colleague with an opportunity to reply. Eamon related the events of the previous night and how he had now taken up clandestine employment as the village gravedigger in order to avoid capture by the Germans. Quite whether this hoax was sustainable was doubtful, but his situation appeared to be inescapable at the present time.

"What are you doing back here at this time?" asked Jonjo.

"Miss Elodie has lost an earring," he explained. "And I was going to have a look for it."

"An earring?"

"Aw, it may be only an earring to you, Jonjo. but to a woman…" He didn't finish the sentence because he couldn't think of a suitable analogy. "I know these things, you see. There's nothing worse than losing an earring."

"Of course there are worse things than losing an earring, you idiot."

"Don't lose your rag, it's just a figment of speech," replied the Irishman.

"It's a figure of speech, not a figment of speech," Jonjo corrected him.

O'Reilly ignored him and examined the collection of objects he had found on the cemetery path. Two coins, a religious medal and a half-smoked cigarette.

Then, just as O'Reilly was about to launch his defence, the door opened again.

"Keep the noise down," Elodie suggested as she stood there holding a bag of food and a jug of hot coffee. Jonjo surprised himself, for he was more pleased to see her than the food and drink. He took the empty mug from her and she poured from the jug. She nearly spilled it as she couldn't take her eyes from his face. Jonjo was expecting tea and wondered if she was trying to poison him when he took the first mouthful. He had never tasted coffee before, but was desperate for a drink, so he finished it and thanked her politely. He had once eaten a coffee cream at Christmas, so he knew what the taste was, but he would have preferred something else, like tea.

"I'm leaving," he said to Eamon, but glanced at Elodie's face to see her reaction.

"Leaving? Where are you going?" asked the Irishman.

"I can't say, but the captain's moved his hiding place and he's given me new instructions. I'd better not say what they are," he continued and they understood that he didn't want to compromise them.

Eamon may have been slow but he noticed the look in their eyes. He apologised for not being able to find her earring and handed Elodie the collection of items he had found on the path. She realised that he was still looking for the imaginary lost earring, but he interrupted her before she could tell him it was simply a ruse.

"I'll keep a look out for Jerry," he said, closing the door behind him.

"Jzonjzo," she whispered and the sound was captured and held forever in his memory, his prize to cherish and extol in the dark days ahead. Each element of tone, accent and harmony was memorised and enslaved for all eternity in his heart. A complete poem in a solitary word, dedicated to a heart made callous and inaccessible by the hideousness of war. They were both a little too embarrassed to speak at first, conscious of the way that Eamon knew they wanted to be alone. So they spoke less about their feelings and more about their fears, about whether he would return and in what circumstances that might happen. Both feared he would not but neither wished to consider this eventuality. The war put everything on hold, the times were uncertain, incalculable. They hardly knew anything about each other and in those few moments they traced around the important questions they each wanted to ask the other and, instead, simply looked at each other and spoke in short sentences.

"You will never age in my mind," he said.

"That's a good thing," she said, smiling.

"But it's unfair. It will only make me miss you more."

"One day we will look back on this day and wonder how it might have been." She spoke with certainty that it could not be as they would wish.

"In different circumstances we would never have met and I wouldn't change that now. We have a saying, at home," he said. "It is better to have loved and lost than never to have loved at all."

The word 'love' hovered in the space between them. She wanted to tell him that she loved him too, but couldn't, for the pain of separation was already too much and she feared that she might start to cry and embarrass herself.

"Some day, when this is all over, you will be at home in England, a married man with children." She was trying to tell him to forget her without actually saying the words.

"I'm not sure I am ready for parenthood," he said. "It seems to me that it's just an excuse to live your life all over again through another person. I'm not sure I want that."

"Don't say that," she said and paused. "Listen to us, standing in this place of the dead talking about new life."

There was a noise outside and they both wondered whether Eamon was coming back. They had but a few seconds to say what was in their heart and Elodie got there first.

"I just want to be with you."

"I'll come back."

"Don't say that."

"Elodie," Jonjo uttered and her fledgling heart awoke to the hushed tone of his voice. All the sonnets ever written could not capture the revelation of first love. He placed his hands on her shoulders and she did not pull away, but stared into his eyes. The intimacy of an enclosed space, the silence of the night and a conviction that this might be their last meeting began to conquer any reticence or inhibitions they may have harboured. The passion he shared with Violet stood eclipsed by this new sensation. No longer the adolescent servant of emotion driven by compulsion or desire, his passion succumbed to tenderness, and youthful craving was subdued by a yearning he had never known. This was a moment chosen from all time, a longing to love, rather than to make love. And yet the shadow of despair hung above it. The danger of being captured and shot as a spy loomed and he suddenly realised he was putting her in danger by delaying his departure.

The intrigue and heroic allusion that accompanied their first meeting had now become reality. It had always been present, of course, but the danger that crouched in the darkness now suddenly stood among them and became a force that would almost certainly separate them. He could not leave without claiming that one kiss to treasure in the worrying times ahead, along with the soft murmur of her voice speaking his name in the quiet of the night. And she would not let him leave without submitting to that same kiss. But the kiss made his departure only more agonising than either of them could imagine or bear. Her heart pleaded silently that he might stay there, like O'Reilly had done. But that same heart knew this was impossible. And, in that moment, both suffered the realisation that they may never see each other again. That agony seized his mind and he pulled her closer to him. She wanted to speak but the words became trapped in her throat, unable to find a voice. If she spoke, she would cry and she knew that must not happen. Tears now would crush them both. They kissed and, as he turned to open the door, it was Jonjo who spoke, assuring her that he would return, he would see her again. Looking at the items clasped in the palm of her hand, she gave him the coins and then looked at the medal that O'Reilly had found on the path outside. It was oval in shape, encrusted with dirt and the size of her fingernail. She rubbed it on her apron and her eyes lit up when she saw the name that could just be made out above the figure of a saint.

"This is the medal of St Jude," she said. "He is the patron saint of lost causes." She tucked it into the breast pocket of his shirt, pushed the bag of food into his hands and, as he walked between the graves towards the rear wall, Eamon handed him two water carriers.

"Go n-éirí an t-ádh leat!" the Irishman said as Jonjo climbed the wall. "It means good luck in Walloon," he explained, "or perhaps it's Gaelic."

Jonjo paused and sat on top of the wall to look at Elodie for the last time. She was crying.

"Don't worry yourself, young lady," Eamon said, comforting her. "I'm sure to find your earring."

Jonjo sped off as quietly as he could and, trying to avoid any animal traps, he melted into the forest. He thought back on how many soldiers had begun this journey. More than six hundred and fifty had landed at Boulogne and now it was just him who was left to fulfil the mission. Ten minutes later he reached the far side of the forest, close to where the captain had injured his leg in the animal trap. This was to be the last time he would look back and consider abandoning the mission.

The density of the trees thinned and then disappeared as the ground sloped steeply downward into a valley. From the edge of the forest he could see fields of wheat leading northeast. He needed to get to the other side of these fields and into the woods, where he might be able to move a little more freely until daylight. Farther along the valley there appeared to be an extensive acreage of maize, which stood sufficiently high to provide good cover. But he couldn't see beyond this and so decided to make for the woods. He had been given the best route based on the latest knowledge that the captain had. However, that information was certainly out of date, so Jonjo needed to make decisions on the move, in order to avoid the German troops.

The radiance of an almost-full moon was shrouded by low cloud. He made his way, as they had done previously, walking along the inside of hedgerows and clambering over wooden fences or through gaps in the hedges where they appeared. It was still dark when he reached the wood on the other side of the valley. It was a steep climb but he had little to carry. The water bottles and the revolver were kept in a small knapsack that the captain had given him. It was the only item that identified him as a British soldier but then, if the Germans found the knapsack, they would also discover the gun.

Just before dawn he came to some open flat land that continued almost to the horizon. The sun was rising and its faint glow produced a thin red line on the skyline ahead of him. About one mile ahead, Jonjo saw a small wood, or copse. He wondered whether it was big enough to hide in for the day. Farther ahead to the north there appeared to be a larger wooded area and he decided to press on towards that spot. But daybreak arrived more rapidly than he remembered and he had to run the last stretch, into the cover and shade of the trees, and then onwards until, out of breath, he sank to the ground deep within its protective grove. He sat up and leaned against a large old oak tree, before closing his eyes and drifting back to his youth for a few moments. He was tired and would need to find somewhere to sleep. But, for the moment, he lay flat on the ground and looked into the boughs of the tree.

The childhood memories of trees were enduring and graphic for Jonjo. A teacher had once told him that trees share hormones similar to humans and a school friend had said that they were the equivalent of elephants, remembering everything that happened or had been told to them by the four winds. It was a childhood of spirited imagination, inspired by adventure stories of pirates or a chivalrous knight who suffered the enchantment of an evil witch. Playing on the streets of London, he became that knight, of course. A templar cursed and transformed into a tree by the evil daughter of deceit and shame, destined to live for hundreds of years, remembering everything he had seen or heard but unable to speak a word. But, for now, Jonjo lay exhausted below its boughs, contemplating the inglorious fate of that good knight, an arboreal prisoner condemned to know all things and to speak of none until liberated by Andrew Martin, the Red Cross Knight.

Rich in sensation, inspired and burdened by the words of the wind, and encumbered by their timeless memories. That is how the trees rested in the mind of Jonjo for, as his mother had feared, he thought about matters too much and lingered too long in the land of fable and fantasy. In science, he'd learned that plants communicated to each other about pest attacks, but he knew that they saw and heard so much more. So much that it weighed upon their consciousness and pressed them into the earth's core. Trees never sleep, he thought, looking up as the light broke through the canopy. They are yoked by an unrelenting duty to remember all things, but unable to speak of what they see and hear.

Jonjo wondered, as he lay beneath the tree's spreading foliage, if it was only he who understood the secret of trees. And, as he did so, the noble oak looked back at him and promised to tell nobody of his presence. The tree was neither British nor German. It knew no master, recognised no borders and yet its largest branch stretched out like a human arm, or road sign, pointing northeast. As he stood up, he imagined it said 'Amsterdam' and he walked slowly off in that direction, deeper into the forest, in search of a badger sett to rest during the daylight hours that were now upon him. Outside the wood, a sunny dawn began to light the world, but here he rested and here Morpheus transported him to a warless world.

Inside the badger sett, the tremors of the earth could be felt more acutely than in the world above. When its vibration woke him from his dreamless sleep, he was released back into the world by a disturbing turbulence. Still lost in the land of his childhood, the shudder reminded him of bath time as a child. His mother rubbing him down with a soft towel after getting out of the tin bath that had previously been occupied by his father. But this time it was mother earth that caressed him, as small shards of soil fell about him, threatening to bury him alive if the trembling grew stronger. But it didn't; the reverberation above him felt too subtle to be a tank; this was more like footsteps marching, there was a rhythm to it. But soldiers were unlikely to be marching through a wood. So they must be close by and there must be many of them. Perhaps there was a path nearby that he hadn't seen in the poor light of dawn. His head was only a few inches away from the opening of the sett. Eventually the earth around him stopped vibrating and he drifted back to sleep.

When he awoke, the thin shaft of light that had pierced the foliage covering the hole had gone and only darkness remained. Through the gorse and ivy he could see it was getting dark, so he crawled out of the hole and, after inspecting the local area, shook himself down, consulted his compass and continued his onward journey towards Amsterdam. In spite of his exertions, it was difficult to sleep throughout the daylight hours, so there was ample opportunity to think about Elodie. He wanted to be with her and wondered whether there may ever come a day when they would be together again. It seemed an increasingly unlikely conclusion to his present, precarious situation. At best, he would get back home, the Germans would be defeated and he might, somehow, return to that small village on the French and Belgian border. At worst, he would be caught and executed as a spy. In between this range of possibilities there were sufficient alternatives to occupy Jonjo's waking hours in a cramped badger sett.

In Cache Moyen another heart shared the same stirring and another young mind dwelt upon the possibility of love. If Jonjo had been captured anywhere close to the village she would have heard about it. The day after he had left, she overhead a discussion between some German soldiers about the sighting of a British soldier in the area. But she couldn't establish whether these were new rumours or simply those that had begun when the imprint of a British soldier's boot was found at the edge of a stream in the forest. It was clear that they were not talking about

O'Reilly, as he had now been accepted in his new capacity as the village gravedigger. Of course, they may have been talking about the captain, but it was unlikely that he had left his hiding place.

There had been other, similar rumours in recent weeks. The most common was that a British soldier had been parachuted in to France or Belgium to reconnoitre the German positions. Shortly after she heard this, there was increased activity around the area of the stream. The stories always referred to a lone operative and Elodie could now only wonder which of the three men would come under closer scrutiny by the occupying forces. Who was in the most danger? Eamon had been accepted as one of the locals but was prone to stupid errors and Elodie worried that he might say something in English one day and they would all be in trouble. But how could anyone believe he was an enemy intelligence agent working behind enemy lines? He was such an unlikely agent provocateur and a very convincing gravedigger. Then there was Egan; the man she had never actually seen but only heard of. He had to wait patiently for his leg to heal, but then what would he do? Germans occupied the land for a hundred miles in every direction, so how could Egan escape? Finally, there was Jonjo, a man who was about to go even deeper into enemy territory and then try to get out again. He could be captured at any time. He would make a credible undercover agent, thought Elodie. He was in civilian clothes and out of hiding. He would be captured, interrogated and shot. The thought of how she and her father might be implicated only casually occurred to her, for she was too busy considering the almost inevitable capture and death of her new love.

That night, before he left, Jonjo had told Elodie where the captain was. He was worried that he might run out of food and starve to death in the hedgerow, unable to move because of his injured leg. So she visited the hideout the following day, walking along the country road, quietly calling until she heard a response. She didn't see him and did not want to pause too long in case the

Germans passed by. She just left some food and whispered to the hidden voice what she had heard the German soldiers talking about. She also told him that O'Reilly had been discovered but had convinced the occupying soldiers that he was a local.

"Be careful," she said. "Some new officers have arrived in the village, who the soldiers speak of as SS." She wasn't sure what that meant but explained that they had taken over the small parish hall adjacent to the church that stood opposite the inn and she believed they had been charged with finding the British soldier that everyone kept saying was in the area. She left, promising to bring him some more food the next day. But Egan never spoke and she was never called upon to fulfil that promise.

On most mornings the German soldiers were on manoeuvres while the officers were engaged in planning their continuing advance. Egan suspected that would be the case so that night, armed with the revolver and a pocketful of bullets, he dragged himself through the forest until he reached the stone wall surrounding the church. He didn't bother to change out of his uniform, there was no point.

On the way he had found a large branch that he could use as a makeshift crutch. The journey took him nearly two hours and afforded him an opportunity to consider his plan. He had no difficulty convincing himself of its merits because it worked on so many levels. Firstly it would convince the Germans that they had found the lone British soldier who was on the loose and thereby provide clear passage for Jonjo and a chance of freedom for Eamon. It also resolved his own position. The injury to his leg was not improving and might even require amputation if a qualified doctor ever got to examine it. He couldn't bear such an injury, nor could he simply sit and wait to be found and captured or killed by the enemy. For all these reasons his plan made sense. All it required for success was the courage of his great grandfather, who had followed the order of Lord Cardigan and ridden directly into the enemy cannon at Balaclava.

"Death or glory," he whispered, as he lay hidden in a large bush by the cemetery wall, close to the road that ran past the inn.

He waited there patiently for his opportunity. He heard the soldiers rise, parade and march off. There were occasional voices but he could tell the area around the inn was now occupied by just a few people. He thought the plan through in his head and crept out of the bushes to survey the surrounding area.

It was mid-morning and the tables and chairs outside the inn were empty. Egan would have loved to enjoy one last pint before charging into the enemy guns, but a lone soldier stood on guard outside the door to the church hall, directly facing the inn. He was about twenty metres away and Egan could see him only if he looked around the corner of the church building where he now lay.

Just then the soldier stood his rifle against the wall and thought about lighting a cigarette. He turned away from where the captain lay and placed his ear to the door of the parish hall. In that second the captain stood up and skipped towards him, propping himself up with the crutch as he did so. He was within five metres of the soldier before the German heard the strange sound behind him and turned around to see the same British soldier that the SS officers were discussing inside the hall. He reached for the rifle but a single bullet to the head killed him instantly and his body slumped backwards, his knees crumpling beneath him. The occupants would certainly have heard the shot so, without hesitating, the captain pushed open the door and, leaning against its frame, began firing at a group of uniformed officers sitting at a wooden table. He killed four of them before a fifth member of the group, standing apart from the others, managed to retrieve his revolver from its holster and return fire. The injured leg slowed Egan down just enough to prevent him from turning to his left and getting another shot off. He fell to the ground, wondering whether he might still be taken alive, so he raised the gun and pointed it directly at the officer who was now standing over him.

Egan had charged the enemy guns. The outcome was not death *or* glory, but rather death *and* glory. His last thought was for the mission, which now rested on the young shoulders of Guardsman John Joseph Thompson.

That guardsman was striving for neither death nor glory. He thought only of each leg of the journey. Getting from one place to another without being seen and, as a consequence, seeing nobody. The evidence of war was largely absent on his journey from Cache Moyen. Travelling at night and avoiding all inhabited places, Jonjo had been strangely detached from any visual manifestation of war. At times, as he lay in a badger sett or rested in a hedgerow or field of wheat, he wondered whether the war had actually ended and he remained in less than blissful ignorance of it. But when he arrived in the outskirts of Amsterdam all the signs of war became apparent. As he walked deeper into the city, the number of streets containing bombed houses increased. Then the number of houses destroyed in each street grew, until entire streets consisted of rubble, debris, doors, wrought iron fences and bricks piled in heaps or strewn across the ground. Dust and dirt hung in the air and the people seemed to have adopted their own detachment from the chaos.

Walking in the desolate streets at night made him feel more conspicuous, not less, so when morning came he continued walking, albeit a little more cautiously. By seven o'clock he was just one of many people on the street who, strangely, seemed to be going about their normal business in spite of the disarray and misfortune that surrounded them. Jonjo applied more purpose to his step, trying to look as if he was going somewhere, which he was of course, except he had no idea where Spaarndammer was. He was hoping to see a sign, when he was passed on the road by a truck carrying timber logs and, remembering what the captain had said, decided to walk in the direction it came from. Eventually he came to a dockland area and found a sign that said Spaarndammer. Locating a street called Elleburgen without attracting attention to himself by asking for directions in English took longer than he had hoped and it was midday before he stumbled upon his destination. It was a fashionable, tree-lined suburban street, which appeared eerily empty and a suspicion took root in his mind that this might be a trap. Perhaps the Germans were watching the house.

After taking a few moments to consider his situation, Jonjo decided to walk briskly from one end of the street to the other, imagining he was a resident going to buy a newspaper at the local shop. As he did so, he closely observed the pathways between each pair of houses and, as he passed number 14, he looked as casually as he could at the windows on the opposite side of the street, which faced the house. When he turned the corner at the end of the street he stopped and, once he was sure nobody was watching him, began evaluating his thoughts. He had noticed nobody in the street, nor had he seen any curtains moving. So he decided to wait for a short time as he didn't want to walk back down the street too soon. It mustn't appear as if he had simply walked to the end of the street and waited, so he strolled around the next block of streets, giving himself time to prepare a plan. Fifteen minutes later he returned and walked towards number 14.

Unhesitatingly, he opened the wrought iron gate, took four steps up to the front door and banged the heavy black knocker twice. Nobody answered the door and there was nothing to indicate that anyone was in the house. He knocked again and waited, but there was still no sound from inside. He was conscious that this might be a trap, or he may be being watched, but this was no time for the faint-hearted. If the mission ended here, then he had done his best.

He bent down and looked through the letterbox. The hallway was tidy and empty apart from a grandfather clock and small wooden unit containing books. He looked up and down the street but it was as deserted as the house. It was then that he noticed a mailbox, standing on a wooden post next to the gate. He opened the small flap and found several envelopes inside. He took them out and looked through them. It did little more than confirm he was at the right house, for they were all addressed to Mr Fleischmann. The name and address on one particular white envelope was handwritten and it had been posted in England. Jonjo wondered if it was from his nephews advising him of their safe arrival there. He put all the other envelopes back in the mail box but held on to the one he believed was from the nephews. He checked it to see if it had been opened and resealed. If the Germans were watching the house, they would probably have examined any correspondence. But there was no indication that it had been opened.

Jonjo was still standing there wondering what to do next when the door of the adjacent house opened and an elderly woman appeared wearing an apron. She spoke to him but he could not understand the language. Her voice was quiet and inquisitive and he hoped she could speak English.

"I'm sorry," Jonjo replied. "I speak only English. I am visiting Mr Fleischmann with news of his family in England, but he doesn't appear to be at home."

Fortunately the woman spoke a little English and explained that Mr Fleischmann had been taken to hospital a few days ago, suffering from a heart attack.

"Not surprising with the bombing and the occupation," she added, as if war had been declared simply in order to cause her the greatest inconvenience. She seemed resigned to the disruption and a little concerned for her neighbour's health.

"Thank you," Jonjo replied. "Do you know which hospital he was admitted to?" He wondered why she did not find his ragged clothing and scruffiness questionable, but over the past two weeks she had seen many people who had lost their homes and sometimes their relatives too. Many were left with only the clothes they stood up in, so this young man's appearance was not uncommon. She simply assumed that this visitor had in some way been affected by all this; she did not consider that he had probably only just arrived from England.

"I have this letter for him," Jonjo added, gaining confidence and not considering that the woman may indeed have checked the mailbox at some time. Fortunately she had not.

"He leaves a spare key with me, in case he ever gets locked out. Would you like it?"

He was taken aback by the offer and, conscious of his appearance, said he would like to tidy himself before going to the hospital. He promised to return the key before doing so and thanked her for her kindness.

Once inside the house, Jonjo ate what food he could find and made himself a hot drink. He then washed and shaved and began looking for clothes to change into. This proved difficult as Mr Fleischmann must have been shorter than he was and with a larger waist. But eventually he found a suitable pair of trousers, let down the turn-ups to make them a little longer and secured the waist with a belt. He looked in the mirror and convinced himself that his new attire made him look Dutch. He picked up a kippa, the platter-shaped cap worn by Jews and put it in his pocket, thinking it might prove useful to gain access to the uncle. It was mid-afternoon before he returned the key to Mr Fleischmann's neighbour and asked for directions to the hospital.

The thirty-minute walk gave him time to consider how he might get to see Mr Fleischmann without having to speak English. He tried to hide his anxiety as he approached the hospital. This natural apprehension was strangely alleviated when he saw how busy the hospital was. Medical staff rushed here and there around the front of the building, but there were very few civilians, other than the patients being stretchered inside. It occurred to him that his best opportunity to find Mr Fleischmann would be at visiting time, but he didn't know when that was. So he waited as inconspicuously as possible until people who looked like visitors began to arrive. He put the skull cap on and joined the crowd, walking directly to the desk in the main hall. He managed to secure a woman's attention behind the counter. She was not in uniform and was probably a voluntary worker helping with the sudden influx of patients. He showed her the envelope he had taken from the mailbox.

"Fleischmann," he said, trying to adopt an accent a little like Elodie's.

"Afdeling zeven," she shouted above the mayhem.

He didn't understand the first word but assumed her answer must have been ward seven and he made his way there as quickly as he could.

Ward seven was a long rectangular room with about twelve beds on each side. They were occupied by patients with a variety of injuries. In some, plastered legs dangled from contraptions above the beds, whereas others contained bandaged heads or patients with severed limbs. Jonjo showed the envelope to two nurses before being directed to a bed containing an elderly Jewish man.

Mr Fleischmann lay, apparently asleep, with a saline drip attached to his arm and a wire running from his chest to a machine that made a regular bleeping sound. His face was wrinkled and, even asleep, his countenance appeared kind and understanding. It helped to diminish the anxiety that Jonjo felt over what he should say to him when he woke up.

Jonjo sat on a chair provided for visitors, which stood next to the bed. In his mind, he repeated the message he had been told to deliver, while he patiently waited for the man to wake. A few minutes elapsed and Fleischmann began coughing, so Jonjo stood up and poured some water into an empty glass on the bedside cabinet. The man felt the presence of someone close to him, opened his eyes and looked intently at the young man who was standing over him. He recognised the clothes he was wearing but not the man himself. Jonjo handed him the glass and he raised his shoulders from the bed to sip from it. They looked at each other, without speaking, as both considered their next move. Jonjo stood upright, smiled and placed the envelope on the bed in front of the old man.

"I have good news for you, Mr Fleischmann," he finally said and waited until he knew he had the man's full attention. "Mutt and Jeff are well and send their regards."

The uncle sat up slightly and his watery eyes scanned the ward suspiciously. He looked at the young man wearing a skull cap and then at the envelope he had been given.

"You don't look Jewish, young man."

"I'm not," he whispered, "but I thought it might allay any suspicions if I pretended to be."

"You haven't chosen the best time to become Jewish," the old man said a little facetiously. The scars of time creased his face and made his grey eyes translucent.

The old man looked at the envelope lying in front of him and wondered how the young man had come by it. It had a postage stamp and was franked, so why was he delivering it by hand? Perhaps he was a German spy trying to trap him. He looked again at the envelope but didn't open it. He knew who it was from and what it contained. He was also quite sure that the words in the letter would not implicate him in any way. The young man who stood over him was wearing some of his clothes and so it was simple to conclude that he had visited his home, found the letter and changed his clothing for some reason. That was not the action of a German interrogator; that seemed more like the behaviour of a British officer sent to retrieve the Gemini and other diamonds in the Fleischmann collection.

"Can I get you anything, Sir?" Jonjo asked.

As he sat up to drink the water, the old man considered his words. "Sit and read to me from that book."

Jonjo had been hoping for a more practical response; specifically, one that indicated that the man knew the purpose of his visit. After all, he had delivered the cryptic message, so presumably the old man should now hand over the cache of diamonds. He paused and wondered if he needed to speak more candidly but decided against such a bold move. He looked again at the man and convinced himself that he understood the true purpose of his visit.

It was visiting time and the ward was busy and noisy, so nobody noticed that they were speaking English. Jonjo picked up the book, looked at the cover and sat back down on the chair. The book was called *Tevyei* by Sholem Aleichem, not that this meant anything to Jonjo, who opened it but did not recognise the language in which it was written. He flicked the pages to see if any of it might have been written in English. It hadn't and he considered what to do next.

"I don't..."

"It is a very interesting book," Fleischmann said, interrupting his visitor. "It took Aleichem twenty years to write it. Patience is a gift that Jews have in abundance, I always think. Tolerance, God gave to the Catholics, but he saved the patience for us."

Jonjo smiled at him and the old man paused and began to believe he could trust the young visitor sitting in front of him.

"Something that is created slowly, contemplatively, has merit don't you think, my friend?" He didn't wait for an answer, nor did Jonjo offer one, preferring to listen and learn from one so wise. "Aleichem considers how much humanity can resist the winds of change without allowing its spirit to be broken. It is both a tragedy and a comedy," he added, smiling back at his visitor.

"But...," Jonjo said, before being prevented from speaking by the quietly spoken and unassuming old man.

"You must start from where the book is marked." The words were chosen carefully and spoken as if they had a special relevance.

Jonjo began to wonder whether they were being watched. The old man's odd behaviour certainly suggested so. So he opened the book where it was marked, taking out the small bookmark. As he did so, he saw something in the man's eyes as they looked backwards and forwards between Jonjo and the bookmark. Jonjo studied the small ticket he held in his hand.

"I think," the uncle said, referring to the book, "that I read it up to the part where Tevye arrives at the railway station." He paused to ensure that the young man understood the relevance of what he had just said, before adding, "Amstel railway station."

Jonjo looked at the frail old man before contemplating the significance of the ticket again. He stared at the ticket and then back at the man before realising that what he was holding was a left-luggage ticket.

"What will happen to you?" Jonjo asked him, but the old man simply shrugged.

"Do you have a return ticket?" Fleischmann asked him and Jonjo understood that he really wanted to know whether he had an escape plan.

"No, unfortunately I still need to get one."

"There is some money in my wallet, if they have not stolen it. Please take what you need."

Jonjo opened it and saw a photo of two young boys. "Mutt and Jeff," he said and realised how fond of them the old man was.

"I never married," the old man said, a reference to his childless state rather than the absence of a wife.

"May I take this?" Jonjo asked, holding up some twenty guilder notes. "I don't know how much these are worth," he added.

"Almost nothing, I'm afraid. The German mark has been the main currency here since last week and the exchange rate is very poor," he added with a smile. "But, please, take it."

Jonjo closed the book, put it back on the cabinet and placed the left-luggage ticket in his trouser pocket.

"Mazel tov," the old man said, smilingly, as Jonjo placed his own hand on the limp, thin-skinned hand that rested on the bed.

"Mazel tov," Jonjo replied, not knowing what he had said.

12

Monday 25 May 2015 – A25, Lille

It was difficult to ignore the lively, yet painfully banal conversation of our passenger as we drove around the city of Lille, turned off the dual carriageway and headed towards Touberge. By leaving Outreau at first light, we were ahead of schedule and confident of arriving at our destination before the coach departed. So, when Brendan indicated that he needed to stop to use the toilet, Tonka decided to pull over on the outskirts of a small town for a coffee. At the risk of unleashing Brendan's horoscope recital on Tonka, I offered to drive for the remainder of the journey. The short break would enable us to change drivers. But Tonka refused the offer in order to avoid the inevitable diatribe.

The small town consisted of little more than a service station, some run-down houses and, a few hundred metres down the road, a cafe. I wanted to ask for confirmation of our route anyway, so as Tonka filled up with petrol, I paid for the fuel and the man in the service station gave me directions. He also told me about the cafe up the road and, as we had left before breakfast was served at the hotel in Outreau, we decided to park the car in a side street and visit it. The attendant in the service station assured me that we were only thirty minutes from Touberge and suggested we took the direct route by turning left after the cafe and travelling through the forest to the famous village.

As we parked the car in the shabby side street and headed off to look for the cafe, it began to rain, so Brendan returned to the car to get his hat. A gang of kids loitering nearby asked him if he wanted them to look after the car, but Brendan told them to bugger off and continued on to find us in the cafe. It wasn't until we were leaving the cafe that he began to tell us about his confrontation with the youngsters.

"I can look after myself, I can," he assured us. "It's all these youngsters understand today," he continued. "A firm hand and the international language of 'bugger off'."

Filled with a little trepidation and expecting to see large scratch marks on the car, I was pleased to find that the now-departed kids had done nothing to it.

"See, didn't I tell you, bugger off works every time."

"I'll drive," said Tonka and we all climbed into the car. Tonka now seemed desperate to offload our new-found friend as quickly as possible and certainly before he began reciting his horoscope to him. As Paul Simon suggested, there may indeed by fifty ways to leave your lover, but we couldn't think of one that could shake off the dogged Irishman.

"Take the next turning on the left," I told Tonka. "Apparently that will take us through a forest and it's about thirty minutes to Touberge. We'll have you there before they've finished their breakfast," I assured Brendan.

I think my friend and I were both now wondering why we had enlisted for this rescue mission. It had seemed the right thing to do at the time. It would take a hardened heart indeed to leave an old man and fellow mourner stranded in a foreign country, separated from his travelling companions and without money or a change of clothes. We were in no hurry to return home anyway, having booked ourselves onto the late afternoon train from Calais. We looked at each other, both assured that we had made the right decision. We were thirty minutes from dropping the old man off and would then have an easy two-hour drive back to the port and be home by bedtime. We had done a good deed. Of course we couldn't have left him alone in that square.

Tonka turned the key to start the engine when, suddenly, there was a loud bang and black smoke enveloped the car. Steam billowed from the bonnet and we all jumped out of the vehicle. It took only a few minutes for Tonka to identify the problem. The street kids had rammed an old screwdriver into the radiator and stuck a French golden delicious apple up the exhaust. So much for the international language of 'bugger off'.

We got out of the car and surveyed the wreckage. Brendan stood in the road, his large hand across his mouth, wondering how on earth such a thing could have happened.

"I didn't have any money to give them anyway," he pleaded.

As Tonka spoke some French, he returned to the cafe to find out where the nearest car mechanic was. The necessary calls were made and we waited patiently by the car for an hour until the recovery truck arrived. The mechanic advised us that he would need to tow it to his workshop a few miles along the forest road and began the long process of securing our car onto the back of his vehicle. It didn't occur to me to ask him to drop Brendan in Touberge on the way. In the confusion, the Irishman's problems had taken a lower precedence and it was only when we arrived at the workshop on the outskirts of a village that we remembered poor Brendan's dilemma. By this time it was nearly one o'clock and the coach would almost certainly have left Touberge. The mechanic suggested that Brendan went to an inn a few hundred yards along the road opposite a church. He could make some calls from there.

"It'll be too late, Brendan. The coach would have left by now," called Tonka. "Organise us some lunch and we'll be along in a minute."

We pushed our car over the pit in the workshop and, after a few minutes, the mechanic suggested that we joined Brendan at the inn and he would come along shortly to let us know how long the repairs would take.

As we approached a bend in the road we could see the top of a church above the hedgerow. When we reached the point where the road veered left, there appeared before us a picture-postcard scene. An old inn, set back from the roadside, stared benignly at the dense woodland on the other side of the road. A few tables were set up for lunch outside, in the space between the inn and the road. Brendan was sitting at one of the tables reading a newspaper. He seemed unconcerned that he had missed the coach party in Touberge, which had now set off for the next destination on their tour. Instead he insisted on reading his horoscope out loud as we sat down and waited for the food he had ordered.

"It's today's," he declared, waving an English newspaper at us. But I ignored his obvious joy.

"Did you ask the innkeeper to find out where your coach was heading?"

"No, I didn't think to ask him that," he replied before adding, "would you look at this?" He then read out his horoscope, undiminished by the fact that he was stranded in the middle of nowhere, with no luggage, no money and no passport.

"'This week's union between Mercury and Uranus will make your mind even sharper than usual. You will spot any opportunities that arise long before anyone else, giving you a distinct advantage.'" He paused and added, "I've ordered us the decongestion menu. I thought that would be perfect after all that smoke we inhaled."

"Firstly," said Tonka firmly, looking at the menu, "we have just had breakfast and the decongestion menu, as you call it, is nine courses long and we'll be here for four hours eating it. Secondly, the word is degustation and it's a tasting menu, which costs ninety-five Euros each. I don't suppose you're paying, are you?" By the tone of his voice, I could tell that the normally imperturbable Tonka was losing patience with our annoying new friend. But his harsh words ricocheted off the thick skin of the exclusion zone that protected Brendan's sensitivities.

"I'd love to treat you boys for all the gracious help you've bestowed upon me but, as you know, I left my wallet in the coach."

The lilt of his voice was persuasive and, as Tonka unravelled his napkin, it was as if he was waving a white flag in surrender. Even the most modest of French hostelries offer a degustation, or tasting, menu and although this was indeed the most modest of inns, it obviously had a long history of providing hospitality to the seasoned traveller. The surroundings were pleasant and tranquil but I couldn't help wondering whether this was one of my regular, anxious dreams, where I can't find my way home and become stymied at every attempt to do so. But it wasn't a dream. Somehow we had stumbled off our planned course and found ourselves reluctantly enjoying a nine-course lunch at a countryside inn situated in rural France, somewhere near the Belgian border. Considering we had only intended to visit Boulogne before returning home with some duty-free booze, it was difficult not to wonder whether this was, after all, a disturbing dream. Brendan was unperturbed, suggesting that the simple, rural life was unbeatable.

"Why do people have to complicate life?" he asked. "What can be more pleasurable than this simple fare? Why do governments have to interfere? Look at the other week, for example. Why do they have to cause all that confusion by putting the clocks forward an hour?"

What confusion?" I asked.

"Well, I mean," he answered, "how do all the wild animals get on when the clocks change? Imagine how much it must confuse them."

I looked baffled, especially when Tonka decided to engage in this stupid conversation.

"They don't know the clocks have changed," he explained. But I was forced to change the subject before I screamed.

"What's happening about your coach?" I asked, wondering why this issue wasn't being given priority.

"The innkeeper said he would make some enquiries with his friend in Touberge," the Irishman answered, with an unruffled tone.

As we waited patiently for our first course, a priest came out of the church opposite and crossed the narrow road, which had not seen a single vehicle pass in the time we had been there. He sat at one of the tables and, after nodding politely, began to open his newspaper.

"Good morning, Father," I said, trying to be polite. "You have a lovely church, how old is it?"

"I am new here," he answered disinterestedly. "But my predecessor would know."

"Where is he?" I asked.

"He's dead," came the brusque response.

"Oh, I'm sorry. What did he die of?"

"He was ninety-three, what do you think?" he answered, as his manner turned from brusque to surly and ill-tempered. The conversation ended abruptly.

I don't know why people always expect priests to be patient and polite. In the main they probably are but, like any walk of life, there are many who are not. This one wanted to be left alone to read his newspaper and I convinced myself that he was guilty of nothing more than that. I wondered about trying to offload Brendan on the priest, after all, he was closer to the Good

Samaritan than I was. Perhaps Brendan could claim sanctuary in the church opposite.

As we were speaking, or rather not speaking, the owner of the inn came out with a tray containing our first course. As he did so, the priest relented, presumably realising that upsetting the customers might affect his immunity against paying for his daily cup of coffee.

"Perhaps Monsieur Tremblay can assist you with your questions on local history," the priest commented, a little more cheerily. "His family have owned this inn for one hundred and fifty years."

"Bonjour," said a stocky man wearing a blue and white striped apron. He was about seventy years old and had a three-day growth of beard. He had overheard the priest's introduction. "Not mine, actually, but my wife's."

"I was just asking the priest if he knew how old the buildings are."

"As the priest says, the inn is more than one hundred and fifty years old and the church is older still, I believe."

Tonka grew a little impatient and interrupted his meal at regular intervals to look up the road to see if there was any sign of the mechanic. "How far is it to Touberge?" he finally asked the innkeeper, as he placed the second course on the table.

"It is just fifteen miles," he answered, pointing in the opposite direction from where we had come.

"So close," mumbled Tonka, dispiritedly.

The third, fourth and fifth courses arrived at a slow pace, in-keeping with the surroundings. Life moved with a languid ease in this secreted cloister of a village.

"I have been busy with your lunch, Monsieur," explained Monsieur Tremblay as he arrived to remove the empty plates that had contained a snail confined within a small profiterole. He directed his comment towards Brendan. "But I will speak to my friend soon and try to find out where your coach has gone."

Brendan smiled back benignly, as if it wasn't the most important issue at the moment. He looked down at the empty plate that represented his fifth course.

"What was that wonderfully flavoured dish?" he asked.

"L'escargot," came the reply and Brendan looked suitably impressed but was too eager to see the sixth course to ask what it meant.

"It's a very quiet village, Monsieur Tremblay," said Tonka, realising that it was too late to worry about reuniting Brendan with his coach party. "What is this place called?"

"Don't delay the man about his business," insisted the hungry Brendan. But the innkeeper was happy to linger.

"Cache Moyen," he replied, adding, "And my name is Baptiste." He directed his comment to all of us and shook our hands. His grip was strong like Tonka's. "It is very quiet today," he continued, "because my family have gone to Charleburg to demonstrate about the closure of a children's hospital there. I don't suppose it will make any difference." He shrugged his shoulders and looked towards the sky. "They will be back later, but you will probably have left by then."

Baptiste Tremblay was a subdued fellow and yet a little cynical, too. He seemed to me like one of life's passengers. It took him where it wanted, with little resistance on his part. He was resigned to accept life's problems and, if the health service wanted to close the local children's hospital, what could he do about it? The ebb and flow of life's tides buffeted him and he would simply continue feeding and watering his customers as it did so, considering himself a tiny link in the history of the inn. He spoke good English and I assumed he had regular visitors to his quaint and typically French country inn. The inclusion of pasta dishes and other Spanish and Italian cuisine provided an international characteristic to an otherwise classic French inn.

Across the road, beyond the church and graveyard, a strong wind whispered as it travelled through the high branches of the trees. I looked at Tonka and we both thought of his grandad. I knew he wanted to speak but he had a stronger desire to simply leave this place and get home to Gabriella. Unnecessary conversations would only delay that process.

I was just commenting on its setting among the densely wooded area of Foret Isole when the mechanic came strolling up the road towards us. There was no urgency in his step and I assumed from his swagger that the problem with the car had been fixed.

"Après-demain," he said, pulling up a seat at the table next to us.

"The day after tomorrow," said Baptiste, assuming we didn't speak French.

"The car won't be repaired until the day after tomorrow?" asked Tonka fretfully, wondering what he meant by 'après-demain', but the mechanic shook his head.

"Non. Bien sur que non," replied the mechanic.

"No, Monsieur," repeated Baptiste.

"Oh, good," I said, assuming he meant it had already been repaired and 'the day after tomorrow' was just a little joke by the mechanic.

The young man shuffled his chair, unconvinced that we had understood him. He looked towards Baptiste but decided to make an attempt at speaking in English himself.

"No," he replied and slowly began constructing the sentence in English. "The piece; the part can be sent après-demain, tomorrow. The car to be fixed in five days."

Having spent the previous twenty minutes mentally criticising Baptiste for his submissive response to life, I was bowled an unplayable ball by the god of providence. It seemed there was nothing we could do to escape our worsening situation. Baptiste sensed our disappointment.

"Sometimes I think these things are meant to happen." He said before seizing the moment. "We have rooms available, Monsieur."

Tonka and I looked at each other and searched for a solution to the problem facing us, but found none. Travelling home by public transport and returning to collect the car later would have taken even longer than waiting until it was repaired. After questioning the mechanic about what action might be taken to speed up the process, it soon became clear that there was nothing that could be done. So we reluctantly resigned ourselves to remaining in this idyllic but isolated village for several days. The mechanic finally left, assuring us he would complete the repair as soon as the parts arrived. Thirty minutes later, our long meal ended with coffees and truffle chocolates, which Tonka and I refused but Brendan gobbled up. Then we sat in silence, still contemplating whether there was any other way out of this maze. When it became obvious there was none, we capitulated to the inevitable delay in returning home and began to think about how we were going to explain this ridiculous mess to Ludo and Gabriella.

The fortuitous Baptiste left us to consider whether we would require rooms at the inn although, to be frank, there was no alternative than to take up his offer to stay in this tiny village. The ensuing conversation with the innkeeper took only a few minutes, during which Brendan's situation was relegated farther down the list of problems to be solved. Indeed, it was only when Baptiste approached us with three room keys that Tonka and I remembered our commitment to repatriate our new-found friend. I took the third key and handed it to Brendan.

"Have you managed to find anything out about our colleague's coach party?" I asked Baptiste.

"I will show you to your rooms and deal with it immediately," the big man said as he led us back into the inn.

The intimate rooms were well furnished and in-keeping with the ageless beauty of the building. The pale blue and oak-timbered exterior continued into the small public areas and the rooms were painted in a pale primrose yellow with the same blue accessories.

Once we had unpacked, we telephoned Ludo and Gabriella to explain our predicament. The obvious questions followed and it was difficult to convince anyone not caught up in this conundrum that it was not of our own making. What were we doing on the Belgian border when we had only been visiting Boulogne, which is situated close to the channel port of Calais? Brendan was a useful card to play at this time. Who among us could simply abandon a penniless, passport-less and friendless old man whose coach had departed without him?

"Couldn't you have handed him over to the local police?"

Now, this was a good suggestion from Ludo and I must admit it was an option that neither Tonka nor I had thought of at the time. The only way to respond to such a sensible question from your wife was to rebut it completely; turn adversity to advantage, introduce a tone of disparagement and bet all you have on a humanitarian putdown. The fact that my wife was half feisty Italian and half self-effacing Roman Catholic gave me an even-money chance of success.

"He's a fellow traveller on God's highway, Ludo," I replied wistfully. "Not a lost purse."

This response expressed altruism and appealed to my wife's religious ideals. I didn't mention the parable of the Good Samaritan, but the analogy was too obvious to miss for an archetypal guilt-ridden Catholic such as Ludo.

"Sometimes, Jack, you can be a kind, patient and thoughtful man."

As she spoke there was a knock on my bedroom door.

"Jack, Tonka," called Brendan from the other side of the door, not knowing whose bedroom it was. "Do you have a spare pair of underpants I can borrow?"

I couldn't quite hear what he was saying, but desperately wanted to shout the internationally accepted response of 'bugger off'. However, I mediated my reply because Ludo was still listening.

"Sorry, Ludo, poor old Brendan is knocking on my door and needs help with something. I'll call you again in the morning when we may have more news about the car. Give my love to the kids. I'll get home as soon as I can."

"I was on the phone," I called as I opened the bedroom door. "What did you ask for?"

"Underpants. Do you have any spare underpants I can borrow?"

"No, I don't."

"Oh, okay, I'll just turn these ones inside out then."

Oh God, I thought, too much information, Brendan, too much information. I reached into my trouser pocket, took out some notes and thrust them into his hand.

"Here," I said, "go and get yourself what you need. Ask Baptiste if there is a shop nearby."

As he departed, with a hearty thank you, I tried to dismiss the thought from my mind of Brendan returning a pair of borrowed underpants. As I walked down the hall and passed the door to Tonka's room, I could hear that he was still talking on the telephone to Gabriella. I didn't want to interrupt him and he would certainly know where to find me once he had finished his conversation.

After the nine-course tasting menu we'd enjoyed for lunch, not even Brendan could entertain the thought of another meal that evening. I sat at one of the four tables outside the front of the building, sipping cold beer on a warm May evening. The narrow road ran directly past the inn, but we were disturbed only very occasionally by a passing car. However, from my room at the side of the building, I had heard a group of people arrive during the afternoon and assumed these were the other members of Baptiste's family.

There were certainly more people working at the inn that evening, not because there were any more customers than ourselves, but simply because this was a family business and it needed to provide employment for all members of the household.

As the sun began to set above the trees in the forest opposite, Baptiste introduced me to the other members of his family. Firstly, briefly to his son, Alexis, and then to his daughter-in-law, Claudia, who were both about my age. Alexis was tall and, although he reminded me of someone, he looked nothing like his father. He was more talkative than his pretty wife, an attractive woman made more so by an endearing, but reluctant, smile. Like the rest of the family, she spoke good English and the attraction of her smile was diminished only by its weakness, for a strange sadness furrowed her young brow. It seemed to me that the cause of her troubled countenance might have been her daughter, Ellie, who I saw only momentarily but who, despite her cheery disposition, seemed delicate and pale. The child rushed out of the inn towards our table, but was led away to her bedroom by her father. Just as he swept her up in his arms and glanced towards me I recognised something in his eyes. There was something about him that I hadn't noticed before, something familiar, but I couldn't place it and dismissed the thought from my head. Just as I did so, another gust of wind rushed through the tree tops beyond the cemetery opposite and the bright, new, green leaves chanted shallow and incoherent incantations to the fading light.

After Alexis had taken Ellie to bed and Claudia had returned to her duties inside the building, an older woman appeared from the pathway that ran down the side of the inn. She nodded to me and sat at a table close by.

"Good evening," she said and asked if I was one of the guests who had arrived today. I confirmed that her assumption was correct and went on to explain the circumstances that had led us to

Cache Moyen. To begin with, she was reluctant to engage in a conversation and seemed to do so more out of obligation or politeness than any personal volition. I understood why when she began recounting the history of the inn and how she had inherited it from her mother. My first impression was that this gift was a burden rather than a blessing, but she undertook her responsibilities with undoubted pride.

"You're Baptiste's wife," I pronounced, realising who she must be and she introduced herself as Julia. From her potted history of the inn, I realised she was, very much, the matriarchal leader of the family, following her mother in that role. As she talked, I became more convinced that the discussion was the product of duty rather than any great desire to know anything about me personally. I suppose she was hoping I would be joined by one of my travelling companions, who might then relieve her from her burden as a host in the absence of her son. But, for the time being, she reluctantly continued our rather superficial conversation and after a few moments, when nobody arrived to rescue her, she began to relax.

Ellie, now dressed in her pyjamas and dressing gown, had escaped her parental guard and ran eagerly from the inn with the intention of saying goodnight to her grandmother, while delaying her bedtime. But she changed her mind and, in an attempt to impress Julia with her inherited hospitality skills, she asked if her nana wanted anything from the kitchen. But there were no late waitressing duties to be performed and, after finally kissing her grandmother goodnight, she left, running enthusiastically back inside the building to report that Nana did not want a drink.

"Bonne nuit, Ellie," the woman called and a small voice returned her words from the passageway of the inn.

After the little girl had left, Julia spoke at length about her granddaughter, who had been named after her own mother. She stopped the conversation abruptly when Ellie ran out of the building once more to see her nana again and sit upon her lap.

Her father called her name from inside. But Ellie ignored him and looked at me with the inquisitive scrutiny of a small child, so I asked her name and how old she was. The little girl spoke to her grandmother in French but responded to my questions in English, her pale complexion providing a worrying contrast against the light olive skin that her grandmother shared with the other members of the family. I complimented her on her English, but Julia replied for her.

"She will run this inn some day, just as I do and my mother and grandfather did before me. We have many visitors from Britain, so she needs to speak the language well."

I didn't reply but simply asked Ellie where she had been today. Julia looked at me anxiously, as if she recognised the questioning tone of a reporter.

"To the hospital," she replied, looking back at her nana for approval. "But I didn't have any treatment today."

I assumed she had attended the protest march about the closure of the hospital, but wasn't sure what she meant about not receiving treatment. I looked at Julia, hoping to receive an explanation, but none was forthcoming and she told the child it was time to go to bed. Her excuse to leave was less than convincing and I reasoned that she didn't want to discuss Ellie's quite obvious illness with a stranger. The child's paleness conjured up a number of possibilities but I resisted any speculation on such a sensitive matter. As they walked away, I could just make out the little girl's plea, in French, for her grandmother to tell her a story.

As I sat there, waiting for Tonka to finish his marathon telephone conversation with Gabriella, I couldn't help thinking about the elegant and intriguing Julia Tremblay. Just like her son, Alexis, there was something about her that I recognised. At first, I convinced myself it wasn't her facial features, because I couldn't remember anyone who looked so sublimely beautiful in their seventies. No, in her case, I told myself that it was her sad countenance that I recognised, because I had seen that forlorn look several times before.

When I first went to work at the sports reporting agency on Fleet Street, the firm employed a team of reporters, including a man named Chris Willoughby. He seemed much older than me, but I was only twenty and he was probably only in his late thirties. He was six feet tall, suave and very handsome. He was the agency's golfing correspondent and so he travelled extensively. When he had more than a couple of newspapers to write for at a tournament, he would take an assistant along and, occasionally, he took me. Chris was a charming man who was attracted to women. He was a declared bachelor, who never considered marriage, but enjoyed brief affairs of the heart. He avoided married women so, in a way, there was absolutely nothing wrong with his activities.

In the beginning, he would say to me: "Go and find me a nice plump virgin, Jack." He was joking, for he needed no help in attracting the opposite sex. He enjoyed, I think, educating me in the mysteries of courtship. He did whatever he could to ensure that the women were single and then, when he first managed to get each one into bed, he restricted the session to petting. He never made love the first time. He said it made the woman all the more eager for a second date. And he never minded waiting because he was supremely confident he would get what he wanted very soon.

I travelled to Scotland with him on three occasions and to Spain on another. He produced fantastic reports for the newspapers who engaged him and, on each occasion, he would leave a broken-hearted woman behind. So, although he was doing nothing wrong, someone always got hurt because he never once met a woman who enjoyed the same detached feelings that he had for such relationships.

So what did that have to do with Julia? Well, it was *that* look that I detected on Julia's face that day. The same look that I had seen on the faces of certain young ladies who had fallen in love with a philanderer. Handsome, charming, single and suave, but a philanderer all the same, that was Willoughby. And so, I convinced myself that Julia had loved and lost heavily before she met Baptiste, who was clearly not a handsome philanderer. No, Baptiste was a provider with a good work ethic and not too much ambition, because Julia was sufficiently ambitious for both of them.

Conjecture and supposition, I know, but the look was familiar. She had met someone in her younger days for whom she had feelings; sensual, rather than sensible feelings in her mind; misplaced romantic feelings that had no place in her future plans. Perhaps he was a gigolo, just like Chris Willoughby. Still, nothing had come of it, that much was clear. She felt too much for her mother and grandfather to jeopardise the hostelry by marrying badly. Her heritage would not be prejudiced by a handsome face, or lost for the sake of love.

Tonka eventually arrived, after making some important telephone calls. The past couple of days had slipped past so quickly, I had forgotten that his father was due to have the operation on his foot tomorrow and Tonka should have been back home to take him to the hospital. Gabriella had stepped into the breach and agreed to undertake the duty. As he was relating the conversation to me, Brendan came walking back from the local shops, so I didn't have time to relate my earlier discussions with various members of the Tremblay family.

"Good evening," said our Irish friend, who went on to tell us that he had not managed to find a menswear shop nearby. He held out the money towards me but I declined, telling him to keep it in case he needed it for anything. "Thank you, thank you," he replied, promising to repay me for my generosity, as he had done on each occasion we'd bought him food or drink.

"The man in the newsagent said he can get me an English newspaper in the morning," said Brendan happily. "He can't get the *Cork Examiner*, so I said anything with a horoscope in it will do fine." He paused. "How would I stay out of trouble without my daily horoscope?"

Not wanting to be drawn into a conversation with Brendan about astrology charts and hoping that Ludo would have more time to talk now she had put the children to bed, I made an excuse and returned to my room. Stepping in from the late, but still bright, sunshine, the hallway on the ground floor was dark. But a shaft of light from a skylight above the door lit up a framed photograph on a bookshelf at the end of the hall. I stopped and stared at the two people in the picture. The immaculately dressed woman was Julia, in her mid-forties and, standing next to her, was a teenage boy, also smartly dressed, who must have been her son, Alexis. It reminded me of the photograph Tonka had of his grandad with the mysterious woman in Paris. As I looked at it, I identified the similarity that I had recognised in Julia's face when we'd met outside. It had indeed been her facial features, for she resembled someone I knew. That likeness was even more evident in the young boy's face, for he looked like his mother, but he looked even more like Tonka's grandad. That similarity, that resemblance I had seen on Julia's face, was especially conspicuous in the boy standing next to her in the photograph.

I wanted to rush back out to tell Tonka. I wanted to compare the two photographs, if only to dismiss the premature conclusions my mind was reaching. But I didn't. It was too incredible; it was a trick of the light. It was dark in the hallway. The ray of late sunlight that had broken through the tree tops and shone through the skylight had moved westwards. Now it was more difficult to make out the detail in the photograph.

Lots of people looked like other people, often more famous people and that doesn't mean they're related. I stopped, realising I was producing a shopping list of reasons to reject my suspicions, or at least prove them wrong. It was just a coincidence, I told myself, adding one more to the list as I replaced the framed picture and left the hallway to go upstairs. But, after I had made the second call to Ludo and returned to that same passageway a little later, I couldn't help dwelling by that picture, pretending to look at the books on the shelf but, instead, staring at the likeness that I had convinced myself had some relevance. I stood there, wondering what had drawn us here to this strange, beguiling place in the middle of a lonely forest.

Suddenly, Baptiste stepped out of the kitchen and I need to move sideways to let the rather large man get past me in the narrow hallway.

"I was just looking at your book collection, Baptiste," I said, as if providing an alibi.

"You might find some in English," he replied. "Visitors sometimes leave them in their rooms and we put them on the shelf."

I went to pick up the photograph, wanting to seize the moment and address the uncertainty and confusion that crowded my brain. But he continued down the hall, calling back to me that the local newsagent also had books in English.

"We like to cater for our visitors in Cache Moyen," he added enthusiastically.

I stood there, transfixed by perplexity, wondering what turmoil and upheaval I would cause by walking outside with the photograph, demanding to know whether Julia was the daughter of John Joseph Thompson. I imagined the heartache I might cause Tonka. The timing was wrong; he had just lost his beloved grandfather and his father was undergoing an operation. Vacillate, my old teacher had called me and he was right. I didn't need much encouragement to avoid causing a fuss and, as usual, I decided to sleep on it.

13

Tuesday 24 December 1940 – Stalag XXV, East Prussia

Sitting on a wooden step with his boots buried in three inches of snow, Jonjo wondered why his first white Christmas had to be spent many miles away from home with few, if any, friends around him. Across the parade ground, on the other side of the camp, a canvas-backed truck pulled up and the driver began unloading parcels and sacks. It was Christmas Eve and it seemed that even the war could not prevent Santa from working. Gifts would be too much to hope for, but a letter from home was all that anyone at the camp really wanted anyway.

He heard the door of the hut open behind him and stood to attention facing it.

"You can go in now, Guardsman Thompson," the officer said as he left and walked purposefully across the snow-covered parade ground towards the main gate, where the delivery was taking place.

Jonjo marched into the wooden building, banged his feet to attention on the creaking wooden floorboards and announced himself as Guardsman Thompson of hut twelve. The colonel put away some papers and looked up at the tall young soldier. As the commanding officer for the British troops at Stalag XXV, he had authority over a disparate group of British soldiers and a few RAF crew, but today he felt like an agony aunt.

"What is it, Guardsman?"

"Sir," he replied loudly. "I wish to request that the gossip and rumour about me is stopped, Sir."

"Stand at ease, Thompson. What gossip and rumour are you talking about?"

"Sir. There is nobody from my company here, Sir and rumours are rife that I am a deserter, Sir, a coward, Sir; which I'm not, Sir, with respect, Sir."

"Look, Thompson, I've got enough to do without dealing with all the back-fence talk that goes on in this place. Just tell them what happened to you, how you got caught and put an end to the tittle tattle."

"With respect, Sir, I haven't told Jerry what happened and I don't think anyone here needs to know either. It might still prejudice the lives of those on active service, Sir." He paused before adding, "Someone still out there, Sir."

The last statement got the colonel's attention.

"What were you doing when you got caught, Guardsman Thompson?"

"I'd rather not say, Sir."

"And that's exactly why there's so much gossip, Thompson."

"But nobody needs to know, Sir, not even you, Sir," Jonjo replied, adding, "with respect, Sir."

"Well, what can you tell me?" he asked, before telling Thompson to sit down.

Jonjo pulled up a rickety wooden chair and sat down.

"You see, Sir, I don't even know which bits of this are true myself and I was there. We were just told things, lies actually, Sir, with respect, Sir. So that, if I got caught by the Germans, I would tell them what I had been told. Which, with respect, Sir, was probably a load of rubbish."

"Like what, Thompson?"

Jonjo explained how he had been told about the mission to rescue the Queen of the Belgians, but found out that there was no Queen of the Belgians, well, not when he was sent to rescue her.

"You were sent to rescue the Queen of the Belgians, Thompson?"

"Yes, Sir and we succeeded. Well, we brought some people back from Belgium, although it wasn't Belgium actually. It turns out it was Holland, according to my captain."

"And who was he?"

"Again, I'd rather not say, Sir."

The colonel puffed out his cheeks and lit his pipe as he thought for a moment.

"So, how did you get captured, Thompson?"

"On the next mission, Sir. It was early in May; we went across to France from Kent, not expecting to find any Germans. After all, Sir, we had been as far as Belgium, or Holland, the week before without seeing them, so we certainly didn't expect to find them camped across the channel in Boulogne."

"Yes, I heard about that one before my lot was captured. Took you by surprise, I imagine. The Krauts came in through Belgium; they went round the Maginot Line instead of through it. Typical Nazi ploy. The Belgian boys put up a great fight, apparently, but they were no match for a Jerry panzer division." He paused and relit his pipe. "Your boys were with the Welsh Guards at Boulogne then. Was that where you were taken?"

Jonjo explained that he was not captured at the battle but found himself behind enemy lines with his captain and another soldier.

"The captain resolved to complete the mission he had been given and so we set off to…," he hesitated. "I'd rather not say where we were going, Sir."

"Very well, Son, very well. Understood, understood. Loose talk costs lives. Quite right, quite right."

"Well," said Jonjo. "Because I was captured weeks after the rest of the Irish Guards at Boulogne, some of the boys here think it's suspicious. They're saying I must have run off or something."

"I see, I see, Thompson," answered the colonel, wondering what could be done. "What would you like me to do?"

"Oh, nothing, Sir," he said firmly to a suitably surprised colonel. "I just wanted to make you aware, Sir, that the next time someone makes a remark like that, Sir, well, I'm going to switch his lights out, Sir. With respect, Sir."

The colonel assured Jonjo that there would be no need for such precipitative action, as he felt entirely able to correct any misunderstanding among the men.

By the time he returned to his own hut, the mail he'd seen being delivered was being distributed. It had already been read and censored by the Germans before being sent on to the camp. There was nothing from his two regular correspondents, Mum and Ivy, just a small parcel that contained a letter and a book. It was from Violet Martin, showing predictable foresight by having posted her Christmas present months in advance. Mum and Ivy would wait until December before thinking about Christmas and their cards, letters and a pair of knitted socks were likely to arrive closer to Easter. He looked at the parcel and wondered whether he should save it, as a present, until tomorrow.

Correspondence from home tended to arrive in batches and Jonjo had received a bundle of eight letters in October. These were the first he had received since his capture. He had recognised the writing and put them in order, according to the postmark, so that he could read them in sequence. There had been three from Ivy, four from his mother and one from Violet. The earliest one, from his mother, was dated August and said that she had received a telegram the previous month, telling her that Guardsman John Joseph Thompson was missing in France. It was another two months before she heard that he had been captured. Jonjo could only imagine the agonising weeks she must have endured between those two messages. The most recent letter had been from Ivy and it told of the relentless bombing of London. Every night the entire east end of London was subjected to bombing that required them to take refuge in London underground stations.

Each letter consisted of two small sheets of paper, with writing as small as the women could make it. Jonjo would read them in a different order each day. Sometimes he would read all of Ivy's letters and other times all of his mother's, or just the one from Violet. The four letters from his mother said more about the way she was feeling than any worthwhile news from home. He could almost imagine the emotional weight placed on the pen as she had written that first letter and yet it had been done swiftly, urgently, as she'd wanted to despatch it as quickly as she could. What it didn't say was 'thank God, you're safe', yet he understood that this was the message it conveyed. By the time she wrote the fourth letter, there were references to Joe Louis successfully defending his heavyweight title, as if Jonjo would be more interested in sport than life at home.

The letter from Violet was less emotional, more practical. She wanted to know if he had been injured, whether he was getting sufficient food, what the weather was like, how the Germans were treating them and whether he needed anything. He had replied, telling her about the very useful Red Cross parcels that arrived too infrequently but at regular intervals. At the time he'd replied it had not yet snowed, which was probably for the best because she would only worry about it. And he would much rather have a book for Christmas than a pullover or pair of socks.

Jonjo rested the parcel on his chest and lay on the bed, thinking. His mother told people that her son thought about things too much. The timbre of her voice was connotative of an illness. She had said it in front of him, while gossiping with a neighbour one day, which simply gave him something else to think about. It was true, of course, for his head was just so full of thoughts. The previous day, his teacher had said something that had made him think and, that morning, Mr Churchill had said something on the radio that made him think, too. The two comments had fused together, like milk and cornstarch in a blancmange.

"What is the greatest gift?" his teacher, Mr Wormley, had asked. "Patience, tolerance, contentedness?" If Jonjo had known then what he knew now, he would have told him what Mr Fleischmann had said. The Catholics were given all the tolerance and the Jews were given patience. But he had remained quiet, believing this was a rhetorical question anyway.

"Or perhaps kindness," the teacher had continued, "kindness to others?"

Mr Wormley was himself a kindly man who encouraged others in the same direction. He had seemed to be looking directly at Jonjo, like God's spy, searching his soul for the truth. But the truth was trapped in a young boy's heart made permeable by the death of the young Andrew Martin.

And then, by some strange coincidence, the same subject had been mentioned on the radio, when he arrived home from school on that same day. Mr Churchill, it seemed, had chosen to answer his teacher's question, even though he obviously hadn't heard it, suggesting that courage was the greatest gift, for it was this gift that guaranteed all others.

"We have not truly lived," Mr Wormley had added, "until we have done something good for someone who can never repay that kindness."

A few boys had attended school barefoot, but all the girls had worn shoes. Mr Wormley had collected old boots and tried to find pairs suitable for those unshod boys. The boys from slightly more affluent families had cycled to school but most children had walked, as Jonjo had done, accompanied by Andrew and two girls who lived in his street. It had always taken them longer to walk home as they invariably stopped at a sweet shop. Not that they had any money. But, occasionally, they would find an empty lemonade bottle and take it back to the shop to get a halfpenny. This would buy two blackjacks, which they would bite in half and share. Ivy had always wanted to share with Jonjo, but he'd never noticed.

Oldfield Road school had accommodated five to fourteen-year-old boys and girls and lessons had begun sharp at nine in the morning. Sometimes they went home for lunch at noon. With just a small bottle of milk for nourishment at mid-morning, Jonjo had always been hungry. The day had always begun with an inspection of fingernails and hair. The boys' hair had to be cut very short and the girls were required to have plaited hair to prevent the spread of head lice if it touched the desk. This had also provided the boys with something to pull on the way home.

Jonjo lay, stretched out, on his bunk and wondered whether to read the letter and just save the book for tomorrow. Any Christmas wrapping had been torn from it anyway, so that it could be checked for coded messages or information about Britain's battle plans, as if Jonjo would be party to such information; he hadn't been told about the plans for the battles he had fought in, so why would he be treated any differently now he was a prisoner of war? Anyway, it wasn't going to be a surprise, but it would cheer him up on Christmas morning. So he put the book to one side and read the letter. It began with news of his family. Violet had never seen herself as a surrogate mother, even if Jonjo believed himself to be the cuckoo's child. The letter said she had met Mrs Thompson in the market and Jonjo's mother had informed her that everyone was keeping well, although they hadn't taken their annual holiday in Kent this year. Jonjo knew that Violet was being polite when she referred to an annual holiday when, in reality, it was two weeks of hop picking.

There was no reference to Ivy in Violet's letter. Jonjo couldn't remember if he had ever mentioned Ivy to her. Nor was there any mention of the war. It was as if Violet knew it would be censored anyway, so she didn't waste paper by commenting on it. Instead she had written about a strange young man she had met in a bookshop. He must have been strange indeed, thought Jonjo, if she considered him so, for she herself was beyond strange, eccentric, unpredictable, as was demonstrated by her choice of subject for the remainder of the letter. Try to guess what someone like Violet Martin would write a letter about and then take as many guesses as you want. She would still surprise you.

When he finished reading the letter, he checked the postmark to see when it had been sent. It was necessary to do this because letters often arrived in the wrong order and, from their content, it was clear that some didn't arrive at all. He began reading the letter again and thought about the holidays he had enjoyed as a boy in Kent. They were working holidays, or they were once you were about six years old, but they were great fun. The fact that the 2nd Battalion had camped in the adjacent field to where he'd picked hops with his parents never ceased to amaze him. He had wanted to tell his comrades about it when they'd begun bedding down for the night there, but they had all been too tired. For them, the temporary army camp set up near the Beltring Hop Farm close to Paddock Wood was simply somewhere to get some sleep. It had actually been the last sleep for some of them. The fond memories of the hop farm would now always be subdued by the vision of that gallant lance corporal who'd lain dead next to the anti-tank gun he'd manned. Memories of that May day held no promise of hot summers in Kent.

There must have been more than one thousand soldiers billeted at Paddock Wood and there were rumours of dozens of such camps across the south of England. All the talk among the men was of a landing in France, followed by a big push against Jerry. The word resonated in his heart. The push was what had changed his life. One might consider it was the push that had defined his life. But that would be wrong, because it had defined who he wanted to be, not who he was at that time. He didn't like who he was and the push had caused him to recognise this. But it wasn't this push, not the push his comrades were feverishly talking about. This was about another push; one made six years ago. The conversion that followed it was as much about other people as it was about himself, just as this push would be.

After six months in Stalag XXV, Jonjo was convinced that if you told a lie often enough, eventually it became the truth, or a distorted version of the truth in your mind and the mind of others. He hadn't appreciated this at the age of fourteen. But months with nothing to do but placate his troubled conscience made it difficult to distinguish between the truth and a poor recollection of the lies he had told in the days following Andrew's death. For this particular lie and the others told to support it would implicate an innocent car driver and corrupt the minds of two young girls.

A lie was such a powerful thing. Once spoken, given life, it assumed immortality. An uncontrollable force from birth. An ever-present shadow of the self we hated. Or at least it appeared so, but it wasn't the lie that consumed Jonjo, it was the truth that he had murdered that haunted his waking nights. That ever present shadow wasn't the lie, but the truth that could not rest in its untold state, like a spectre of an unborn child, denied life by one moment of weakness, when a lie was easier to speak than the truth. That was what had driven Jonjo to consider hanging himself that day. That lie had caused the driver of the car to be arrested for dangerous driving. That lie had been forced on Ivy and Lily, who were coerced into corroborating it for Jonjo's sake.

He rested his head on the thin pillow, held the St Jude medal in his hand and gazed at the wooden rafters above him. Those childhood days seemed so long ago and so far away. Walking to school alongside Andrew, with the girls just ahead of them, close enough to hear their conversation, most of which was ignored of course. Girls were not interested in hearing how Manchester City had beaten Portsmouth in the FA Cup Final, or even about the first sighting of the Loch Ness monster, like boys were. But their antenna was never turned off; multitasking was an ancient skill of women and these two could walk, talk and listen at the same time.

"Have you had any under and over?" asked Andrew, nodding towards Ivy.

"Not likely," Jonjo replied, "she was May Queen last year. Sees herself as the Holy Virgin till she marries, does Ivy."

"Yer right there, Jonjo," she called back, having overhead the boys' comments while holding her own conversation with Lily. "My mum says I need to keep my hand on my ha'penny when you're around."

Jonjo ignored her. Somehow boys knew instinctively if a girl fancied them and he was certain that Ivy held a candle for him.

"You?" he asked Andrew a little more quietly while raising his eyebrows towards Lily. Andrew smiled and nodded.

"There, you see," replied Jonjo a little too loudly, while trying to suppress a laugh. "Proves my point. Typical strewer is your Lily."

"Don't push your luck," Lily called back.

The four friends had made this walk together ever since they joined Oldfield Road School as toddlers. Jonjo had continued to do so with the girls, even after Andrew's untimely death. For the first few months it was in a sombre mood, with Jonjo trailing behind, unable to talk about it. And they never did discuss it, other than to correct their stories to ensure the driver of the car was not imprisoned. Jonjo had assumed the girls would tell the truth after he had hanged himself. Instead he went to the police himself, without speaking with his parents first. He didn't have to tell the girls because the story spread as quickly as news of some knocked off scotch from the docks. It was Mrs Martin who had brought about his change of heart, of course, not that her visit was ever mentioned. But her unsolicited and unconditional forgiveness was a gift so rare, so unexpected, that it gave him the courage to accept the consequences of his action.

But the strange episode with Mrs Martin had not ended there. Shortly after his confession to the police and while the gossip-mongers were at their most animated, the incredibly surprising Mrs Martin had called at the Thompson's house, this time when she knew that Jonjo's parents would be in. She told them what a very brave thing their son had done by going to the police and that she fully accepted that Andrew had died as a result of an unavoidable accident. Then, just when they had expected her to take her leave, she said she wanted to ask them something, as a favour to her.

"Of course, of course," Jonjo's mother answered gratefully, even before hearing the request.

"I was wondering," she asked, looking backwards and forwards between Mr and Mrs Thompson, "whether John might accompany me and my husband on holiday?" She spoke so deliberately, enunciating each syllable and then waited for the response with a smile.

Mother was speechless, so Mrs Martin removed a glove and continued. "Bill and I have booked a coach holiday to France in July and, of course, Andrew had been going to accompany us. So I was just wondering if John would like to..." she hesitated, not wanting to say 'take his place'. "If he would like to accompany us?" she said instead.

Jonjo agreed, of course, for he saw it as part of his redemption. It was cathartic more than therapeutic and Jonjo appreciated that Mrs Martin felt the same way. This was not a healing process but one of emancipation for them both. And that was when the weekly visits began. The following Monday, on the way home from school, Jonjo visited Mrs Martin to accept her kind invitation to join them on holiday. He returned the next Monday to receive details of the holiday and a list of what he should take with him. And when he arrived the week after that, she had already prepared tea and cake for him. The significance of Monday was never mentioned but both knew it was the day on which Andrew had died.

Each Monday, after school, he would accompany Ivy and Lily for a short distance before turning right and heading off towards the Martin's house. Ivy had asked where he was going on that first week and again on the second week. But, after that, she stopped asking because it annoyed Jonjo. It became a pilgrimage, his personal journey of salvation.

When his parents went hop-picking that summer, Jonjo set off on a Bartlett's Motor Coach tour to France and he brought back a photograph of himself standing in front of the Eiffel Tower with Mrs Martin. It was never framed, or put on show; it would have prompted too many awkward questions from visitors. So Jonjo had kept it in his room.

The first Christmas after her son's death, Violet had given Jonjo a book of poems by Rudyard Kipling, pointing out that Mr Kipling and Mr Yeats had shared the Gothenburg Prize for Poetry earlier that year. *Barrack Room Ballads* became Jonjo's introduction to poetry and to soldiering, and the enigmatic Mrs Martin had given him a book of poetry every Christmas since.

~~~~~

The following morning was a mixture of unfamiliar merriment and profound forlornness as the inmates of Stalag XXV contemplated their first Christmas Day there in contrasting ways. Most were still hopeful as they queued for their daily ration of burgoo on that bitterly cold morning, but some, like Ebenezer Scrooge, saw a vision of Christmas future. A lifetime of consuming watery porridge and Red Cross parcels, as they themselves were consumed by the wintry winds of East Prussia.

Jonjo returned to the hut and read the letter from Violet Martin again. He skipped the opening lines about meeting Mother in the market and reread Violet's recollection of meeting a young man working in a bookshop in London.

'I'm not sure why he is not serving his country; I didn't like to ask but assume he was deemed unfit to do so. His name is Arthur Tessimond. He is a strange character.'

'He told me that he had a book of poems that was published back in 1934 and the year registered with me for obvious reasons. He was such an interesting man I felt obliged to purchase a copy of his book. He was a strangely self-effacing man and, when I asked if he would have another book published, he said, in all humility, that he had not produced anything of merit and that he was surprised the first book had been published. On a subsequent visit to the shop, he kindly gave me some handwritten poems that he had been working on but that have not yet been published. I have written the best of these inside the back cover for you. I hope you enjoy reading them. I think of you often and pray that you will return to us soon, when this terrible war is over.'

Jonjo picked up the book and turned directly to the poem inside the back cover. He could understand why she thought 'Not Love Perhaps' was such a joy to read. He had certainly not read the like of it before. It was not the bawdy, rollicking verse of Rudyard Kipling and was much more unobtrusive than Yeats. To his unsophisticated palate, it reminded him of the little he had read by the Romantic poets.

The book was slim enough to slip under his pillow. The men were encouraged to donate all books to the camp library so that everyone could enjoy them. But Jonjo looked around the cold room and wondered how many of his fellow prisoners would appreciate the subtle emotions of this volume of poems. If it was discovered, he would plead its sentimental value to him. But for now, on this cold Christmas Day, it would remain beneath his pillow.

With a weekly ration of just two small sheets of notepaper, Jonjo had to decide each week whether to write a short letter to two people or one long letter to his mother or to Ivy. But this week, he had to use at least one sheet writing to Violet Martin, to thank her for the present. He considered asking his mum to pass on his thanks, but he wanted to hear from Violet again, so he used one of his valued sheets and wrote a polite thank-you letter. In it he expressed his concern that the winter could be harsh at the camp. It began snowing in November and he could barely remember a day in the past few weeks when it had relented. He assured her that he was keeping well in spite of a poor diet. His biggest regret was the shortage of books, which was why he was particularly grateful for her gift. Poetry, he wrote, had a great advantage because it could be read over and over again, with the joy of discovering new facets with each reading.

Jonjo had grown up reciting poetry and he related stories with that same melodic, lyrical voice. And so he did with his comrades at the camp, when they asked him why he had not been sent to the same stalag as the rest of those captured with him. Instead of keeping quiet, as he had done since his arrival, he simply told them a story. It was never the truth, it hadn't been the truth when it was told to him but, in the end, even Jonjo himself had begun to believe it. By the end of the war, he didn't remember very much about the truth of what had happened back in the spring of 1940. He remembered the hanging attempt in 1934, when he had wanted to put to flight the dark shadows of guilt. He never thought of it as suicide, it was more an execution. But it was a weak thing to do. It was a compromise instead of facing the truth. Compromise was the virtue of the weak, he remembered Violet Martin saying once.

The influence that Violet had over Jonjo was subtle and, to a large extent, went unnoticed by him. But he did recognise himself as a cuckoo's child, as he had written in one of his rare attempts at poetry. He had continued to visit Mrs Martin every Monday after school and the significance of Monday continued to be ignored by them both. He would tell her about the things he had learned at school and she would listen patiently. She was less interested in the science subjects than those with artistic merit. Sometimes Jonjo would read her an essay he had written or show her something he had drawn. She was always praising his work and telling him what a success he would be when he grew up.

To begin with there had been blancmange or scones, then a bar of chocolate to eat on the way home. His mother knew where he'd been and she always asked politely how Mrs Martin was. But she didn't discourage the visits because she felt so sorry for the woman's loss and was unable to deny her the chance of seeing a boy grow into manhood as her own son would have done. Later, as Jonjo grew towards adulthood, he put away childish things and yet he still continued to visit her every Monday after work. It was an obligation he could not resist and the conversation was more mature than at home. They would discuss politics, music and even foreign affairs. As a result he acquired the sophisticated tastes that Violet had directed him towards, such as jazz, literature and the arts. She liked Billie Holiday and Benny Goodman and he preferred Fats Waller and Tommy Dorsey. She influenced him towards Chesterton and Greene, although he had a penchant for Wodehouse. Sharp differences between home and the Martin's house became glaringly evident. They conversed and debated rather than argued and gossiped. She surprised him with her views on the abdication and they often laughed together.

At Christmas, when he was sixteen, they had discussed the merits of King George VI and considered how he might be influenced by the death of his father and abdication of his brother all in the same year. As they did so, carol singers outside began singing 'We Three Kings' and they both laughed out loud, realising that the country had, indeed, had three kings in that one year.

Jonjo rarely saw Mr Martin, who had withdrawn into himself when Andrew had died. He sold life assurance for the Prudential Assurance Company and he had a large area of east London to cover. So he met a lot of people, many of whom knew of his loss.

In those early days, condolences greeted him at every door he knocked on. Every 'sorry for your loss' was another nail in the barrier that began to separate him from the world. Eating, sleeping, even working became ritualistic and Jonjo was never convinced that Mr Martin shared his wife's view of his own absolution. Mr Martin often worked in the evening, in order to collect premiums, which his customers paid weekly or monthly, but even if he arrived home before Jonjo had left, he retreated to another room, avoiding anything that might remind him of his lost son.

One day, Jonjo arrived at Mrs Martin's house as usual. It was four years since that fateful day when her son had died. They were sitting, drinking tea and she offered him a biscuit. Then, in the same casual manner, she said, hesitatingly: "Bill, my husband," as if Jonjo wasn't aware who Bill was. She paused. "He hasn't been able to make love since Andrew died." Her casual tone masked the change in the content of their rather mundane conversation, although she wasn't casual, she was extremely tense. He could not recall her speaking to him on the subject of sex before, although he was now nearly nineteen years old.

She waited, staring absent-mindedly, before adding, "Guilt, I suppose. Or some form of guilt." She appeared a little wayward, emotional.

Naturally, Jonjo was unsure how to respond. She just sat there, a picture of contradiction, looking so sad, so abandoned, in a bright red dress with white spots. A row of white buttons ran down the centre of the dress. He wasn't sure if she was crying but thought he noticed a teardrop run down her cheek. He stood up without speaking and walked over to her. Examining his handkerchief and noticing it was still folded, he offered it to her. She looked up at him as he stood in front of her. Ignoring the offer of the handkerchief, she put her arms around him and pulled him towards her. She remained seated and her face was now pressing against his stomach. Her arms wrapped around his youthful backside. The pair leaned against each other in support and her fingernails gripped the soft flesh of his buttocks. He stood there for a while, looking down at her dark brown hair, not wanting to move. He stroked her hair and slowly her hands began to explore his lower body. It wasn't fear that transfixed him, nor was it her age, for she was only thirty-eight.

Previously she had embraced him like a mother but this was different. She loosened her grip and released him for a moment. He remained standing there, as she undid his trousers and felt inside for the taut flesh of his manhood. Jonjo reached down and began to undo the white buttons at the front of her dress. Neither of them spoke. He reached down into her blouse and felt inside her bra. They never kissed and the only word spoken was 'please' as she pulled him into her and lay back on the couch.

It was the first time for Jonjo. It seemed like a betrayal to Andrew, but the more Jonjo thought about it, the less guilty he felt. It was not something either of them wanted to do, nor were they doing it simply because they could. They needed to do it, him through excessive youthful testosterone and she through sexual frustration. Violet seemed unconcerned that her husband might walk in at any moment.

When it was over, nobody spoke. They simply dressed and then hugged each other as they had done many times before. This time the goodbye lingered a little longer and she didn't seem to want to let go.

He stepped out of the front door, conscious of the neighbours skulking behind their net curtains. He felt different as he passed the children playing in the street and the four women talking at the gate of number 31. In his mind, they all knew his dark secret whereas, in fact, nobody did. Not even the perceptive young Ivy Frampton ever learned of what had happened that day.

When the following Monday came, Jonjo didn't visit Mrs Martin. He simply walked around the shops so that his mother did not become suspicious of his motives for getting home earlier than expected. The following day he received a call at work. Violet had looked up the number and asked the switchboard operator to put her through to Mr Thompson.

"Hello," she said, recognising his voice.

"Hello," he replied nervously.

"It's okay," she said quietly.

"I know," he said, "I know."

She put the telephone down and the visits resumed the following Monday. But they never made love again. Jonjo didn't reach maturity that day. That would come much later when he reflected on the events of that day.

'This is not Love, perhaps,' he read, *'Love that lays down its life, that many waters cannot quench, nor the floods drown, but something written in lighter ink, said in a lower tone, something, perhaps, especially our own.'*

The book of poems was placed under his pillow as Jonjo made the swift journey from that summer evening to an ice cold Christmas Day. In ordinary times, people made informed decisions that impacted on their lives and those of others. But these were not ordinary times. In times of war, decisions were frequently ill-informed, or, when serving His Majesty's Army, uninformed. On the first mission, he had been told that they were to rescue the Queen of the Belgians. They had been told that because, if they were caught by the Germans, that was what they would tell their captors. He knew that because that was exactly what he had told them. And he was quite surprised when they told him that the Queen of the Belgians had died in a motoring accident in 1935. There hadn't been another one since, so he certainly hadn't been rescuing her.

He should have guessed this from what he had found out about the second mission, which had ended for most of them at the Battle of Boulogne. They had been going back to retrieve the queen's crown jewels, which she had forgotten to take with her when they had rescued her at the Hook of Holland. Jonjo had actually found out the truth regarding the 'mission' before he was told by the Germans of the first lie. Captain Egan had had to tell him.

"We need a plan," said Axe.

"What we need," answered O'Reilly, "is a concrete bed to hang our hat on."

Jonjo and the captain had grown accustomed to O'Reilly's barbaric mistreatment of the English language and chose to ignore him as usual.

What sort of a plan had any chance of producing a satisfactory outcome? Egan was lying with his right leg smashed by an animal trap, unable to walk. O'Reilly was an idiot of the highest order and Jonjo was little more than a raw recruit with no language skills and little experience of fighting. Surrender appeared to be the only reasonable option. He had to make a decision and he knew that life was simply about the decisions people made, or rather, the consequences of those decisions. The most trivial of decisions could change the direction of your life. Indeed, it was rarely the momentous decisions that did this. Life was often determined by one insignificant moment of madness, one poor judgement that reshaped your life to its own inclination. The decision to push, in jest, his friend, Andrew, on the way to school one morning had unbalanced Jonjo's life. His friend had stumbled and was struck by a passing car, which had glanced him and caused him to fall. The sound of his head hitting the kerb revisited Jonjo for the remainder of his time on earth.

One ill-considered action had created another. He had coerced the two girls who had accompanied them to lie. He had convinced them that the car was driving too close to the pavement. He had never intended for the driver to be arrested for dangerous driving but lies grew like a tumour, they ate away at you, generating other lies until any return to the joyous, truthful, innocent world you previously inhabited was impossible.

Had Mrs Martin not chosen to visit the Thompson household that day; had her own doggedness not taken her into the backyard; had she run away when she heard someone in the outside lavatory, then perhaps Jonjo would have succeeded in hanging himself; he wouldn't have served in the war; he wouldn't have been captured by the Germans and he wouldn't be spending Christmas Day in a freezing cold prison camp. Good and evil were equally balanced and for all the self-condemnation, the self-loathing, Jonjo was overwhelmed by the kindness of Andrew's mother, the redoubtable Violet Martin. "We all live on the edge of madness," she said that day and she spoke with inner certainty, as if she, herself, had visited this terrible place that he now inhabited. She didn't tell him that it was pre-ordained or out of his control. She didn't offer absolution, just a compassionate response and shelter from the storm.

Life itself began in a moment of improvised passion and could end as abruptly, in an instant, through ill judgement or maligned intent. Life was not predetermined, but a game of chess, with a million pieces and an infinite number of moves. That was what Jonjo concluded because he needed to take responsibility for his own actions. If the opposite was true, then why did he carry such a burden of remorse?

Captain Anthony Xavier Egan, of the Irish Guards, had taken two soldiers and gone off to look for Germans to the south of Outreau, near Boulogne. He didn't realise they were surrounded by the enemy. He made that ill-chosen decision and it changed the lives of many others as the tentacles of consequence reached out.

Jonjo had had six long months to think about that mission, to reflect on the deception and falsehoods. He found it difficult to say the word 'lie'. You didn't call a man a liar in those days, it just wasn't done. Being a liar was tantamount to being a killer, but had less credibility on the street. He knew, of course, that he was being lied to for his own good. The truth was a dangerous commodity in the war and foot soldiers were rarely entrusted with it. The Germans employed people whose singular mission in life was to extract the truth.

So believing he was on a mission to retrieve the Queen of the Belgians' crown jewels was essential for his own safety. Knowing the truth would have got him killed if he had been caught. So, once he did learn the truth, he wasn't going to tell anyone. Jonjo's interrogation was long, arduous and painful. Deprivation of food and friends were harbingers of the anguish to follow. But, fortunately, after his ramblings about the Queen of the Belgians, whom the Germans knew to be dead, the enemy concluded that Guardsman John Joseph Thompson knew nothing of interest to them. So what he did know was best forgotten.

Whether it was the spirit of Christmas or an instruction issued by the colonel, the attitude of the other soldiers towards Jonjo changed that day. Perhaps it was as Arthur Tessimond wrote: *'A need to reach out, sometimes, hand to hand, And then find Earth less like an alien land'*.

14

Tuesday 26 May 2015 — Cache Moyen

The only thing I felt truly certain of as dawn broke on our first full day in Cache Moyen was that certainty itself did not exist. For everything considered to be a certainty in life there was a contradictory doubt; for every wholesome truth, there was incontrovertible scepticism. 'Quid est veritas?' 'What is truth?' Pilate asked when he questioned the witness of truth. I felt the same agnosticism about truth, the same suspicion of certainty. Something I was positive about appeared, on the face of it, to be impossible, or at least irrational. In my mind I was entirely sure that Tonka's grandfather was also the father of Julia. There was no other explanation for the unmistakable similarity between Grandad and Alexis when they were both in their teens. Photographic evidence might not be as conclusive as DNA or a fingerprint but it was enough for me. Enough, but it still didn't quite fill that little space between conclusive and dubious. There was still room for misgivings.

The poetic chorus from the nearby forest was broken by a rattling of bottles as the morning delivery of milk was made just below my bedroom window. I was the first to arrive for breakfast and decided to sit outside in the fresh air, waiting for Tonka to come down from his room. I heard him showering and knew he wouldn't be long. But Baptiste mistook my intentions and arrived with a tablecloth and some cutlery, assuming that I wanted to eat outside on this cloudy May morning. I hadn't considered it, having noticed that the small dining room had been prepared as I passed by it on my way out. But I didn't object, knowing that Tonka would prefer to dine al fresco. There were too few opportunities to do so at home in England and certainly not as early as May.

After laying the table, Baptiste asked what I would like for breakfast and I said I would prefer to wait for my companions. I resisted asking him about the photograph on the bookshelf in the hallway, even though it had played on my mind throughout the night, wondering if I was the only person to have noticed the likeness between members of the Tremblay family and Tonka's grandad.

Just as I was thinking about him, Alexis came out of the inn, into some sunshine that broke from behind a cloud. He said good morning and walked to the edge of the road. He looked up and down but there was no traffic to poison the silence of such a fresh morning. The tranquil and pleasant ambience of eating breakfast on the patio area at the front of the inn made it easy to picture how this scene must have looked in the distant past. Even though I had never been here before, it was clear that so little had changed over time.

The parish hall opposite and the inn itself had been painted at intervals, but the place was timeless and I conjured a sepia image of Julia's grandfather waiting on tables, just as her son Alexis was preparing to do now. I stared intently at his face as he turned to walk back and he returned the look, expecting me to say something. But my silence hung in the air.

Across the country road that bordered the area outside the inn, the lych gate leading to the cemetery behind the church stood, unaltered by time. What oaths had been sworn within its holy realm? How many devoted couples had pledged their love? How many damaged souls had met their maker within the hallowed walls of the graveyard?

I was just about to say something about the photograph in the hall, when Alexis looked past me and spoke.

"Good morning," he called to someone behind me.

"Good morning," replied Tonka, who stretched his legs as Alexis had done, looked off into the forest and then joined me at the table.

"No answer from home," he commented as he sat down. "They must be on their way to the hospital." He sounded guilt-ridden and obviously wished he could have been with his father on the day of his operation.

"It's not a serious operation," I said, hoping to placate his troubled conscience. "Gabriella will ring you soon to update you."

Alexis felt he had loitered long enough and stood next to us to take our order.

"We'll wait for Brendan," I said, wondering how late they served breakfast.

"Your friend has already eaten," Alexis assured us. "He walked into town to buy a newspaper."

In his absence, we ordered a generous breakfast and I wondered whether the moment was right to discuss my business plan for the investigative reporting agency with Tonka. But I couldn't spoil such a beautiful day, for it was too early for a discussion on work. So, I chose to postpone it until another time and considered, for a moment, mentioning the photograph in the hallway. Had Tonka noticed the likeness between his grandad as a child and the picture of the young Alexis? Even now, as he walked between the kitchen and our table, I could see a family similarity. Surely nobody could fail to reach the same conclusion as me once they were able to compare the two photographs side by side. Quite how I would bring that situation about hadn't yet occurred to me, but I was certain such an occasion would arise, it just needed to be done with guile and tact.

I decided not to raise the matter with Tonka. I would wait until he saw it for himself, or an appropriate opportunity arose with Alexis or Julia. For the moment, we spoke of his father's operation and continued to recall our childhood memories of his grandad.

The original purpose of our visit was never far from my thoughts. The many distractions we had suffered had not succeeded in deterring us from remembering John Joseph Thompson. In many ways, certainly for me and I am sure for his grandson, the old man was making this journey with us. He sat laughing to himself on one of the vacant chairs at our breakfast table and watched as I struggled to assemble the pieces of a very old, but complicated, jigsaw puzzle.

The likeness in the photograph I had seen yesterday evening haunted my thoughts. If Julia and Alexis were indeed direct relatives of Tonka, then my suspicions made sense; the pieces of the jigsaw began to form a picture, which, however irrational, provided an explanation for those suspicions. If this was the case, there were some pieces missing and providence, it seemed, or perhaps Grandad, was providing an opportunity to find them.

And then, of course, there was little six-year-old Ellie. What illness made her so pale and her smile all the more endearing? I resolved to find out and to compensate for my prevarication on all the other matters. I decided to act immediately.

After breakfast, Tonka went back to his room to call his mother again, whereas I lingered in the dappled sunlight turned to shade by the new leaves of the many old oak trees opposite. Lost in a dream and recalling something Tonka's grandad had once said about oak trees, I was startled back into the present by Alexis, who wanted to know if I needed anything else. My resolve to ask about Ellie diminished, so I explained that I was simply sitting enjoying this glorious setting and he picked up our empty plates to return to the kitchen. As he turned to leave, I regretted my lack of will power and suddenly seized the moment by asking a question that I immediately regretted, as it intruded too much into the personal life of a relative stranger.

"What's wrong with Ellie?" I wanted to apologise for asking but thought this might give him an opportunity not to answer.

Strangely, and to my relief, Alexis didn't seem to mind the question. In fact, I think he secretly wanted to discuss it with someone outside the family. It must have been the subject of many family conversations and they would all have stepped delicately around the issue, unable or unwilling to hurt each other with the truth and almost inevitable conclusion of their fears. Alexis was about the same age as me and, like me, had been married for about eight years. Perhaps it was this that made him relax and speak so candidly of their only child, Ellie and explain how she was suffering from a very serious illness. I had never heard of polycystic kidney disease, or PKD as he referred to it, but I was left in no doubt about the possible consequences of the condition. The illness had been discovered when she was hospitalised with pneumonia at the age of four. She was acutely unwell and resistant to anti-inflammatory drugs. Unbeknown to doctors, one of her kidneys had been inoperative since birth and the disease had caused hundreds of small cysts to grow quickly on the one remaining viable kidney. It soon became apparent that a kidney transplant would be necessary if Ellie was to live a normal life and a close relative was thought to provide the best chance of a successful organ donation. However, Claudia, Alexis and Julia had all submitted themselves to tests but none were found to be suitable. In the absence of a matching donor, Ellie required twice-weekly haemodialysis treatment at Hôpital Saint-Joseph, a children's hospital in Charleburg and, after two years, the routine had taken over her young life.

To make matters even worse, Alexis and Claudia were found to be carriers of PKD, although they were unaffected by it themselves. This, of course, only added to their overwhelming sense of guilt. Julia, Ellie's redoubtable grandmother, could not accept the inevitable outcome of the illness and had devoted her life to finding a solution.

To add to their anxiety, the hospital providing Ellie's care was now threatened with closure due to financial cuts and she would need to travel to another one much farther away for her twice-weekly treatment. The medication she currently received, he told me, was not a cure but amounted to only palliative care. It enabled her to live at home while she waited, in vain it seemed, for a suitable transplant donor to appear. It didn't have to be a relative for the transplant to be successful but the chances of finding a suitable donor from outside the family were remote.

Alexis drifted from the emotional aspects of the situation to details about her medical condition and, as he spoke, he appeared liberated by the opportunity to talk openly about his daughter's suffering. Every member of the family had taken the tests but sadly, in each case, there was no match or the organ was unsuitable for transplant.

"It's Ellie's seventh birthday on Sunday," he declared despondently. "I don't think any of us can bear the thought of the hospital closing and Ellie having to travel hundreds of miles for treatment. So we're actually thinking of selling the inn and moving closer to the new hospital."

I could tell by the tone of his voice that this would be an incredibly difficult step to take. Apart from losing their income and employment, the inn had been in the family for generations.

As Alexis spoke, he could see his mother approaching. "Please do not say anything to my mother," he pleaded. "It distresses her so much."

I knew how much the inn meant to Julia. This was her heritage and she wouldn't give it up for many things, certainly not some handsome gigolo. She had continued the family line, managed and kept the inn going; rejected advances from anyone who might not share, or even support her commitment to the family business to which she had dedicated her life. And yet, she would give it all up willingly and without hesitation in exchange for the healthy life of her granddaughter.

Conscious of the way my intrusive questioning had driven her away the previous day, I pretended I had not noticed her sitting at a nearby table until she had been served a coffee by her son. She sat reading a newspaper and sipping the coffee for a few moments before I turned in order to engage her in conversation.

"Your granddaughter is such a beautiful little girl, Madame," I commented. "If she takes after her great-grandmother as you say, then your mother must have been a very beautiful woman."

She nodded politely, acknowledging my clumsy compliment.

"And, your father a very handsome man, I imagine. Is he still involved in the business?" I wondered if she had detected the interrogative nature of my question. A clumsy compliment followed by an even clumsier question caused her to shuffle on her seat.

She looked about her, as if searching for an escape route. "No," she said, sternly, as if she was referring to her unwillingness to engage in conversation as much as comment on her father's involvement in the business.

"He has a business of his own?" I asked.

"You really must excuse me, Monsieur, I have so much to do."

She stood up, tucked her newspaper under her arm, ignored the cup and saucer, and walked into the building behind us. Her evasiveness was intriguing and served only to fan the flames of my suspicions. At that very moment, Tonka passed her in the doorway, nodded politely and wondered why she was rushing away from me.

"You certainly have a way with women," he said, quietly, before suggesting we walked down to the mechanic's workshop to hopefully get some news on the car. I agreed and as we approached the grubby old workshop it became clear that good news, bad news jokes had reached the more rural parts of France, but they hadn't improved with age the way some wines did in this country.

"I've got some good news and some bad news," the mechanic said, cheerily, as if he had been practicing his English for the past twenty-four hours.

"Has the part arrived?" I asked, trying to deflect him from his well-rehearsed jest.

"That is the good news," he answered, before trying to construct the next sentence in English. "The good news is that the part has arrived."

I wanted to move this conversation on, as it was now clear it was going to end badly. "And what is the bad news?"

"The bad news is that it is the wrong part. Well, the right part, but for the wrong car model. I have telephoned them already and the correct part is being sent today. I will have it tomorrow. So good news 2–bad news 1," he reported.

"And how long to complete the repairs?" asked Tonka.

"No more than two days. So tomorrow is Wednesday. Depending on what time it arrives, your car should be ready on Friday or Saturday."

"Splendid," I said and my feigned joy was immediately doubled by the arrival of Brendan.

"You were up early, Brendan," Tonka commented.

"Trying to keep fit, boys," he said smilingly. "My horoscope last week said I had to keep fit, so I've been doing a bit of walking and even some exercises too. Nothing too strenuous, of course."

"Of course," I replied.

"Anyway, I think I must be getting taller, because I used to be able to touch my toes, but now I can't."

We ignored his joke but couldn't avoid his company as we walked back to the inn, realising on the way that it wasn't a joke and he really did think that he was getting taller. Our misery was added to as we sat down outside the inn and Brendan began reading his horoscope to us.

"Today," he announced, "Mercury, the planet of knowledge and Uranus, the planet of genius, unite, making your mind razor sharp. Nothing will escape your attention and everything you learn will be put to good use. Don't neglect your superior intelligence."

"And that's *your* horoscope?" asked Tonka, disbelievingly.

"Good advice," I said, trying to deflect an insult from Tonka. "You definitely shouldn't ignore your superior intelligence, Brendan."

"Does it say anything about you being reunited with a coach party?" asked Tonka, a little cynically.

Brendan ignored Tonka and agreed with me before seeking out Baptiste to see if he had heard anything from the coach tour operator.

In the shade of an apple blossom tree sat Julia, who had returned to the patio area after I had left. I could see she was thinking about leaving again, clearly to avoid my questions, but she remained; hopeful, I suppose, that I would be occupied with my friend.

Tonka and I sat in silence, contemplating the quiet beauty of the French countryside and wondering how we were going to occupy ourselves for the next few days. Well, Tonka was, but I was concocting a plan. I took up a position at the table where I could see Julia and asked my friend if he had the photographs of his grandfather on him. He handed them to me and I was relieved that he didn't ask why I wanted them. I sat looking at the old black and white pictures of Jonjo while, occasionally, looking up and making comparisons with Julia. She sat reading her newspaper, reminding members of her family about specific jobs that needed attending to as they passed by her table. She, herself, did little more than to occasionally deadhead some flowers that provided colour to the edge of the patio. As she did so, I sat piecing together my opinion of the woman, using a combination of experience and speculation.

Julia was an elegant woman who glided, rather than walked, through life. She certainly didn't run. She was a woman designed to be waited upon rather than one who waited on others, which was strange for someone who had inherited an inn. Her mother had managed the hostelry single-handedly after the death of her father, Henri Poirier and hadn't wanted to hand over the reins until late in her life when she became physically unable to continue. Her mother, Elodie, knew Julia better than anyone else and knew she would need to marry wisely if the inn was to continue in the family.

Julia had inherited her mother's natural beauty and could have had her choice of the young men in the area. In the end she didn't need her mother's advice. She had known Baptiste from her schooldays and was convinced of his suitability as a husband. He demonstrated a good work ethic, he was strong, loyal and fell deeply in love with her the moment she showed any interest in him. Convinced that her mother had never known love and, having never experienced it herself, she was entirely happy to marry for more practical reasons than the elusive and perhaps illusionary concept of love.

If I was right about Julia then she was probably susceptible to a charm offensive. I concluded that I could probably get her to show me a photograph of the young Alexis in two moves. The first of these relied heavily on the assumption that every parent or grandparent carried one or two photographs of their children in their purse or wallet.

"Ellie must have been a very beautiful baby," I said, as she passed our table on the way back from her deadheading. Step one succeeded and she returned to her table to retrieve a photograph from her handbag. She handed it to me and I placed Tonka's black and white photographs on the table. Showing an appropriate level of enthusiasm at the baby photo, I managed to disguise my true intent and launched stage two of my plan.

"She really is beautiful, Madame. And I bet Alexis was a handsome young chap when he was a boy, too."

It worked. She removed two more photographs from her handbag and handed them to me. One was of Alexis and the other was of an elderly woman.

"Alexis," she said, handing me the first. "And this is my mother, Elodie, who little Ellie was named after. I also have some old black and white photographs of my grandfather, Henri Poirier, who owned this inn during the war. He was a charming man."

She placed some more photographs on the table and sat down next to us as Tonka joined me in examining them. I sat and watched as he did so and could see the slow realisation dawning on his face. I felt a sense of relief when he picked up the old photo of his grandfather with the mysterious woman in Paris. He still held the photograph of Alexis in his other hand and, after comparing them both, he looked at me. He knew I had already reached the same conclusion and wondered why I had not said anything. He looked at Julia and remembered her walking away from me earlier on.

Tonka placed the photograph of his grandfather on the table, next to the photograph of Alexis. They were about the same age and the likeness was undeniable. Tonka showed none of my vacillation and pushed the two photographs across the table towards Julia.

"Do you know this man, Julia? This boy," he said, correcting himself, tapping his finger on the figure of his grandfather. To help her, he moved the photograph of Alexis alongside it. She looked at the two photographs and then looked at each of us, as if we were fraudsters of some kind.

"Is this some kind of trick?" she asked, picking up her photographs and putting them back into her handbag. She stood up and, closing her handbag, walked back towards the inn.

"Tell me about your father, Julia," I called.

"I never talk about him. I didn't know him."

As she left, Tonka stood up and went to follow her, but I grabbed his arm and told him to sit down.

"What's this all about, Jack? What's going on?"

"I don't know, Tonka," I answered, truthfully.

"No, Jack," he replied. "I've known you a long time and you knew. In fact, I think you manufactured that little conversation and you also knew what the outcome was going to be."

I had to admit he was correct but assured him that I had noticed the likeness only the previous evening and had wanted time to think about my suspicions. I then took him through the pieces of the jigsaw I had found so far.

"Look, Tonka, I know none of this makes sense. It didn't make any sense to me last night when I looked at the photograph in the hall. But now I've had time to think about it and, even when you put all the pieces together, it still doesn't make sense."

I tried to explain the conclusion I had reached but it was impossible to support that theory with any rational argument. Julia was unable or unwilling to tell us who her father was, so we couldn't rule out the possibility of it being John Joseph Thompson. But how Tonka's grandad had managed to visit this village during the war was a mystery. Even if he had been held here as a prisoner of war, or had been interrogated here, how had he managed to form a relationship with and get a young local woman pregnant?

Tonka leaned forward and rested his elbows on the table. He spoke quietly and I joined him in a huddle.

"Perhaps we're on the wrong trail," he said quietly. "What if it wasn't Grandad, but his father, who may have been here in the First World War? There were many British soldiers around this area in World War One. Perhaps it was Julia's grandmother and Jonjo's father? Maybe that's where the family likeness came from?"

"But the resemblance between the photos of Jonjo and Alexis at the same age is so great. They are identical. Everything points to it being your grandad, Tonka."

It seemed incredible that someone who had told us so many fascinating stories had never made reference to this extraordinary period in his life.

"We need to find out about Julia's father," whispered Tonka.

Suddenly we were both startled from our quiet head-to-head parley by a voice behind us.

"Now we shouldn't get beside ourselves, boys," said Brendan, loudly. "We mustn't walk before we can run."

From his comment we realised he had heard everything we had said and, strangely, he had understood it, even with only half the evidence on the table. He picked up the photograph of Grandad as a teenager.

"I saw the photograph in the hallway, too," he said. "But don't eat your chickens before they're cooked. I've known many people in my life that looked like someone else. My cousin is the spitting image of the Iron Lady, Margaret Thatcher. Didn't make her very popular back in Ireland," he added sarcastically. "And mighty dangerous for her, too. She took to wearing dark glasses and, as she's got older, she's grown a moustache, too."

"Look, Brendan," Tonka declared in a serious tone. "Don't go mentioning this to anyone until we get to the bottom of it."

"How are you going to get to the bottom of it without mentioning it to someone? In fact, how are you going to get to the bottom of it without getting Julia to confide in you? Anyway, I think you boys are going to need my help. Don't forget what it said in my horoscope this morning. 'The planets of genius will unite making my mind razor sharp. Nothing will escape my attention.' That's been proved right already, hasn't it?"

I had to admit that it was true to a certain extent. Our very private conversation had not escaped his attention. But it didn't encourage me to rely on his help in this delicate situation, so I tried to dissuade him from contributing anything to our investigation. My words fell on barren ground. Brendan's weekly horoscope in Sunday's newspaper had advised him to avoid reading too much into other people's words this week because they don't mean what they say.

"'The chances are,' it said, 'that you're not thinking straight yourself at the moment and will overreact to even the most minor criticism.' So, I'm not going to do that. I'm to ignore you boys and, using my razor-sharp mind, I'm going to help you two out. I owe you that much."

He walked around the patio area for a few moments, looking skywards and contemplating a plan.

"Now, I think we need to consider your horoscopes, boys," he said enthusiastically. "Jack, you're a Gemini, aren't you?"

He then went on to tell me that Saturn was in retrograde this week and this had created the unsettling and confusing events of the past few days. "'Things don't go as you anticipate. Go with the flow and you will be pleased with the outcome.'"

"Thank you, Brendan," I replied and held my breath in the certainty that he was about to ask for Tonka's star sign again.

I could hear someone silently counting to ten, when the Irishman asked the inevitable question.

"I'm Capricorn, Brendan, Capricorn." He paused. "The goat."

And, I must say, I truly thought he was going to butt him, except Brendan was up out of his seat punching the air.

"I knew it, I knew it," he shouted. "You're a typical Capricorn, very private, introvert, sceptical, keep yourself to yourself. I'd already looked that up because my mammy is a Capricorn."

He then read excitedly from the newspaper. "'With your ruler, Saturn, in retrograde, expect confusion in your life. Even at your most shrewd, you could not anticipate the unexpected events now happening. Do not try to anticipate the outcome of recent developments.'"

"Well," replied Tonka, "in fairness I'm not sure anyone could have guessed what has happened to us over the past couple of days."

~~~~~

That evening Brendan joined us for dinner and I could see Tonka was losing his patience with the man. After a couple of hours of unsuccessfully trying to find the magical mystery tour, neither of us was desperately seeking his company. But forcing him to eat alone would have been tantamount to drowning a kitten, so we sat trying to distract him from the subject of horoscopes. This wasn't proving to be as difficult as I thought, but then Brendan was keen to collaborate with our efforts to establish whether Julia was the daughter of the recently deceased John Joseph Thompson.

"Do you know, boys," he declared as dessert was served, "this is the best fun I've had in my life." He then went on to tell us that he hadn't really made any friends on the coach trip, which is probably why he had wandered over to us in the square in Outreau that day.

After we had plied Brendan with brandy, Tonka opened up a long and incredibly boring conversation about his dad's operation. It was deliberate, of course and the only real risk was that Brendan would ask what Joe's star sign was. But Operation Bunion succeeded and, eventually, Brendan retired to bed, leaving Tonka and I to finish a bottle of red wine together.

"I was wondering the other day," I said to Tonka, as we both relaxed in the old man's absence, "whether there were any clues in your grandad's bedtime stories."

"What, about this place?"

"Yes, well, maybe a person, a character, or a situation that was prompted by his experiences here."

"If he ever was here," Tonka corrected me.

"Well, if he wasn't here, speculating about it won't hurt, will it?"

"It might hurt Julia and her family, suggesting that her mother played fast and loose with my grandad."

"Fast and loose," I blurted with a smile. "I haven't heard that expression for years."

"That expression was something else Grandad used to say, I suppose. His words certainly seemed to stay with you." Tonka paused. "The stories were so far-fetched, Jack; I can't believe any of it was true."

"Not true, but based on a true experience. Maybe not even the experience, perhaps a character."

"Well," Tonka replied, "Oscar and Dolores were real."

"What, the parrot and the cat?"

"The parrot and the three-legged cat were the two doctors at our local surgery. I didn't realise until I grew up and learned their first names. I knew them only as Doctor Cummins and Doctor Grant but, later on, I found out their names were Oscar and Dolores. And, what's more," he added, "he had a lisp and she had a limp."

Neither of us was quite sure how this information might help our cause, but at least it confirmed that some of Grandad's characters had been based on real people.

"Can you remember any others?" I asked.

"Deacon Tull, he was a real bad hombre."

"Bad hombre?" I replied. "Another of Grandad's expressions?" Tonka nodded.

"Perhaps we're looking for Deacon Tull."

"We're not looking for anyone, Jack."

"Well, what else could Colonel Elton want?" I sighed, revealing my true demon. Then, in an effort to vent my frustration, I tore off at a tangent and ranted on about prisoners of war being held for decades in the Soviet Union.

"They were German," Tonka declared. "The war on the eastern front was incredibly barbaric, Jack. After Stalingrad, the Russians couldn't and wouldn't forgive and, yes, they did capture and imprison hundreds, perhaps thousands, of Germans and, yes, they never set them free, they died in captivity. But that was Siberia, Jack. Cache Moyen would be a lovely place to be imprisoned."

His argument couldn't alleviate my fears about the colonel. I was convinced that his arrival at the Legion had been no coincidence and, whatever Tonka said, I knew he was behind our current predicament, lurking somewhere in the shadows.

Tonka tried to convince me otherwise but, by now, I truly suspected that this entire situation had been created by Elton. To what end, I had no idea. And, as yet, I had not worked out quite how he had prompted the detour from Outreau, caused a group of delinquent kids to sabotage our car and then ensured we arrived at Cache Moyen. However, all of these random incidents were referred to by Tonka, when he declared I was now clinically paranoid.

"Anyway," Tonka asked after a long pause. "What do you mean, looking for Deacon Tull? Who was Deacon Tull a caricature of?"

"Well, perhaps there are still some German war criminals about, needing to be found."

"What, you think Hermann Goering or perhaps Manfred von Richthofen are holed up in Cache Moyen?"

"Well, maybe some lesser-known Nazi," I suggested, quietly, realising how stupid my suggestion sounded.

"Oh," declared Tonka. "Herr Deacon Tull, head of the SS, you mean?"

I had to concede defeat and changed the subject in order to avoid any further embarrassment. "So, how is your dad after his operation?" I asked.

"I think we covered the subject of bunions in sufficient detail earlier on, Jack. Come on, let's turn in."

It wasn't until I was lying in bed that night that inspiration finally struck. While considering all the possible negative aspects of our dilemma, I had missed the one very positive outcome that it could create. I sat upright and wondered why it hadn't occurred to me before. Little Ellie required a transplant and the best possibility of a match was through a relative. If my suspicions were correct, then Tonka was a relative and may be a match. If Tonka was willing to part with a kidney for Ellie's sake, which I was sure he would be, then the consequential DNA test would prove whether my theory had any foundation.

As I lay back down again, wondering whether to call Tonka, I realised it still wouldn't explain how Tonka's grandad had come to be in Cache Moyen or how he had managed to father a child there. And by this time it was three o'clock in the morning and Tonka was fast asleep in the room next to me.

15

Wednesday 24 December 1941 – Stalag XXV, East Prussia

It wasn't a carol that ordinarily reduced men to tears but, combined with the freezing conditions, an uncomfortable seat and a homesick, lovelorn heart, this was the emotional outcome following a particularly poor rendition of 'We Three Kings'.

After his first white Christmas the previous year, Jonjo had prayed he would never see another. But in this part of the world a cold winter was as inevitable as death and taxes. There had been little respite from the snow since November and the bitter eastern wind that blew in from Siberia provided little opportunity for exercise and confined everyone to the draughty wooden huts for the greater part of the daylight hours. Such internment was incompatible with socialising or recreation and, in any case, nobody in hut twelve could replace the wit and conversational skills of Violet Martin nor supplant the simple pleasure of exchanging first names with Elodie Poirier.

Basketball, football and tug-of-war had been replaced by indoor activities since the snow arrived and the close proximity of so many men began to irritate even those of a more conciliatory disposition. So Christmas provided an opportunity to replace chess, draughts and whist with activities such as amateur dramatics and, on this particularly cold Christmas Eve, a carol service. Jonjo was sitting at the back of the wooden canteen building, close to the door, which kept opening and closing as people came and went. It was his own fault, he had wanted to finish the final chapter of the book he was reading. Unfortunately it wasn't Chesterton, Greene or Wodehouse, but Zane Grey's *Riders of the Purple Sage*, possibly the most popular work of fiction on the camp. It held little appeal for Jonjo, but it was one of the few books he hadn't read from the small lending library made up of gifts sent by loved ones.

The camp library held a disparate collection of books that had been sent to the prisoners, although many of them had poor reading skills. Jonjo had volunteered to work in the library as this provided the opportunity to peruse any new donations before they became too ragged and worn to read. Often he would read half a book before realising that some individual had found a more urgent need for the pages while visiting the latrines. There were many children's books sent to help those who had limited reading ability and Jonjo read the best of these, including Kipling and Robert Lewis Stevenson. In the early days of his imprisonment, when there had been very few books, his lively imagination had often invented follow-on stories for adventures such as *Treasure Island*.

Of the adult books, westerns were the most popular and none more so than Grey's tale of the two-gun hero, Lassiter, in *Riders of the Purple Sage*. Woe betide anyone who tore a page from this book, even in the most dire situation, because there wasn't a soldier on the camp that didn't read the tale of gunfighter Lassiter and the evil Mormon elder, Deacon Tull.

Jonjo donated all the books he received, after writing inside the cover: 'This book belongs to JJ Thompson'. All, that was, except the book of Tessimond's poems sent to him by Violet Martin. Only he could appreciate this slim volume of poetry and, in any case, it was too precious for him to share. If he wasn't reading it, the book remained under his pillow, as it did now while he sat in the cold wooden building listening to Christmas carols.

The choir fielded a predominance of Welshmen and a man needed to be a soprano, contralto or possess exceptional talent to be admitted unless he originated from, or had a close family relative living in, the Valleys. The audience was, of course, encouraged to join in. After all this was, primarily, an exercise in keeping warm and nobody was anticipating a summons from Noel Coward to appear in *Cavalcade*.

It was only when someone called for something a little more rousing than 'Silent Night' and the choir began singing 'We Three Kings' that Jonjo began to feel emotional and had to leave the building in case he embarrassed himself by crying. Only Fats Waller had achieved this previously with 'It's a Sin to Tell a Lie', which was, unfortunately, played on the radio at home on the first anniversary of Andrew's death.

Once outside in the empty parade ground the tears could not be contained. It was Christmas, freezing cold and anyone he had ever loved was a thousand miles away. Well, one was probably less than that, but it was still too far to walk, even if he had known which direction to walk in. He hadn't demonstrated an aptitude for geography at school, so he had no idea where East Prussia was. What he did remember was being pushed into a cattle wagon somewhere in Belgium or France and being sent to this godforsaken place. The journey had taken many hours; there were no toilet facilities on the train, nor any food or water, just some straw for bedding. And, when he and a wagonload of British soldiers had fallen out, filthy, stiff, aching, starving, dehydrated, unshaven, infested and unloved, he'd had no idea where he was. When someone had told him it was East Prussia, he thought he had been captured by the Russians, who were allies the last time he'd read a newspaper. But the sign on the gate confirmed he had been transported to Stalag XXV in a place called Marienburg, somewhere near the Baltic coast and the uniforms were unmistakably German. It may have been near the coast, but there was no sea air to be enjoyed and the first few days had been spent queuing, waiting for dog tags, Red Cross registration and, if you were lucky, food.

'We Three Kings' rang out heartily from the canteen as Jonjo walked back across the yard towards hut twelve and his thoughts recalled the pleasant company of Violet and the now-forgotten experience of laughing. For a second he was sixteen again, enjoying an adult conversation with the remarkable Mrs Martin and wondering when he would begin shaving like his dad. He hadn't donated his book of Tessimond poems to the camp library. Instead, for the past year, it had slept under his pillow, a gift from one woman that reminded him of the love he felt for another. He yearned for a letter from that someone else, a special someone else, even though she could not possibly know where he was.

The following morning, the Red Cross parcels were distributed. Jonjo's contained a tin of condensed milk, which he detested but could swop with someone who had never been weaned off milky tea as he had been, initially by Violet Martin but, more recently, by necessity and good taste. There was also a small packet of tea, a tin of pilchards and a packet of pilot biscuits. There wasn't a soldier on the camp who was tougher than a pilot biscuit. Unbreakable and, some thought, uneatable, pilot biscuits were built to travel well, rather than taste well. Imperishable, incorruptible and inedible. Jonjo had realised why pilot biscuits were designed for durability only after his mother tried to send him a packet of custard creams. He received a wrapper and enough crumbs to feed a small sparrow.

He unpacked the Red Cross parcel but what little comfort and Christmas joy it offered was offset by the absence of any mail from home. In the end, he had to make do with rereading the previous correspondence he had received and revisiting the text of last year's Christmas present from Violet. It was strange she had not sent a gift this year. She made a fierce enemy for her gossiping neighbours and, yet, someone who had caused her enduring pain and anguish was pardoned and treated as the son she had lost at his hand. The holiday in France had been the first of many signs of her generosity towards him. He had hoped she might repeat her benevolence the following year, maybe even visiting the new Butlin's holiday camp that had been built at Skegness, rather than the sedate countryside of France on a Bartlett's Motor Coach tour again. But something had happened to Mr Martin after the holiday in France. He became detached, pre-occupied and Jonjo heard he had suffered a breakdown. The boy saw him occasionally and there were no physical signs of an illness except, perhaps, the transfixed and absent look in his eyes. He had rarely spoken to Jonjo prior to the breakdown, so it was difficult for him to notice any difference.

Jonjo sat up, looked around the hut and comforted himself with the hope that a batch of letters would probably all turn up together, as they had done previously. He removed his socks, examined the holes and decided to darn them again if he could find someone who had some thread. He was hoping for another pair of socks from mother but these would probably turn up once the snow and bitter winds had turned to summer.

Of course, mail was frequently lost, that was apparent from the postmarks and the content, which often referred to events that had not been mentioned previously. Or letters arrived out of sequence, delayed for many months or damaged by the weather. The rain made the ink run, words dissolved in transit and often arrived only partially legible. Among the last batch, Mother had written about attending a funeral of which Jonjo was clearly supposed to have been aware. Perhaps she had forgotten to mention in her previous letter who had died, or maybe that previous letter had been mislaid or delivered incorrectly to some other lost soul.

The same arbitrary handling of letters applied in the other direction too, of course, although Jonjo needed no help in producing cryptic correspondence. In one letter to Ivy he had informed her that he had 'told someone' and, although she knew he was referring to his part in the death of their friend, Andrew, she wrongly assumed he meant he had told someone at the camp. He meant he had told someone before the war had begun, for he had never spoken to Ivy about his strange relationship with Mrs Martin and she was never bold enough to ask. He had certainly never mentioned the hanging attempt to Ivy or the subsequent conversation that had taken place with Mrs Martin. 'It helps to purge one's soul', he wrote in the letter to her and Ivy was pleased that he had a close friend at the camp in whom he could confide his innermost guilt.

Ivy never found out that it was Violet Martin who her beloved Jonjo could place his trust in. Ivy closed her eyes to anything that might hurt her, especially in her relationship with Jonjo. To her, their friendship was a delicate, fragile piece of china that would break if she upset him. So she avoided confrontation or any discussion that might result in a quarrel. Andrew Martin was rarely mentioned, especially on the anniversary of his death, when Jonjo disconnected himself from his friends and made an excuse to spend the day in his room. She often dreamed of marrying Jonjo but knew it could never happen in the month of May or on a Monday.

No mail arrived that Christmas or in the New Year. In fact, heavy snow and freezing conditions prevented any mail from arriving for several weeks. But, eventually, Jonjo received eight letters in a single bundle and he was so eager to hear news from home that he didn't pause to put them in order. He could tell from the handwriting that they were all from Ivy and his mother, but what he hadn't noticed was that some were much older than the others. Neither did it register that there was no parcel from Violet Martin.

The first letter he read was from his mother and was dated October 1941. It showed her address as Beadsman's Cross, near Evestown in Hertfordshire and, for a moment, he thought he had received the wrong letter. But the address was correct and the letter told him that she was settling in to their new home. It didn't explain why or when she had moved, so he opened another letter in the same handwriting. This one was older and had her former address at the top. It gave no indication that she was moving house but did refer to the relentless bombing of London. A third letter from Mother said she was sorry to tell him that Mr Martin had committed suicide the previous week.

Jonjo was in a hurry to find out the circumstances that had caused his mother to move home. In his heart, he knew the house must have been bombed, but where was the letter telling him that? Just as he went to discard the third letter he stopped as a fragment of the next sentence registered in his mind. *'He hadn't been the same since the death of his wife when their house was bombed'*. He looked at the date of the letter and realised that the funeral Mother had written about previously must have been that of Violet Martin. He began to cry and tried to conceal his grief. This was not an uncommon sight when the mail arrived and it wasn't always bad news that prompted the tears. Sometimes it was simply that events were happening without your participation, such as family weddings. More often, though, it was a family bereavement. He knew that people wouldn't understand if he was asked who had died. 'A neighbour' wouldn't quite capture the true sense of their relationship and he certainly wasn't going to tell them that this relationship had developed into something inappropriate, carnal, something that diminished their friendship rather than defined it.

Once he had stopped crying he read the other letters then put them in order and read them again. Ivy covered the same ground as Mother. The Blitz bombing of London that had begun in September last year had continued unremittingly until May, shortly before the letter was posted and occurred nearly every night. But neither of the women explained why it appeared to have stopped. Examining all his correspondence from home over that period it was clear that some letters were missing. He spread them on the bed and began joining the dots to get the whole picture. He concluded that Nelson Street, where they lived, had been hit around April that year and most of the residents, including his family and Ivy's, had been relocated to Essex, close to the Hertfordshire border. The destruction of the street where the Martins lived must have happened before this. It wasn't clear how Violet had died but it was presumably as a result of the bombing.

His next letter to home was a difficult one, comprising mainly questions. It was a hard task with his miserly ration of two small sheets of notepaper, as he had to explain that some of their letters had failed to arrive and another had been badly damaged by the rain. A joint letter sent to Mother's new address seemed to present the best solution, provided it began *'Dear Mum and Ivy'*. He tried not to dwell too long on the death of Mrs Martin as he knew, in his heart, that his mother was a little jealous of the relationship he'd had with her and probably Ivy was, too.

After he had finished writing the letter, Jonjo sat on his bunk pushing and pulling a needle through his sock until the hole was replaced by a scar-like ridge of yellow thread near the toe. He looked at his poor workmanship and remembered how hot it had been on the last day he saw Axe Egan. When difficulties arose, Jonjo let people down. It had happened with Andrew, Ivy and every other person whom his sad life had touched. So, why had Egan thought he would be any different? The captain had had such certainty in his own ability and yet he was forbearing towards the failings of others, a rare quality in any leader.

The onward mission to Amsterdam had allowed for no mistakes whatsoever, working behind enemy lines in civilian clothes made sure of that. The fearfulness and trepidation Jonjo had felt was in spite of Egan's courage and belief, not because of it.

It was his own lack of ability and track record for failing people at times of crisis that had caused such restless foreboding. Could the captain not see the yellow thread that held this lowly guardsman together? The memory of a penitent man was seldom reliable, for truth was dissipated by remorse, but Jonjo could never forget that day, not now he knew how events had panned out.

"Amsterdam. Have you any idea how far that is?" barked Jonjo.

"I know exactly how far it is," answered Egan, pulling a map from his tunic pocket. "It's two hundred and thirty miles from Boulogne, where we started this mission and we're nearly halfway there, Thompson. We've skirted Calais, Dunkerque, Lille and made it to Cache Moyen. We're now on the Belgian border and from here we need to go to Brussels, Ghent, Antwerp, Breda and then on to Amsterdam."

Jonjo did not question Egan's liberal use of the word 'we'. The captain wasn't going anywhere. Anyone who fell by the wayside was still part of the mission, still part of its success, that was the captain's firm philosophy. The 'we' was more compatriot than royal.

"You, Thompson, have just got to carry on what we've been doing. You need to travel at night and avoid built-up areas. Certainly don't go to any of those towns or cities I just mentioned. You travel through fields and forests, and rest during the daylight hours. You walk thirty miles a night, every night and you will arrive in Amsterdam in six days' time."

Egan made it sound simple, as he always did, because he could visualise himself doing it. In reality it was impossible to walk thirty miles each night. The nights were getting shorter. Jonjo wanted to protest, he didn't feel capable of completing the mission alone, but he knew the captain wasn't fit to travel. Ultimately, it wasn't the words that persuaded Jonjo he should go to Amsterdam, nor was it the conviction in the voice that spoke them. Axe Egan was a leader who led his men by example. When the three of them had arrived at the stream near the village — that was the moment that had won his heart and mind. As he had approached the stream and led them across, Egan had instructed them to step in his footsteps, to follow him precisely as they forded the small river. He knew he needed to convince the Germans, if they found the imprint, that only one British soldier was in their midst. And Jonjo had walked in the captain's footsteps ever since. Throughout that journey to Amsterdam, Egan was only ahead of Jonjo on the road, just as he was in life.

Now that Jonjo knew what had happened to Egan, he knew also that the captain had always planned it that way. He was always going to be the lone soldier who confronted them. That brief incident that rested easily in his mind was also the moment that Jonjo realised he was on the winning side, for he had witnessed the true leadership qualities and courage of the legendary Captain Anthony Xavier 'Axe' Egan.

That legend grew, not as the result of inspirational words, but simply because he never considered anything but success, he never thought he'd lose, he only thought he'd win. Where Jonjo saw adversity in the lengthening days, Egan saw the approach of summer as an advantage, as the greening hedgerow would conceal his presence. The white flowers of the blackthorn hedge would soon fill the air with its jasmine-like bouquet, he'd insisted, and provide cover for you to continue your journey through dusk and dawn.

And so, in spite of a great sense of foreboding, Jonjo picked up the gauntlet offered by Axe Egan. When the clouds of the eastern sky looked impotently at a dawning sun, he walked on until those clouds drifted aimlessly across a perfectly blue sky, trekking through forest and field, only taking to the hideout of a badger sett for a few hours' sleep or when the earth vibrated with the sound of marching troops. And yet, in spite of all the hardships, through providence and imagination he reached Amsterdam.

For poor Jonjo, though, in retrospect he saw only failure. Apart from his moments with Elodie he recalled only the bad times. In his mind it was all destined to fail. In truth, his mother was right; he did think about things too much. But, where excess lived, balance was essential, for he thought too much on the past and too little on the future. And there, in that statement, was his great fault. He lived too much in the past and feared too much for the future and this weakened his resolve. Self-fulfilment of his own fears and insecurities overwhelmed him when his escape became impossible. When he found every escape route blocked by German troops, instead of seeking out sympathisers or trying to locate the communist resistance, he allowed himself to be seduced at the gate of Elysium, choosing to return the way he had come, through the backwoods and farmland, instead of heading east along the coast towards Ostend or Dunkerque. Never questioning the rationale or consequences of his actions he was bewitched by love and determined to see Elodie one more time. Oblivious to the chariots of war that lay about him and blind to the danger at the edge of each forest and over the brow of every hill, he made the difficult journey back towards Cache Moyen.

Of course, that is how Jonjo recalled it, after he had spent eighteen months dwelling on the events. In reality, escape had been impossible, but his guilty conscience and poor memory denied him that small comfort. The delay caused by Egan's injuries had lost them too much time and the evacuation of the British Expeditionary Force at Dunkerque was completed one week before Thompson stood on that high hill looking out to sea and witnessed the overwhelming might of the German army below him. He had seen Boulogne fall and now he saw before him a closed gate. And, in his despair, he turned towards the last place he had felt safe, Cache Moyen. But he would never forgive himself for his failure. He had let Egan down.

He arrived back in Foret Isole before dawn two weeks after he had left, with just enough time to search the various hideouts he had shared with Egan, just enough time to hide in the hedgerow where he had left his captain. Here he found a rifle, some old bloodied bandages and an empty water bottle, but no sign of Axe Egan. He slept for five or six hours and then waited for darkness before making his way cautiously towards that place where the forest met the wall at the back of the graveyard.

There appeared to be fewer German soldiers than before but he could still hear the voices of those who remained beyond the church as he sat against the stone wall waiting for them to return to their camp. Just before eleven o'clock he climbed the wall and crept quietly towards the wooden shed. Its crumbling structure was barely visible under the rampant ivy, lichen and moss. Inside there was a mattress and an old blanket on the floor. Some water bottles stood on the rickety wooden shelves and he drank from them before looking around the small shed for evidence of Elodie, Egan or O'Reilly. But he found none.

He waited until the noise from the inn fell silent and the soldiers began returning to their camp. His intention was to visit the inn. He knew the danger, of course, but he desperately needed to see Elodie again. Just as he had finalised a plan in his head, he heard movement in the graveyard outside. He had already checked his revolver before leaving the hideout, but he took it out and again checked it was loaded, not knowing what he would do with it. Shooting one German soldier would only lead to his capture.

The sound outside grew louder. He believed it was an individual because there was no talking or whispering. It was too risky to open the door, so he waited and hid behind it as the footsteps came to a halt outside. The door creaked slowly open and someone looked inside, saw the empty mattress and closed the door again. Suddenly, he recognised the scent and pulled the door back open quickly. The sharp movement startled her and, as she turned around, her eyes smiled and yet she began crying. She had visited the little wooden hut every night and sometimes during the day too, in the seemingly forlorn hope of ever seeing him again. Each day she searched for Eamon to find out if he had heard anything at all about his lost comrade. But, as each day passed, there was no news and less hope.

Without speaking they went back into the shed and he took her in his arms. They kissed and, without letting go of his hand, she laid down on to the mattress that covered the floor. He lay next to her on the mattress and they continued kissing, caressing each other's bodies. The night was hot and he undid her thin blouse. Eventually he had to stand to discard his own clothing and he looked down as she lay there on the mattress, her large dark eyes reminding him of a famous painting he had once seen. And now here she was, a beautiful young woman lifted from the canvas into his life. Her nubile body was covered in the unseen silken down of youth, made cinnamon by generations of harvest suns. Her body lurched at his first touch and he felt, rather than heard, a quick intake of breath. She looked nervously into his eyes and, for a moment, he expected her to ask him to stop. But she didn't. She leaned forward and kissed him again on the lips.

The passion that engulfed their lovemaking was nothing like his experience with Violet. Only the urgency that crushed all their inhibitions remained. Yet, this urgency was now accompanied by a new intensity, a warmth, rapture and affection he had never felt before. And, for Elodie, this was an untrodden path, the first fruits of love, the undefiled response of true love and the fulfilment of a desire that only requited love can satisfy.

Afterwards, as he lay next to her, he felt guilty for his selfishness, for not enquiring about Axe or O'Reilly. They were an afterthought; his return to Cache Moyen was all about Elodie. So, when he heard of the ultimate sacrifice that his captain had made, he realised just how much he had let him down, just as he had let down Andrew Martin all those years ago on the way to school.

Jonjo took the St Jude medal from his pocket and offered it to Elodie.

"Keep it," she said. "It's kept you alive this far."

He knew how hazardous his position was. Miles behind enemy lines and Germans present in greater numbers than previously.

"The patron saint of lost causes," he said, quietly, knowing how much he qualified for such help.

16

Wednesday 27 May 2015 — Cache Moyen

There was a statue of Fortune at the Vatican in Rome, a strange place for faith to be challenged by the goddess of good luck. In more secular states, such as the United Kingdom, she was blindfolded, which was itself a strange depiction of justice, as that country saw the same figure. The personification of Fortune was both good and bad luck and, in Roman times, good luck would manifest itself only through virtue or courage.

It occurred to me at around six o'clock the following morning, having been woken by birdsong in the oak trees opposite, that we had been taken on a wondrous journey over the past four days by this strange goddess. Our sails had truly been swollen with favouring breezes and betwixt it all stood the strange character of Brendan Donnelly, who appeared like the messenger of Fortune herself.

Much as I ached to reject and discredit the ramblings of his horoscopes, there was a mystifying accuracy to his prophetic conjecture of the future. From his first reference to his mistress's foretelling, when he had warned that we could reach our goals only if we enlisted the aid of those who shared our aims and ambitions, he had been proved right. We were not even aware we had aims or ambitions on this mundane journey to a memorial service at Outreau. Yet it was certainly true that the discoveries we had made could not have been achieved alone. And forasmuch as we ridiculed his constant references to his genius and razor-sharp mind, nothing had escaped his attention when he had overhead our huddled conversation on the parentage of Julia. And, finally, he had foretold that we would find ourselves among total strangers but we would get along as if we were long-lost friends. Long-lost relatives might be truer.

In spite of our initial assessment, Brendan was proving to be as interesting a character as Tonka's grandad. They both seemed to live in an enchanting world of harmless truths that for a short time, like any convincing story or play, took on an enigmatic realism that beguiled the onlooker.

Grandad was never one of those old people who went on endlessly about how poor he had been as a child. Poverty did dominate his childhood, of course. Most children of working class people could not afford shoes and ate very basically. Yet he rarely mentioned such matters, choosing instead to take us into his world of storytelling. On the few occasions he had made references to growing up in the east end of London, it still represented a different world to the one Tonka and I had known. His parents couldn't afford to buy him sweets, so he would mix cocoa powder and sugar, lick his finger and dab it in the mixture. For some strange reason I was reminded of this when I went downstairs to enjoy a generous breakfast with my friend. As we finished our meal, Baptiste was preparing to drive to a local farm near Touberge in order to purchase provisions. So we asked if he could drop us off near the neighbouring village in order that we could buy some toiletries and perhaps some presents to take home.

The drive provided an opportunity for me to reflect on Julia's reaction to the photographs. It also gave me time to consider whether to tell Tonka about Ellie's illness and how he might be a possible organ donor. It was also Ellie's birthday on Sunday and I was eager to buy a card and a present for her, even though we hoped to have left this strange and bewitching place by then.

We left Brendan back in Cache Moyen, trying to locate his tour operator but, when we returned, he had learned only that they were in transit that day and were not contactable. However, Alexis had found out the name of the hotel they would be stopping at the following day and promised to make contact with them.

That evening I phoned Ludo and considered whether to tell her about Ellie but decided not to. There was a chance that she might tell Gabriella, who would tell Tonka and I wanted to be the one to do that. So I went to bed that night regretting that I had not told Tonka about my thoughts and resolved to do so the following morning.

~~~~~

As the sunlight burst through the branches outside my bedroom, I awoke from a deep sleep, eager to share with Tonka everything that Alexis had told me about Ellie's illness on Tuesday. I showered, dressed and knocked on his door but there was no answer. I had slept heavily but I was certain his shower would have woken me. Confused by his apparent absence, I ran downstairs and looked in the dining room and outside on the patio. Baptise appeared behind me.

"Is something wrong?" he asked.

"Have you seen my friend?"

"He went jogging twenty minutes ago. He ran off that way," he added, pointing in the direction of the mechanic's workshop.

I smiled at him, took a seat in the warm sunshine and declined his offer of breakfast, choosing to wait for Tonka to return. It was an opportunity to consider what I was going to tell him and to remind myself not to present him with a finished plan. One of my failings in our relationship was that I didn't seek his opinion often enough. I also needed to consider all the pieces of the jigsaw. And I needed to persuade myself that this wasn't all a coincidence. Tonka had thought of at least one other scenario, so perhaps there were more.

After a few minutes of sitting at the empty breakfast table, convincing myself that there was no such thing as coincidence, Ellie came out of the inn and sat on a chair next to me. I was a little surprised but then she was probably more used to people than my own children were. She was a couple of years older than my son, Giacomo and was a little more confident with strangers. But she was nearing the age of reason and less inquisitive than my own children. This was the age, I reminded myself, when common sense began to overwhelm childish innocence and literal compliance with rules succumbed to a more considered view. I prepared myself for some off-the-cuff questions.

"Hello," I said and she smiled.

"Do you know any stories?" she asked without hesitation and I recalled her pleading with her grandmother for a story when she was taken to bed two evenings ago.

"Lots," I answered, but she was unfamiliar with the term.

"What's lots?"

She had an incredible grasp of the English language for one so young, but some colloquialisms had escaped her everyday use.

"Lots means many, hundreds."

"Hundreds *is* many," she confirmed and asked me to tell her one.

"I'm only beginning to learn girls' stories," I explained. "I have a daughter who is just one year old, but my son is four."

"What are their names?"

"Elissa and Giacomo."

"That's a funny name."

"It's Italian. Their mummy, my wife, is from Italy, you see."

She thought about what to say next. "A boys' story is fine, if that is all you know," she conceded after considering her options.

I sat and told her the story of Captain Axe Egan, the Crimson Pirate, who sailed the seven seas looking for treasure, then buried it.

"Why did he bury it?" she asked.

"So only he would know where it was hidden and nobody could find it but him."

"How did he remember where he had buried it?"

"Well, he drew a map and on the map he drew a cross. X marks the spot," I told her, recalling one of Tonka's grandad's old adventure stories.

Alexis came out to relieve me of unsolicited babysitting duties, but I simply waved to him and assured him it was fine. I missed my own kids anyway and this was, at least, some consolation. So he left us alone and just checked on us occasionally.

My storytelling was interrupted at regular intervals by questions, mostly about the Crimson Pirate and his ship, but sometimes Ellie would think back to the beginning of our conversation and ask me about Giacomo or Elissa again. How old were they? Could they speak French? Did they go to school? Why were they not with me? I wondered about the last question, myself and it prompted some unspoken questions of my own, like, what were we doing here? How did fate cause us to arrive at this small village situated in the middle of the same enchanted forest that featured in so many of Grandad's old stories? Like Odysseus, I felt buffeted by fortune's whim. I was sure Tonka was accustomed, through his service in the SAS, to being sent to strange, remote places, but this journey seemed even more wondrous than that.

I sensed that Tonka held the same suspicions as I did. But, at the moment, it seemed too coincidental that we might have stumbled on the very village that Jonjo Thompson had in the late spring of 1940. Surely he had been captured by the enemy at

Boulogne, so how had he arrived here? Unfortunately, there was nobody left alive who could answer that question, or even confirm that our wild imaginings were totally incorrect and we were being misled by some Puck-like prank of the fairy king of this forest. Foret Isole, the isolated or lonely forest and this, Cache Moyen, a tiny village in the middle of that enchanted wood.

If he had been here, Grandad had never spoken of it. Or perhaps he had forgotten it. After all, he spent five years as a prisoner of war, followed by four months on the 'long walk' as it became known, traipsing around in circles as the Germans tried to avoid confrontation with the allied troops. He had endured all kinds of suffering before he was repatriated. Maybe he thought he had imagined his experience in this illusory place. And yet, if he had fathered a child here, as I suspected, he could not possibly have forgotten that. It took only a few seconds for me to realise that he would not have known about it, for he was certainly captured in late June or July and Julia's mother would not have known she was pregnant at that time.

Perhaps it was a brief encounter. Maybe that's why Julia was so evasive about her father. If it was Jonjo Thompson, an escaped British soldier, Elodie had probably wanted to keep that to herself.

All this was speculation, of course. The photograph of Alexis only resembled the young boy and soldier in the black and white photos of Tonka's grandad. As Brendan had said, lots of people looked like other people, famous people sometimes. And some of them made a living out of it. They weren't related to them. It was just a coincidence. 'Tonight, Matthew, I'm going to be John Joseph Thompson.'

Eventually, Claudia appeared and took her daughter off in a car. I hadn't really noticed that Ellie had a school uniform on and, as she had visited the hospital for treatment only the previous day, it was sensible to conclude she was going to school. My mind was in such turmoil that I couldn't say, with any certainty, that this was the case. Doubt seemed to fill my head, even on the most mundane of matters, such as whether or not Ellie was going to school. I was desperate to latch on to something that was certain, absolute. What I needed, as Brendan had said, was a concrete bed to hang my hat on.

I was dwelling, absent-mindedly, on the sad twist of fate that had caused this poor little girl to be born with such a terrible illness when the priest came out of the churchyard opposite and sat at a nearby table for his mid-morning coffee. He was a little earlier than usual and I realised I was feeling quite hungry.

"Bonjour, Monsieur," I said and he responded politely before opening his newspaper. Alexis came out with a cup of coffee and a croissant, said good morning to the priest and went back into the inn. Why the priest could not make his own coffee in the presbytery and read his newspaper there was a mystery. Perhaps he was less likely to be disturbed here. Convinced that this was his intention, I decided not to make conversation.

Just as I was thinking about ordering my breakfast, Tonka came jogging along the country road and assured me he wouldn't be long, before rushing upstairs to take a shower. In the clear light of day I wanted to discuss my suspicions with him, but felt it was too early for such an emotional conversation. I needed to speak further with Julia as I was convinced she knew more than she was saying. I was still hesitating about telling him of Ellie's illness when he returned and we ordered breakfast.

"Tonka," I began, "there's no easy way to break this idea to you, but I had a long conversation with Alexis the other day." I wondered whether the priest could hear our conversation but he seemed to be fully occupied with his newspaper and his grasp of whispered English could not have been that good, judging by his lack of conversational skills. Just then my mobile phone rang. Behind a newspaper, the priest tutted his disapproval, so I got up and walked across the narrow country road before answering it. I wondered about wandering around the small cemetery but thought the priest might object, so I stood against the wall of the old parish hall and told the unknown caller my name.

"I know who you are," stated Colonel Elton, impatiently. "I have some interesting news for you."

What the old government intelligence officer told me next felt like two large jigsaw pieces slotting into place and forming a photograph of Tonka's grandfather standing in his uniform in the village of Cache Moyen. Firstly, after questioning me about the stalag number in which Jonjo had spent five years of his life, the colonel confirmed that Tonka's grandad could not have been captured at the Battle of Boulogne. He had carried out checks and was now certain that all the Irish guardsmen from that encounter were taken to Stalag XXII. Stalag XXV, where Grandad was held, wasn't built until June 1940 and the first prisoners were not admitted until later that month. This suggested that he had not been captured until at least one month after the battle.

"Perhaps he was held and questioned somewhere else and got separated from the others," I said. But the colonel was certain that this was not the case. Apparently none of the officers or guardsmen who fought in that battle was taken anywhere else other than Stalag XXII.

"It's more likely," said the colonel, "that he failed to get to the port area to join the escape and managed to evade the enemy for several weeks before being captured. I'm looking through the files to see if anyone might have escaped capture with him."

"But surely they would have ended up in Stalag XXV too."

"Not necessarily. I'm searching through the list of killed and missing."

I was still assimilating these facts when the colonel sent another piece of interesting information in my direction. He told me he had discovered what the purpose of the mission to Boulogne had been. He was still putting the details together but it seemed that a small unit within the 2nd Battalion of the Irish Guards had been charged with recovering a cache of diamonds from Amsterdam. It was unlikely that a raw recruit like Jonjo would have been allocated to such a team unless he had spoken fluent French, Dutch or German. As this was not the case, he would have needed some other talent to secure a place on that team. I couldn't think of any and wondered whether to ask Tonka. But the colonel was in a hurry as usual and said he would call me when he had further news.

The line went dead abruptly and I walked back towards Tonka. I had the distinct feeling that the colonel was not telling me everything he knew. Indeed, that last piece of information had been delivered in such a way that, to me, it seemed he had always been aware of it and was simply giving me clues to a puzzle he needed to solve. Why had the colonel turned up at the British Legion club that evening? I knew this man. I had worked for him at Woolly Fold Manor five years ago and he played his cards close to his chest. In my opinion, he never told anyone everything he knew, he simply told them what they needed to know to get the job done. It suddenly occurred to me that I was inadvertently working for him again. There was a purpose in all this. It was just another battle for the colonel and I had become one of his foot soldiers.

Tonka was used to thinking about challenges in terms of strategy and tactics, much as the colonel did. So we sat together to assemble the facts, or rather the probabilities and possibilities. We concluded that perhaps John Joseph Thompson had avoided capture at Boulogne as the colonel had suggested. Maybe he had followed the special force group and got lost in Foret Isole, as this was a route they could have taken to Amsterdam.

"The forest covers many square miles," said Tonka, "and it would have been easy to lose one's way. He wasn't trained in tracking people, so he could easily have got lost."

"And then what?" I offered. "He stumbled upon the village, got a young woman pregnant and was eventually captured by the Germans?"

"Maybe," answered Tonka, "but four or five weeks is a long time to be lost in enemy-held countryside. You need training to stay free and alive for that length of time." He spoke from experience and I had to concede to his intimate and expert knowledge of survival.

I told Tonka of my suspicions that we were simply working for the colonel, being fed small pieces of information, until we came up with whatever it was he was looking for. But Tonka was a pragmatic soul who was less convinced about the shortcomings of others in spite of his many years of service in the SAS. He accepted that the colonel had his own agenda and his arrival at the British Legion club just before our departure to Boulogne had been no coincidence, but he couldn't believe this entire situation we now found ourselves in had been the grand design of Colonel Elton.

When I resigned from my position at Woolly Fold Manor, I was actually employed by the Army. Colonel Elton tried to talk me out of leaving. He had never praised me, or spoken highly of my work, but I think he quietly admired me. In fact, when I left, he said he hoped we could work together in the future. I asked him why and he said he could always use someone who was "innately suspicious of the world". I never considered myself so, although it was true that, by nature, I distrusted most people until I had known them well for many years. The fact that I knew Ludo for ten years before we settled down together was evidence of this. And the absence of close acquaintances, apart from my childhood friend, Tonka, also supported the colonel's theory. In God we trust, everybody else can form an orderly queue. Except, I wasn't even sure about God or religion anymore.

Since my churchgoing mother died, I had thought less about religion. Ludo attended mass every Sunday with the children but, all too often, I would find an excuse to be somewhere else. My father, or rather, the man I knew as my father, died when I was a child; my real father died before I was born. So Tonka's parents and grandad were like family to me. I trusted them as I did Ludo, Sebastiano and Tonka. But outside this small band of close friends, everyone was guilty until proved innocent in my book. The colonel was right, then. I was suspicious of the world and that included him.

Tonka and I agreed that the only link with the generation that Grandad had lived in was Julia. Perhaps she, like the ancient oak trees that Grandad spoke of, was laden with knowledge that she could never impart. She was the only person who might be able to recall the character John Joseph Thompson, through the memories of her mother.

Alexis came over to our table, cleared our breakfast plates and asked if we wanted anything. After ordering some more tea, we asked if he knew where Brendan was this morning.

"Oh," said Alexis, "he has gone to the local store to buy an English newspaper."

We both knew what the purpose of this was and wondered if we might escape before he returned.

"Any news of his coach party, Alexis?" I asked, with only a hint of hope in my voice.

"Yes," he replied. "I managed to track them down and made contact with his tour representative by telephone. Brendan spoke to her this morning. It is all arranged."

"Are they coming here to pick him up?"

"No," answered Alexis. "Mr Donnelly told them to proceed without him. They are sending his luggage over by courier later today."

As he spoke, Brendan arrived back at the inn, reading his newspaper as he approached.

"Brendan," Tonka said with some alarm, "why didn't you meet up with your coach party?"

"I couldn't leave you boys stranded here, after all you have done for me," he declared. "No, no, no. I don't run out when it gets cold in the kitchen."

Before we could intercede he was sitting down at the table and assuring us that the stars supported his decision to stay.

"Listen to this," he said confidently. "'You have been deflected from your chosen path.'" He nodded towards us knowingly. "'The Sun, allied with Neptune, is pointing towards a new direction in the company of strangers. Follow your intuitive wisdom towards the new challenges life presents.'"

Tonka and I rose to our feet and told him that we were going to visit the mechanic to see if there was any news of the car.

"I'll come along with you," he declared. "I know a little bit about cars," he added ominously and the opportunity for me to tell Tonka about my conversation with Alexis had passed, because I certainly didn't want to discuss such a matter in front of Brendan.

There was no news of the car parts and it was late afternoon before we finally managed to shake off Brendan. A van arrived with his suitcase and hand luggage and, once he had left to unpack, I took the opportunity to talk to Tonka. The day had turned cloudy, although rain seemed unlikely, so we decided to take a walk through the woods where, undisturbed, I might relate to him the details of my conversation with Alexis earlier in the week.

By starting at the beginning, rather than the conclusion I had already reached in my head, it gave Tonka the chance to reach the same outcome.

"So, you think I should put myself forward as a potential organ donor?"

"That's ultimately your decision, Tonka, but it could prove whether Julia is related to you."

"That's what bothers me, Jack," he commented, dejectedly. "I don't want to do this for the wrong reasons. And I certainly don't want to build up the hopes of these poor people and then be responsible for destroying them when it is found we're completely wrong in our assumptions."

"Well, perhaps we need to let them make their own minds up about that, Tonka. Let's just push Julia a little further about your grandad's possible liaison with her mother and not mention the prospect of the organ donation until it is all we have left."

Tonka agreed and that evening we waited for an opportunity to confront Julia. Unfortunately Brendan was with us at the time and we were both worried that he might manage to sabotage our plans. But, in the end, it was him that broke the ice.

Having read our daily horoscopes to Tonka and myself, Brendan then broached the subject with Baptiste by asking what his star sign was. The big man failed to understand the question and so Brendan asked when his birthday was. Baptiste was too courteous to refuse and, after the Irishman had explained what good fortune awaited him, he turned to Baptiste's wife. Julia seemed a little annoyed but, having been set an example of politeness by her husband, could not really refuse.

"I'm not sure," she answered. "Scorpio, I think."

"When is your birthday?"

"The twenty-sixth of March," she answered, trying to remain aloof from such inanities.

"That's incredible," said Tonka in an astonished tone. "That was my grandad's birthday, too. What year were you born?"

"You shouldn't ask a lady a question like that," Brendan corrected him. But Julia answered anyway.

"1941."

"Are you sure you were born in March?" I asked.

"Yes, of course I am," she replied gruffly.

"Ah, you'll be a Pisces then," interrupted Brendan and he began reading her horoscope.

"'There is no guarantee that what you are about to get involved in will work out, but don't be afraid to swim against the tide. Someone new to your circle will produce a strange but welcome outcome.' Do you see how clever that is?" he added. "Pisces is the sign of the fish and it says 'swim against the tide'. Clever, isn't it."

I looked at Tonka and realised he had already calculated that, to be born in late March, Julia must have been conceived in June, not May. Even if his grandad had made it to the village, as he suspected, he would need to have stayed for more than one month if Julia was his child. But it was still possible and Tonka could not resist seizing the moment.

"Julia," he pleaded, "I know you don't want to talk about it, but I need you to tell me about your father."

"I didn't know him," she answered as she stood up.

"Well, just tell me what you do know about him." He paused. "Please, Julia."

She sighed, sat back down and looked into the darkening sky beyond the trees opposite.

"I have only a childhood recollection of my mother telling me that my father was a brave soldier who died in the war. I asked if it was the brave soldier buried in the cemetery. But she said it wasn't him."

"Do you know how long your father was in the village?"

"The first time or the second time?" she answered.

A shiver went down my back. "What do you mean, the first time or the second time?" I asked.

"My mother said he left but came back to the village to see her one last time before he was killed."

"What, after the war? Is that when he returned?"

"No, I don't think so. I'm not sure what she meant but I think perhaps he escaped and came back. But not after the war. I think she meant it was much sooner than that."

Julia's date of birth suddenly took on a different significance. Jonjo had left the village and returned at a later date, managing to evade capture. Everything began to make sense, although what Jonjo had been doing for a month was still a mystery.

"Look," I said and wondered how best I could raise the matter of Tonka being a potential organ donor for Ellie. But Tonka sensed my intention and intervened. He shook his head, indicating that it was too early to build her hopes up.

"You said your mother mentioned another soldier who was buried in the cemetery," said Tonka. "Who was he?"

But she confessed she didn't know. She only knew that, even into her old age, her mother had continued to place flowers on that grave regularly, which was why Julia had wondered if this person might have been her father.

As we were speaking, a car drew up and Claudia and Ellie got out. The little girl ran to her grandmother, asking why she was crying. Julia did look tearful but was resisting such a public show of emotion. She was clearly not enjoying revisiting old memories of her mother.

Like everyone else seemed to be doing, Tonka stood up. "Can you show me this grave?" His request was directed at Julia, who was now resisting her daughter-in-law's attempts to comfort her.

"Yes, of course," Julia replied as she stormed off towards the lych gate on the other side of the road.

Just then my mobile phone rang. It was Colonel Elton.

"Listen, Jack, the special force's mission was to recover a cache of diamonds from Amsterdam before the Germans got their hands on them."

"Yes, you told me that."

"Well, that cache included the Gemini diamond, which was, at that time, the world's most valuable stone. Two Jewish brothers named Fleischmann, who were preparing to cut the diamond, were rescued with the Dutch Government at the Hook of Holland. It was the Fleischmann brothers who told the British where to find the diamonds."

As he continued speaking, I followed the small crowd of people across the road and into the cemetery. We snaked along a pathway and there, set back two or three graves in from the track, was a worn, grey headstone. A beautiful brimstone butterfly rested upon it. It's once sun-like wings of spring were now beginning to take on the paler hue of ghostly white and showed just a hint of the sulphur yellow that had burned in its youth. Then, in an instant, it flew away and I was left staring at the gravestone with the name 'Anthony X Egan' carved on it. The letter 'X' was strangely larger than the others.

"A guy called Egan," the colonel continued, "Captain Anthony Egan, known as Axe Egan, led a small unit to recover the jewels. But he was killed in the battle at Outreau. Well," he continued, correcting himself, "he was missing in action, presumed dead and his body was never recovered."

"I'm looking at his grave now," I stuttered into the phone.

"What?" blurted the colonel. "Are you drunk?"

"No, Colonel. I'm looking at Egan's grave right now. I'll call you back." It was time for Colonel Elton to be kept waiting.

We stood, in silence, looking at the ragged and slightly lopsided grave. Julia, Claudia, Tonka, Brendan and I stood looking down at the grave, along with Baptiste and Alexis, who had heard the noise outside the inn and followed us across into the cemetery. The priest, too, had joined the group and looked puzzled at the small crowd that had gathered around the old grave. They had all heard my last statement to the colonel and were now looking directly at me, wondering who on earth I was talking to. Then suddenly, as the talking stopped and the rustling of the leaves above our heads ceased, the eerie silence was broken by a small child's voice.

"Look," Ellie shouted excitedly, pointing at the headstone. "X marks the spot."

The same thought had just occurred to me and I asked if anyone had a spade.

"What for?" the priest asked.

"We need to dig it up."

"Dig it up?" he bellowed. "Are you mad? You cannot exhume a body without permission from the authorities."

"We're not exhuming the body," I shouted. "We're just going to dig down a few inches."

"We need to tell the police," demanded the priest.

I called the colonel back on my mobile, to let him know of my suspicions and that the local police were about to get involved. At the insistence of the priest we waited for someone in authority to arrive, but nobody left the scene, everyone wanted to know what was going to happen next.

When two local policemen arrived from Touberge an hour later, they were mystified as to why they had been summoned. The cemetery began to look like a crowd scene from a Puccini opera, with me simply wanting to remove a few inches of soil from the grave. Inertia reigned for another thirty minutes until, suddenly, a phone rang in the pocket of one of the policemen. He apologised and stepped to one side to take the call. It quickly became apparent that the call referred to the grave and I began to suspect that the colonel had pulled several important strings to get matters underway. The call ended and the policeman instructed his colleague to dig down about fifty centimetres. The younger officer protested in French but his older colleague assured him that the body was at least two metres below the surface. The younger one asked if they should put a scene-of-crime screen around the grave. He was told, in no uncertain terms, that this was not the scene of a crime and was instructed to do as he was told.

As he began slowly removing the grassed-over soil from the top of the grave, his colleague asked if there was anyone living in the village who was alive when Anthony Egan was buried. The priest said his predecessor may have been, but that he had died earlier this year. Anyway, he wasn't sure he had been in this parish since the war. Julia confirmed he had not.

"There are many older parishioners in the farming community hereabouts," added the priest as he reflected on the demographics of his congregation since his arrival. "But it is difficult to tell their age. Some thrive on the hardships of rural life and look younger for it, whereas others are worn down by the demands of the land, as their weathered faces testify."

"A few stop here for coffee after mass," said Julia. "Although most will not waste what little money they have on such extravagances."

"It is true," nodded the priest. "Many are poor, barely self-sufficient. The collection at mass on Sunday is much smaller than in my last parish."

As they were talking, the policeman lifted another spadeful of earth from the ground and an object appeared in the dirt. It was a velvet bag, encrusted with soil and tied with a piece of cord. I reached down to pick it up but was prevented from doing so by the older policeman. He bent down and took the bag in his hands before carrying it off, as if it was a fragile antique. Walking out of the cemetery, he crossed the road and went back to the area outside the inn. The small crowd followed him, speculating on what it might contain. He placed the bag on a table and looked directly at me.

"What's inside the bag?" he asked, presumably wondering whether it was an explosive device or poisonous spider.

"I believe it may contain some diamonds," I answered and, as I did so, he undid the cord and poured out, on the table top, a dozen diamonds including one very large one. There was a group gasp and Ellie shouted that it was buried pirate treasure.

"Now," said the policeman, adopting a more authoritative tone, "we just need to establish who owns them."

I was able to help in this respect, telling him that they were owned, at the outset of the war, by a Dutch diamond merchant in Amsterdam named Fleischmann.

"By now, the British authorities will be speaking with their French and Dutch counterparts about this matter and I suggest you keep the jewels very safe until you hear from them."

The policemen left with the diamonds, saying they would return tomorrow with some news.

That evening, after dinner, I told the Tremblay family all I knew and what I suspected about the diamonds. But I still wasn't sure what John Joseph Thompson's role had been.

The most likely scenario was that Axe Egan had led the mission and recovered the diamonds from Amsterdam before being killed, presumably by Germans, in the village. But who had then buried the diamonds remained a mystery. Perhaps he had asked Elodie or her father, Henri Poirier, to bury them in his grave.

"Perhaps we will never know the whole truth," I told them.

"But we can be confident about one thing," Tonka said, cheerily. "My grandad was almost certainly involved and he was here in May or June 1940. It also seems very likely," he continued, "that Julia is his daughter. As I am his grandson, I'm not sure what relation that makes us," he said, pausing to look directly at Julia. "But I'm pretty sure we are family. These photographs," he added, while handing out his old black and white photos, "support that theory."

The other members of the family began looking at the photographs and comparing them to Julia, Alexis and Ellie.

"And," Tonka added slowly, "even if there is only the slightest chance we might be related, I would like to visit the hospital to see if I might be a suitable kidney donor for little Ellie here."

It was clear from her reaction that Julia had not thought about this possibility. She stood up, walked over to Tonka and, as she embraced him, she began crying. Ellie ran to her nana, demanding to know what was wrong.

"Nothing, Ellie. Nothing at all," she replied.

17

Friday 19 January 1945 – Stalag XXV, East Prussia

The floorboards of hut twelve creaked under the feverish movement of its unusually animated occupants. Malnourished and thin-limbed, they gathered up their limited belongings. Jonjo's hands struggled to prise the lid from the empty Red Cross tin. What would he give for a pilot biscuit now? It had been months since the last parcels had arrived at the camp.

His precious letters, still in their envelopes, were lovingly stacked inside the tin and he looked around for anything else that might be kept in there. The book of poems was too large for the tin and he couldn't find a pocket large enough to accommodate it either. Rumours had been circulating for days that something was about to happen. Exactly what that something was had been sacrificed to speculation but those who still continued to hope believed it was their release. Others, like Jonjo, thought otherwise. For him, once hope had departed, trust soon followed and in its place suspicion reigned, casting dark shadows on fellowship and certitude.

After so long away from home, it was difficult to visualise his friends and family anymore. Their images had grown dim with absence and the passing of time. The seed of suspicion had taken root in every aspect of life and distrust of all things and all people had begun to make Jonjo doubt even the words in the letters from home. For him, release was an event he did not dare to imagine. Perhaps he would spend the rest of his life here, in this godforsaken place.

Unshared fears found shelter in silence and cast dark shadows across truth and virtue. So much of the text of the letters had been deleted of late and so much could be read into those black marks. They rose from the page and crushed what little faith remained. The mail arrived less frequently now, there was less food to eat and the winter seemed harsher. Hardship and torment contrived to make Christmas pass almost unnoticed. Nobody wanted to acknowledge that five years had been wasted and they had lost what should have been the best years of their lives. So the day itself passed not so much unnoticed as eschewed, disowned. It evoked painful recollections of times that needed to be forgotten, times when families gathered together, times of great joy and fond memories. With each Christmas that passed, hopefulness and optimism diminished and in their place despair and separation thrived in the cold and hunger that swallowed up his life at Stalag XXV.

Jonjo thought about Elodie a lot. They had shared so much in those few days before his capture. He could remember her face less than the sound of her saying his name. And the sweet smell of her presence as she'd opened the rickety shed door had lasted only a few months. A fragrance, it seemed, required a stimulus in order to arouse the senses and evoke memories of times passed. He convinced himself that she had forgotten him, for why would she waste her time thinking of someone she had not heard from for so many years? For his part, he didn't want her to think about him, he didn't want her to see what had become of him. Thin, dirty, bearded, bedraggled and, hopefully, unrecognisable as the person she had known. The world had changed. Perhaps she was married now. He hoped she was.

He could not persuade himself that she still thought of him. He had never mentioned her to anyone at the camp, nor had he written about her in his letters. At first, he had justified this through his vow of silence on all matters related to the mission. But he had always known the truth behind his silence. Ivy thought of herself as his sweetheart; this was clear from her letters, not in words of course, but inferred, implied by tone or suggestion. The assumption, on her part at least, had always been that they would marry when he returned from his detention. He thought about that last word; today it did not feel as if he was simply detained; today it was beginning to feel like he would never return home.

Ivy was the only girl he had known before he joined the army and his imprisonment had denied him access to anyone else. Then, on that now distant day when the first bundle of letters had arrived for him at the camp, his mother's letters had been accompanied, perhaps not unsurprisingly, by some from Ivy asking him to write to her. And, although words like love and sweetheart were never used, it became an irreversible truth. Jonjo didn't notice it at first, perhaps, but everything she wrote was in the terms of a fiancé and even his mother's letters spoke of Ivy as a daughter-in-law, although never in those words, of course.

No, Elodie did not exist in Ivy's world. She survived only in Jonjo's heart, for love, it seemed, was indestructible, even in the cruellest of environments. Ivy's letters provided comfort and support in his lonely existence and soon affection and friendship turned in her heart to devotion and love.

Gradually, over time, all the gifts spoken of by Mr Wormley succumbed to the anguish of prolonged captivity. Tolerance and contentedness departed, along with empathy, mercy and goodwill, leaving a strange pale, plebeian sister of patience and the residual kernel of love, made indestructible by the divine will of God. And, in the frozen waste of January, when the last and most enduring of God's graces left the camp, its soothing presence was replaced by a dark foreboding. It may have been the rumours that some prisoners were being moved, or it may have been the realisation that this was how life would be for all time. It was the harrowing quintessence of despair that one should fear both something happening and something not happening, but that was how it was that harsh winter, for any expectation of good had long since passed. Jonjo was both sceptical and envious of those who clung to hope more fervently than he did. And, for those fortunate few, while love and faith receded, hope was never entirely extinguished, even in the depths of despair. Like an eternal light on a distant horizon it prevailed, as did its lesser siblings of endurance and trust. But it was not so for Jonjo.

When the moment came, the prisoners were told to leave everything behind, but few did. Who could leave their precious letters from home, or the few belongings they had collected? Jonjo put on his ragged and threadbare greatcoat and the once colourful scarf that his mother had knitted for him, then picked up the tin of letters and put what remnants of food he had in his pockets. The fact that all the inmates were being summoned to leave alarmed him, although he could not imagine a worsening of his current situation. Even death could be met with tearless acquiescence.

The icy wind outside made it difficult to think logically and he could make no sense of events. As he joined the queue of men waiting to leave by the main gate, it reminded him of the evacuees he had seen at the Hook of Holland on that terrible day all those years ago. As the column of refugees had fled towards the port, carrying their belongings, their wounded and even their dead children, German aircraft had swept overhead, machine gunning them as they would an advancing line of soldiers. Jonjo resigned himself to the same fate and saw the immense anxiety on the faces of the others. Some men had large boxes and bags of personal belongings, but realised after less than an hour of walking that such a burden could not be carried through the snow. He trudged through the deep drifts, treading in the footsteps of the man in front, just as he had done that night in the forest outside Cache Moyen. Occasionally he would look behind him and see a trail of personal effects that had been cast aside by men who could no longer carry them. He looked at the small tin under his arm and wondered how much farther he could carry it. His fingers and toes were frozen and only the numbness produced by the piercing chill winds neutralised the pain. They walked until nightfall, when they came across a church on the edge of a village that had recently been bombed. The wind had dropped and, when the inhabitants of the town learned the men were British soldiers, some of them came out into the streets and threw stones at them. The guards did nothing to prevent the attack but simply led the men into the church to sleep for the night

The inside of the church was only moderately less cold than outside. Senses numbed by the icy winds failed to recover before sleep overtook them. Jonjo woke in the night and tried to open the tin box. It took some time to do so, for his fingers failed to respond to his directions. Eventually he managed to prise off the lid, chose two letters at random and pushed them into a pocket. He then crept over towards the Lady Chapel of the church, knelt below the statue of Our Lady and placed the remaining letters in her care. He prayed and, as the feeling slowly began to return to his hands, he felt about his person for a cigarette. He was desperate for a smoke but his pockets were empty.

"Have this," a voice said from the shadows and a young soldier held out a cigarette. He was shivering violently and his gift fell to the floor. "I can't hold it anymore, let alone light it," the boy said through chattering teeth. "I don't want to sleep. I keep thinking I'm not going to wake up."

Jonjo managed to light the cigarette, drew on it and placed it between the boy's chapped and blistered lips. They sat in silence and finished the cigarette. Jonjo took off his mother's scarf and wrapped it around the boy's head and neck, then pulled the shaking body towards him and wrapped his arms around him. They lay there, beneath the serene gaze of the Virgin Mary.

"Sleep," said Jonjo, feeling the St Jude medal in the palm of his hand. "I'll make sure you wake up again."

"Sei still," called an elderly guard sitting in the corner. Over the past year, any young or middle-aged guards had been replaced by older men, as the younger ones were sent to the frontline. Subtle clues like this were lost on the prisoners, who thought little about escaping. Few had any idea of where they were situated in relation to England, or even France and, although some might know what direction to walk in, nobody had the willpower to escape anymore. Exhaustion dulls the brain and, on that first night out of the camp, resting in the church, all the men slept, pleased to be out of the bitter wind.

Nobody was able to find out where they were going. When they awoke the following day and continued their march, a second group of prisoners, of even greater number, joined the column. They, too, had walked from their camp the previous day. With so many prisoners, it would have been easy to overpower the guards. They were armed, of course and there would have been some casualties, but the prisoners were younger and outnumbered them by at least thirty to one. This thought occurred to most of the men but none chose to give the idea life. They remained silent and submissive, even as the food ran out and the weather claimed more victims, whose bodies were left to freeze in the snow.

After they had been walking for several weeks, being joined by more prisoners as they went along, the guards began to struggle to find any food and, when the group stopped walking each day, the prisoners were largely left to their own devices. If they passed a farm, they might find some raw turnips. And, such was their hunger that, if they managed to get close enough to a farmhouse without being shot at, the men would forage through the trough of pigs' swill and wash what they could in the snow before eating it. Jonjo often reflected on the words of Axe Egan that night he had been refused permission to light a fire. What would he give now for a raw rabbit or even a bone to gnaw on as he remembered O'Reilly doing that dark night in the forest? Yes, a raw rabbit did seem as a feast before the war was over.

Egan had been right of course. Jonjo had wanted to intervene and kill a few Germans but Axe had seen the bigger picture. Nothing would stop him completing his mission. Axe had feared failure, not death, and yet Jonjo had chosen to exchange the success of the mission for one last meeting with Elodie. Or at least, that is how he remembered it, for memories fail and, in his mind, he held himself responsible for the failure of the mission. He had not tried hard enough to return to England after visiting Amsterdam. Dunkerque and Ostend had both fallen but maybe he could have continued west and found a port that would have enabled him to return home. In himself, he never regretted the decision to return to Cache Moyen, but the longer such memories had to fester, the more the responsibility for failure gravitated towards Jonjo. Remorse and self-recrimination were his daily penance and Violet Martin's words frequently returned to haunt him. "There is no immunity to failure, John," she said, in an echo from the past.

In reality, so many miles behind enemy lines and with no escape possible, he had had little choice in what to do next. Even if there were groups of resistance fighters beginning to form in France and Belgium, how would he find them? He could only approach someone he knew he could trust and who trusted him. So the return to Cache Moyen had seemed the most viable option available to him. At least there were people he could trust there. The fact that it would give him an opportunity to see Elodie again had encouraged him towards that end. And it was this selfish act, as he now saw it, that persuaded him of his guilt.

So he had gone back to that tiny village on the edge of the forest. That walk had seemed such a long way back then. But now, as he looked down at the ragged boots that covered his sore feet, it was a stroll. He couldn't take his boots off now, fearing they would never go back on again. He could only picture what his feet looked like from the pain that almost overwhelmed him.

For weeks he felt he had been walking around aimlessly in large circles. Everywhere looked the same and he had lost track of the days. When the snow stopped and the weather improved slightly, he saw the first signs of spring as they passed a large wood. He thought about escaping into that forest and surviving as he had done all those years before. But he had been stronger then and he knew he was unlikely to live longer than a few days if he attempted the same thing today.

The sun set later every evening and the dawn appeared earlier, but each day was much the same as the previous one, simply a line scratched on the wall of his prison. Hunger and the pain of hunger gripped his body. They must have been walking for three months and he had lost half his body weight. He survived such harsh penance because he saw it as just that, penance for his failure to complete the mission. Death walked alongside him every day and slept beside him every night. Each morning, Jonjo wondered whether to bless or curse the God that shielded him from harm through the dark night and counted himself lucky if one of their numbers had not died as he slept.

Their greatest enemy was uncertainty. They had walked for four months, stopping only to clear areas that had been bombed by British or American aircraft. They would be accosted by German officers in disarray as they tried to clear bricks and rubble from railway tracks or roads. Then their guards would lead them back to the road, where they began walking again, endlessly walking. Just as death was the harbour he had sought as a boy of fourteen, so it was now; he almost didn't want to wake in the morning.

At the end of April, the group that had increased as other prisoners joined them and decreased as countless died, were marched by their German captors into an advancing American infantry division. One US soldier gave Jonjo some bread with meat inside it. He tried to eat it but couldn't. Neither his teeth nor his stomach was capable of eating anything other than porridge or soup. In spite of all they had seen, the US soldiers were brought close to tears by the condition of the British prisoners and some of their rescuers began asking if anyone had been mistreated, for it was difficult to imagine how life could have inflicted such anguish unaided. A German prison guard was identified as someone who regularly took delight in striking and kicking prisoners. He was summarily shot in the head without comment or question. Jonjo was shocked for, like many of the prisoners, he had been spared the sight of violent death that the Americans had seen in recent days. The memory of Boulogne and the Hook of Holland seemed like experiences from a previous life, another world, a world that he had been shielded from for five years.

The prisoners were rested and fed over the next few days and then, one day at the beginning of May, Jonjo was resting by a US Sherman tank, waiting to be sent home, when a voice on a radio nearby declared the war was over. "Victory in Europe," the man said, but it didn't feel like it to Jonjo. Suddenly it was all over and all he could think of was going home. Many of those gathered around began cheering, clapping and laughing, but Jonjo simply cried.

18

Friday 29 May 2015 — Cache Moyen

I awoke early on another Friday morning in May, realising it was very different from the ones Tonka's grandad had woken to all those years ago. Cache Moyen may have changed very little, but our experiences had been different. I lay for a while, separating what I knew from what we believed or suspected had happened all those years ago. We knew that John Joseph Thompson had joined the Irish Guards and they had been sent to mainland Europe, not to rescue the Queen of the Belgians as he had believed, because she had died several years before the war. The 2nd Battalion of the Irish Guards had, however, rescued Queen Wilhelmina from neighbouring Holland, along with members of the Dutch Government.

Then, he was sent to France, where his unit were forced back to the harbour by the advancing German army. He, however, did not return with the majority of that early British Expeditionary Force. He was captured, not seemingly with his comrades, but several weeks later, more than one hundred miles from where the battle was fought.

There came a time in everyone's life when their childhood seemed light years away, like a previous existence. That sunny, post-Chernobyl day of my youth, when Tonka and I had visited Woolly Fold Wood, certainly seemed so today and perhaps there was a time when, for Jonjo Thompson, Cache Moyen dissolved into such a fictional state and he began to doubt some of the things that had happened to him.

Of course, we couldn't be sure exactly what had happened to him in that distant month of May in the early days of the war. After five years of captivity and hardship, it wouldn't be surprising if those few weeks in 1940 had resembled one of the fictional tales he'd created for me and Tonka. Nevertheless, it was difficult to understand why he had never returned to the village in his later years. Or, maybe he had, but told nobody, choosing to take it to the grave, like everything else that had happened in that long-lost month all those years ago. But, if he had, he would have found Elodie and the world would have been different. No Joe, no Tonka and nobody to help me out when I got into a fix.

I got up and decided to call Ludo. She might be a truculent and feisty soul, but she was often pragmatic and logical in difficult situations. I convinced myself that she would know what to do.

"Hi, how's everything? I'm not disturbing you, am I? Are you getting Giacomo ready for school? Or feeding Elissa?"

"No, Jack, it's not eight o'clock over here yet."

"Good, because I need to talk to you about the situation over here. Something has happened."

"You've found someone else."

"No, of course not. Don't be ridiculous."

"Well," she countered, "it's just that you went away for a weekend and you're still away a week later. What am I supposed to think?"

"Well, not that. I love you, Ludo and I miss you and the kids very much and I will be home in the next couple of days."

"Good."

"I've stumbled on something, Ludo."

"Well, you should look where you are going. I'm always telling you that you rush around too much. What have you broken this time?"

Sometimes Ludo failed to understand certain English expressions. After living in the UK for over five years, she spoke and understood the language very well, but sometimes its idiosyncrasies bewildered even the best student.

"No, not stumbled as in fell over, stumbled as in *uncovered* something, something very strange."

"Oh, Jack, you are always uncovering strange things and they always seem to lead you into trouble. Can't you, for once, ignore it and come home?"

"I can't come home until the car is fixed, Ludo. And this isn't something that is going to cause any trouble."

I went on to tell Ludo all that had occurred the previous evening.

"So you see," I concluded, "Tonka's grandfather was here, in this very village, in 1940. And it looks almost certain that he had a relationship with a woman here. And, that relationship led to them having a child, a daughter."

"Had a relationship? My god, Jack, you English will do anything to avoid using the word 'sex'. He had sex with a woman and they had a daughter."

"Yes, a very charming and beautiful woman, Ludo."

"Ah, so you *have* met someone."

"No, I haven't met someone; well, I have met someone, but not in the way you are suggesting. Jesus, Ludo, she's seventy years old."

"But charming and beautiful," she countered.

"Yes, yes, okay. But, more importantly, she had a son and that son had a daughter. That daughter is Elodie, or Ellie and she was named after her grandmother; the grandmother who had..." I hesitated. "Okay, who had sex with Tonka's grandad...before he was a grandad, of course."

It all sounded a bit bizarre, but I continued and told her about the little girl's illness and how Tonka might be a possible organ donor.

"God," Ludo shouted down the phone, "you two will be there for months."

"No, no," I insisted. "We will be coming back at the weekend and Tonka will return for the operation, if he is found to be a match."

I thought about playing the holier-than-thou card again, but even I couldn't use poor little Ellie's condition simply to win over my fractious wife. Nor did I have to because, as usual, Ludo left me to my own devices. She knew, she said, that I would always do the right thing.

For Julia, this precipitous and unforeseen development was like the proverbial light at the end of the tunnel. The possibility that Tonka may be a relative and a realisable kidney donor for Ellie was nothing less than miraculous. Certainly as miraculous as discovering a large fortune of diamonds in the church graveyard and, to her, of much greater value. The disconsolate look of hopelessness had disappeared from Julia's ageing, yet beautiful face the following morning and she was as animated as her little granddaughter.

I showered, dressed and went downstairs to sit in the dappled sunlight. Claudia joined me as I waited for Tonka and told me about her new hope for Ellie. She had telephoned the consultant surgeon at the hospital in Charleburg the previous night. He had treated Ellie since she was diagnosed with PKD three years ago and he had become almost a member of the family. In return, the family trusted him implicitly and he understood their anxiety and fears. Claudia had explained to him about the strangely fortuitous visit by Tonka and his suspicions that his grandfather could be the great-grandfather of Ellie. If the tests proved those suspicions to be correct, it was entirely possible that this providential stranger could be a match.

Realising it was Friday the next day and the required staff might not be available again until Monday, the surgeon had told her that he would find a slot for the necessary tests on Friday afternoon and promised to fast-track the blood and other samples taken from Tonka so that their anxiety would not be prolonged unnecessarily. He had spoken to Tonka directly and instructed him to make his way to the hospital around lunchtime. He would ensure that all the arrangements for the tests were in place. Ellie did not need to attend with Tonka, but Alexis insisted on accompanying him to the hospital and the rest of the family could do nothing to prevent Julia from going too.

Like me, I'm sure Tonka thought back to his mother's words when we were last at his house. Jonjo had survived the Second World War and a five-year stretch in a prisoner-of-war camp. Jonjo's father had survived the First World War and the influenza epidemic that had swept England shortly after. "The Thompsons are made of stern stuff," Ann had said and, if it was true, then Ellie had the same gene.

After enthusiastic goodbyes and hugs with every member of the family, Alexis, Tonka and Julia drove off and Claudia joined me for a coffee. She spoke to me of the regular treatment Ellie received and her fears about the planned hospital closure, if Tonka was not a suitable donor and Ellie's care needed to continue. It was unlikely, she explained, that if the hospital closed as planned, her doctor would be offered a position at the one Ellie would transfer to. He lived in the opposite direction and this just added to the frustration felt by all the members of Ellie's family over the closure. It was clear from her comments that she didn't want to place too much responsibility on Tonka. The family had been disappointed so many times in the past that she considered it unwise to build up her hopes.

If the hospital closed, the trust created with the surgeon over the past three years would be lost and little Ellie would find herself being treated by strangers. All the campaigning appeared to have had little effect on the decision by the regional health authority to close Hôpital Saint-Joseph through lack of funding.

"Perhaps that will no longer be a worry," I suggested, which brought a reluctant smile to the face of Claudia.

Later that day, as we waited patiently for Julia and the two men to return from the hospital, I received a call from Colonel Elton. The owner of the diamonds had been traced and he was busy trying to determine exactly what had happened back in 1940. The most likely scenario, he believed, was that Captain Egan had made his way to Amsterdam and recovered the diamonds as planned. He must have been caught and killed in Cache Moyen as he tried to make his way back, through enemy-held country, to Britain.

"But how did the diamonds come to be buried in *his* grave? Someone else must have put them there?" I asked.

"I've checked," the colonel replied. "But all the other members of the elite group of commandos were rescued with the other soldiers after the Battle of Boulogne. Nobody else knew about the mission."

"That doesn't make sense," I answered. "He must have had an accomplice and Tonka's grandfather looks like the favourite to me."

"No, Jack. They're two separate incidents, I think. Egan must have given the diamonds to someone for safekeeping and they buried them in his grave, perhaps without even looking at them."

I wanted to refer the colonel to the 'X' on the gravestone. I wanted to tell him that Jonjo Thompson had often referred to 'X' marking the spot for buried treasure. But I couldn't say any of it. It was romantic speculation; it was what I wanted to have happened all those years ago.

The colonel assured me he would continue his investigations and, in the meantime, the diamond owner's elderly son, who now lived in Manhattan, had been informed of the discovery of the Gemini stone.

"Get yourself back here with Tonka and we'll try to put the pieces together."

"We can't do that, I'm afraid, colonel. There has been another development here and I think we're not going to be back until after the weekend."

"Look, Jack, leave the car. Hire another car and get back here."

"It's not the car," I explained and went on to tell him the full story of our strange and beguiling visit to Cache Moyen. He listened patiently while I told him about Ellie's illness and how John Joseph Thompson may have been her great-grandfather. I also told him where Tonka had gone and explained that, to make matters even worse, the hospital treating Ellie may be closed due to cost cuts.

"All our hopes are on Tonka," I told him.

~~~~~

It was early evening when Tonka, Julia and Alexis arrived back at the inn. The surgeon had specifically asked for the results of the tests to be sent to him at the earliest opportunity. He was also aware that it was Ellie's birthday on Sunday and he wanted to do everything in his power to deliver the perfect present of life for the little girl.

Brendan provided added cheer when he read Julia her horoscope. 'Someone new to your circle will produce a strange but welcome outcome' proved entirely accurate when the news arrived. Of course, the Irishman had convinced himself that *he* was that new person to her circle and was content to take all the credit for the welcome outcome. He was the talisman, the conduit that had made all this possible and, while he had to agree that

Tonka would be donating the kidney, none of it could have happened without his unwitting and fortuitous intervention.

So, on Saturday morning, when a motorcycle courier arrived at the inn with a letter, we all assumed it would contain the results of Tonka's compatibility tests, even though we knew the consultant had promised to telephone us as soon as he had them. There was a sigh of disappointment, followed by some strange looks from everyone, when the motorcyclist asked for 'Jack Daly'.

"Why have the test results been sent to Jack?" they all asked.

"That's me," I replied from the back of the small crowd that surrounded the courier.

I grabbed the envelope and tore it open. It wasn't the anxiously awaited news from the hospital, but rather a letter that had been sent by courier around the world from Manhattan in the USA. David Fleischmann, the seventy-year-old son of Mendel Fleischmann, had been sent my contact details by Colonel Elton. Fleischmann's father had been preparing to cut the Gemini diamond when war broke out and the stone had gone missing, presumed to be in the hands of the German occupiers of the Netherlands.

'The British Government,' it began *'has informed me of your discovery. The Gemini diamond was expected to become the most valuable jewel in the world, once it had been cut. When my family fled the Netherlands in 1940, the diamond went missing, with a collection of other, smaller, but very valuable diamonds. It is wonderful news for the Fleischmann family and, indeed, the world that this great jewel has been found. I believe we have you and your friends at Cache Moyen to thank for its recovery and I hope I have the opportunity to meet with you in the near future to pass on my thanks personally. In the meantime, if there is anything I can do for you, or your friends, please let me know.'*

As we sat with the family, discussing the letter, the workshop mechanic came ambling along the road with news that the car would be fixed in a few hours. We were free to leave this strange place but decided to wait until Sunday morning, in the hope that news would arrive from the hospital. Tonka and I made several telephone calls throughout the day and he assured his family that we would be back home in time for the funeral.

On Saturday evening, as the sun slowly set beyond the trees opposite the inn, Baptiste began cooking our meal. But he, like everyone else, was distracted, continually looking at the telephone in the hallway, waiting for it to ring with news from the hospital. When the call did finally come, all the family members hesitated, wondering which of them should receive the news first. It was Claudia, of course, who took the call and held her breath. The rest of us stopped what we were doing and gathered as closely as we could in the small passageway where Claudia stood, intently listening to the caller and uttering, "Oui, oui." Then she spoke quietly into the handset and I asked Baptiste what she had said.

He shrugged. "'Yes, we know that person,' is what she said." Everyone looked a little bemused. Then, as slowly as the sun rose in the morning, the expression on Claudia's face changed and a smile as bright as that same morning sun lit the hallway. Her eyes smiled too as she looked at Tonka and nodded. We soon learned from her that the compatibility tests proved Tonka was a match. Even the rather grumpy priest, who had been sitting reading his newspaper outside, joined in the celebration.

Once the hugging and kissing had stopped, Alexis remembered to ask his wife what else had been said by the consultant.

"Oh," she shouted, as she suddenly remembered something important from her conversation. "He asked if I knew someone called Jack Daly and I confirmed that I did." She looked directly at me. "It was about the man who wrote to you this morning, Mr Fleischmann. Apparently, you spoke to him on the telephone this afternoon to tell him about the hospital closing due to lack of funds," she said. I nodded, wondering what she was going to say next. "Well," she continued, "he has promised to provide any immediate funding requirements the hospital has and to arrange an endowment sufficient to secure its long-term future."

As the night sky darkened, nobody was going to bed, except Ellie of course, who was excited about her birthday the following day. Everyone knew that Tonka and I would have to return to England tomorrow to attend his grandfather's funeral, but he assured them that he would return as soon as the hospital could make the arrangements for the operation to take place.

In the quieter moments, later that evening, we sat around discussing the strange acts of providence that had led us to Cache Moyen and we speculated, too, on the circumstances of Jonjo Thompson's visit here seventy-five years before. Why had he never mentioned the village and his relationship with Elodie Poirier? Why had he never considered returning? Tonka was just expressing his disappointment that nobody remained in the village who might remember those desperate times in the early months of the war, when the priest got up and said goodnight to everyone. As he went to cross the narrow road that divided the churchyard from the forecourt of the inn, he turned and stroked his chin.

"As I mentioned to the policemen, I have many older parishioners in the local farming community. They are early risers and most will attend nine o'clock mass in the morning. If the opportunity presents itself, I will ask them if anyone lived here during the war."

"Or even if they were told of local events in the war," I commented, grasping at any chance to solve the mystery.

"Some stop here for coffee before heading home," added Baptiste. "Perhaps you will be able to question them yourselves before you leave."

~~~~~

I was awoken from a deep but dreamless sleep by the sound of church bells across the road. They were accompanied by the excited screams of a little girl. There were few things as pleasurable as the sound of church bells on a Sunday morning in the countryside and anyone guilty of disturbing that unique experience was likely to reap my anger. But this was an exception. Ellie was seven today and nobody wanted to consider the possibility of her not reaching her eighth birthday.

When Ellie opened the present from Tonka and me, she found a bright, shiny but very small medal. She looked at the man's face on the front of it.

"Who's this?" she asked.

"That's St Jude," said Tonka. "He's the patron saint of…" But he stopped speaking, not wanting to utter the words 'lost causes'. "He's the patron saint whose job is to look after the people we love."

"What, like a super hero?"

"Yes, just like a super hero."

"What does he do?"

"He takes on all the most difficult jobs."

"What is he doing now?" she asked.

"He's saving the world," replied Tonka.

"Saving it from what?"

"Saving it from becoming a world that your mummy, daddy and nana wouldn't like."

"What about you?"

"Me too. He's stopping it from becoming a world I wouldn't like, too."

The local jeweller in Touberge had cleaned the old St Jude medal until it shone like silver and then hung it on a matching silver chain, just long enough to go over Ellie's head.

The church bells stopped ringing and the priest walked from the church to the lych gate to welcome his parishioners. Ellie walked around the patio area showing off her first piece of jewellery and, as she did so, an old man aided by a walking stick made his way slowly towards the church. In her eagerness, Ellie reached the priest just before the old man did and was showing him her special birthday present. As the old man went to pass through the gate he looked down and saw the medal. He stumbled at the shock and reached out against the flint stone wall to prevent himself from falling. Tonka rushed over with a chair so that he could sit down, for it looked as if he might faint.

"What is it?" we cried in unison, as Tonka placed the chair behind him and a crowd gather around.

When he heard we were English he looked surprised and stuttered a few words that none of us could understand. He sat for a moment, as if he was trying to remember the English words for what he wanted to say.

"Medal," he uttered eventually and reached out to look at it.

Julia stepped out of the crowd and spoke. "I know this man. I have known him since I was a child. He is Monsieur Aurelie. He lives in the hills above the town."

"Monsieur Aurelie," the priest asked. "What is it about the medal?"

In a trembling voice, he explained how he had found that very medal in the cemetery behind the church and had given it to Julia's mother, Elodie Poirier. Elodie had given it to a friend of his. He was sure that Elodie had known what it was and what its significance was, too.

"It is the face of St Jude on that medal," the old man declared quietly. "The patron saint of lost causes. She gave it to my friend to keep him safe and now it hangs around the neck of this little girl here with the same purpose." He recollected that the evening was as clear to him now as when it had occurred.

"What evening?" everyone asked.

The medal had been dropped by someone visiting the cemetery, he explained. But providence had caused it to find its way into his friend's pocket. Hopefully St Jude had completed his first mission successfully and was now to become the guardian angel of another lost cause.

"There was no escape for him," he said, a little ambiguously, in a strange combination of English and another language that I could not identify. "The only alternatives were death or capture. Egan had it in his genes to charge the enemy lines and in doing so there was some purpose in it. But the other one didn't feel inclined or able to sacrifice his life by taking a few enemy lives with it."

We were all struggling to understand the old man's words and Julia could see our frustration.

"Monsieur Aurelie speaks mainly in a Flemish dialect, which is probably now extinct," she explained. But it was intermingled with some English and we could just make out the meaning of his words.

"I recognise that language," Brendan declared loudly as he stepped forward to look more closely at the man. "That's not Flemish, that's Gaelic." As he spoke, Brendan studied the old man's features.

"What is your name?" he asked.

The old man finally answered in a language he had not used for many years. "I'm Aurelie, the gravedigger. I haven't seen any British soldiers."

It took a few minutes for Brendan to realise but, even in his old age, Monsieur Aurelie looked sufficiently like his sister, Brenda, to cause him to declare: "Not Aurelie, but O'Reilly! This is my Uncle Eamon."

The old man stood up, placed his hands on Brendan's shoulders and looked as if his mind had been swept to a distant land.

"Brenda," he said and began to cry.

A group of about twenty local people, who had been waiting patiently inside the church for mass to begin, came out to see what the delay was and the old man insisted that the priest should continue with the service. There was a sigh of disappointment from those gathered around, as they were anxious to hear the rest of the old man's story.

Certainly neither Tonka nor I were going anywhere until we had found out more about Monsieur Aurelie, so we too went into the small church and sat at the back. As we did, we were joined by the entire Tremblay family who, judging by the expression on the priest's face, were not regular attendees at mass. Whether it was divine intervention, the act of a merciful god or simply good fortune, we all knew that something remarkable had happened in this tiny hamlet encased by ancient woodland.

As we stepped outside after the service, having given thanks for our good fortune, a sudden breeze rustled the branches on the trees above our heads. The newly budded leaves glowed brightly and the catkins hang down like church bells summoning the faithful to acknowledge a tiny, yet magnificent event.

Everyone who left the church walked across the road and sat around the tables to listen to Monsieur Aurelie's strange and previously untold tale of heroism and stubborn British grit. He took us back to a May day in 1940 and, with all the ability of a landscape artist, recreated the place where we now sat and set it in a sepia background. Henri Poirier came to life for his descendents, as did the beautiful Elodie and the man he remembered as Axe Egan. The old man's only failing was that he could not remember his other colleague's name.

"It was a long time ago," he sighed. "I can't remember," he added, recalling how to speak in English again after so long. "It wasn't his real name, it was, you know, made up, a nickname, like your friend, Tonka, here."

"Jonjo?" Tonka replied.

"Yes, that's it. Jonjo Thompson."

"And the person buried in the cemetery? Captain Egan; you served with him?" I asked.

"Oh yes, Captain Anthony Xavier Egan, 2nd Battalion Irish Guards. Axe was famous."

Both Tonka and I remembered the name from the childhood stories that Grandad had told us. Captain Axe Egan, pirate ship skipper and Yankee officer in the American Civil War. Axe Egan had been a real person. Maybe not a pirate or a civil war hero, but a hero all the same.

The old man enchanted us with his strange tale of a time when this village had been occupied by German forces, at the beginning of a long and cruel war.

The Germans knew there was a British soldier in the area, he told us. But they thought there was only one lone straggler because Axe had outwitted them. They had seen the footprints of one man crossing the stream at the edge of the forest. And they had found evidence of the same man living under the grain barns. It was only a matter of time before they found him. Eamon explained how, incredibly, he had convinced the German soldiers that he was a local, although he did eventually confess that Elodie had played a major part in the deception.

"When Axe sent Jonjo off to complete the mission, there was a risk that Jerry might pick up his trail and Axe had to ensure the mission did not fail. I was absolutely convinced he would do something but I couldn't risk going to the hideout to see him. In any case, he was moving from one hedgerow or badger sett to another. Then, one day, a convoy pulled up in the village and some senior officers, who they called SS, arrived. They billeted themselves in the parish hall of the church. The villagers assumed they were either passing through or had been drafted in to locate and possibly torture the British soldier who was known to be in the area. Even before there was such an organisation as the French resistance, the Germans knew how dangerous it would be to have anyone behind their lines. But they didn't have to look far."

Eamon was given a drink and went on to tell us that one day, while the German infantry had been searching the dense forest, the SS officers were sitting in the parish hall discussing their plans. It was a hot June morning and they had been laughing about the exchange rate they had introduced and how cheap it now was to buy beer in France. He knew all this, he said, because he had still been working in the graveyard, cutting down the gorse and bramble. Suddenly, Axe had appeared from nowhere, hobbling along on a stick with a gun in his other hand. He had shot the German soldier on guard outside the hall, then kicked the door open and began shooting the SS officers.

"It was a suicide mission, of course. The Germans had wanted him captured in order to find out what he knew, but Axe wasn't going to be taken alive and he was going to take as many Germans as he could before they killed him. Seven, he killed, including four of the five SS officers. It was the bravest and most selfless act I had ever seen."

"So who put the headstone on the captain's grave?" I asked.

"Jonjo, of course. When he came back he told Elodie what the headstone should say and he particularly asked for the initial X to be carved larger, deeper."

"But you said that Jonjo had left before the captain had been killed. How could he have arranged the headstone?"

"No, not the first time he was here. When he came back, after he had been to Amsterdam."

His words were like a thunderbolt.

"Jonjo came back?" Tonka and I said, disbelievingly.

"Yes. I didn't see him, but Elodie told me. He managed to hide in the forest for another week but she told me not to look in case I led the Germans to him." The old man paused. "I don't think he wanted to leave. By that time the Germans occupied the whole of France, Belgium and the Netherlands, so there was no escape for him. I suppose it was only a matter of time before he was captured. I think he stayed away from me to ensure I didn't get caught, too."

And so the mystery of the mission, the diamonds and even the medal was resolved through the recollection of old Eamon O'Reilly. He had never returned home. Irishmen who had served the British in the war were effectively excommunicated back in their homeland. No jobs, no benefits and no home. So he had decided to stay. After five years, everyone he knew lived close to Cache Moyen and he wasn't sure if he still had any family back home. He became Monsieur Aurelie, the lonely, reclusive self-sufficient hermit who lived on a distant hilltop six miles from edge of the lonely forest.

Brendan decided to stay a little longer with his newly discovered uncle, so Tonka and I went back to our rooms to pack. We had four days to get home and attend the funeral of John Joseph Thompson before Tonka returned for the operation that would save little Ellie's life.

For all the disappointment Grandad must have felt, the mission had been a success. Diamonds, like gold, were the only currency with any true value in the war and the Gemini diamond would certainly have helped to fund that war for the Nazis. Unable to return the Gemini stone to England, Jonjo had done the next best thing; he had denied the enemy ownership of this most valuable diamond.

It seemed to me, as I packed my suitcase for the journey home, that Colonel Elton had investigated the case of the lost diamond in the past and its disappearance had still baffled him. Presumably the British and Dutch governments believed it had fallen into the hands of the Germans. Had it not been for the unique size and quality of the Gemini stone, the collection may indeed have remained lost. But the jewel had never surfaced after the war and locating its whereabouts was just the kind of challenge Elton enjoyed.

The anniversary of the Battle of Boulogne had raised the mystery of its disappearance once more and I assumed that when the colonel had heard of my connection, he'd thought it was at least worth making contact. He could not have predicted the remarkable series of events that would lead to the diamond's eventual discovery. Or could he?

It was late morning before Tonka and I had said our many farewells. Brendan and his uncle Eamon stood beside Julia,

Baptiste, Alexis, Claudia and, of course, little Ellie as they waved goodbye. A strong wind stirred the heavily laden branches of the oak trees opposite the inn. The gust was of sufficient strength to rock the church bell close by. The muted toll of the bell finally gave voice to the wind and it spoke softly of the strange events it had seen.

Follow me on Twitter Peter Larner @Opuswriter

Made in the USA
Charleston, SC
27 February 2015